TRICK MY TRUCK BUT DON'T MESS WITH MY HEART

Also by LuAnn McLane

Dancing Shoes and Honky-Tonk Blues
Dark Roots and Cowboy Boots
Love, Lust and Pixie Dust
Wild Ride
Hot Summer Nights

TRICK MY TRUCK BUT DON'T MESS WITH MY HEART

LuAnn McLane

A SIGNET ECLIPSE BOOK

SIGNET ECLIPSE
Published by New American Library, a division of
Penguin Group (USA) Inc., 375 Hudson Street,
New York, New York 10014, USA
Penguin Group (Canada), 90 Eglinton Avenue East, Suite 700, Toronto,
Ontario M4P 2Y3, Canada (a division of Pearson Penguin Canada Inc.)
Penguin Books Ltd., 80 Strand, London WC2R 0RL, England
Penguin Ireland, 25 St. Stephen's Green, Dublin 2,
Ireland (a division of Penguin Books Ltd.)
Penguin Group (Australia), 250 Camberwell Road, Camberwell, Victoria 3124,
Australia (a division of Pearson Australia Group Pty. Ltd.)
Penguin Books India Pvt. Ltd., 11 Community Centre, Panchsheel Park,
New Delhi - 110 017, India
Penguin Group (NZ), 67 Apollo Drive, Rosedale, North Shore 0632,
New Zealand (a division of Pearson New Zealand Ltd.)
Penguin Books (South Africa) (Pty.) Ltd., 24 Sturdee Avenue,
Rosebank, Johannesburg 2196, South Africa

Penguin Books Ltd., Registered Offices:
80 Strand, London WC2R 0RL, England

First published by Signet Eclipse, an imprint of New American Library,
a division of Penguin Group (USA) Inc.

ISBN-13: 978-0-7394-9320-5

To Billie Jo and Yvonne.
Your relationship as sisters was the
inspiration for this book.

ACKNOWLEDGMENTS

I would like to extend a special thanks to all of the readers who have taken the time to drop me a note. Knowing that I have made you laugh or touched your heart means the world to me.

Thanks to my editor, Anne Bohner, for continuing to push my creative buttons and for keeping me on task.

As always, thanks to my agent, Jenny Bent. Your encouragement and knowledge is highly valued and appreciated.

1

Somethin's Just Not Right . . .

I'm waving out the car window as I drive down Main Street in Pinewood, in a pretty good mood as I sing along with Carrie Underwood's "Before He Cheats." That song just gets me all fired up. "I took a Louisville slugger to both headlights!" I belt out as I stop for a streetlight, one of only two in my tiny hometown. "Maybe next time he'll thiiiink"—I raise my fist for drama and then sing it really low, the way Carrie does—"before he cheats . . . ," but the end of the song dies in my throat when I suddenly realize that nobody is waving back at me. "Now what's up with *that*?" I say with a frown. "Maybe I shouldn't sing so loud," I mutter, and turn off the radio because I know that if a good song comes on I won't be able to resist singing loud and proud . . . and unfortunately off-key.

Since it's a Saturday morning, many townsfolk are out and about scurrying here and there . . . well, I take that back. People in Pinewood, Kentucky, don't scurry; they sort of meander. Now, in Chicago, where I've been living for the past two years, people scurry. Glancing right and left, I start waving again with no results.

Why isn't anyone waving to me? People in small towns greet *everybody*, even strangers, and I'm not a stranger, doggone it. I've lived here all of my life—well, except for the past two years—and I definitely deserve a wave or a *Hey there, Candie!* I can't help that when I'm by myself in the car I tend to sing as though I'm performing on *American Idol!*

The light turns green but I ignore it and wave one more time, thinking that maybe I was mistaken since I was so caught up in the Carrie Underwood cheatin' song, and thus not really paying attention. Pasting a cheerful smile on my face, I zone in on Mrs. Walker, who is waddling across the street, right smack in front of me. She's the cashier at Pat's Bakery, where I've bought countless cheese Danish and smiley face cookies. She clearly sees me sitting here in my blue Camry, flapping my hand and smiling as though I'm in a parade, but she turns her nose up and waddles on by.

Well!

Of course I'm sort of ticked, but then a creepy feeling of unease settles over me. "This is weird," I whisper, and do a tentative little finger wiggle over at Mrs. Evans as she comes out of the hardware store. She taught me, okay, *attempted to teach* me how to play the piano, but I get the same nose-in-the-air treatment and maybe a bit of a sneer. "Ohmigod, am I being, like . . . *shunned*?"

I'm racking my brain for a reason *why* when a honking horn startles me into realizing that the light is green again. I glare into the rearview mirror at a rumbling pickup truck and briefly consider flipping the bird until I notice that there's a cute cowboy behind the wheel, so I refrain as I ease my foot down on the gas pedal. Flipping people off is really more up my twin sister Sarah's alley anyway, although I have to admit that my two years of city dwelling have made me a tad more aggressive. But anyway, I'm a sucker for cowboys, so I don't flip him off.

Okay, they're not really cowboys since we have farms here in Pinewood, not ranches, but they're close enough in my book. Granted, the metrosexual men in Chicago had a certain appeal, but I missed my country boys. With a sigh I flick another glance in the mirror and smile. Maybe he'll wave back. But after giving him a flirty little wiggle of my fingertips I suddenly feel silly and lower my hand to the steering wheel. And then a thought hits me: Am I that starved for male attention that I stoop to wave at random men? Okay, he was a cowboy, but still . . .

The short answer is *yes*. I can't, however, resist a peek in the rearview mirror and get giggly when the cowboy tips his hat! Squinting, I try to place him, but with the hat brim shading his eyes I can't really see his face. In my imagination though, he's very hot with blue eyes and—"Whoa!" I jerk the steering wheel in order not to clip a mailbox and decide I had better keep my eyes on the road instead of mooning over a man. I hope he's not laughing at me but decide not to risk taking a look.

After turning off Main Street, I head toward the two-family apartment building where I'll be living while I help Sarah get Daddy's used car dealership back on its feet. After Daddy's heart attack, his used car business has suffered and I plan on doing my best to get it back on track. I subleased my apartment in Chicago and took an extended leave of absence from the ad agency where I work, so I basically have a green light to take as long as I need. Family is more important than a job but, although Mama is hoping otherwise, I do plan on returning to Chicago by the end of the summer.

Unlike Main Street, nobody's out and about back in the neighborhood except for a few people mowing lawns, so I can't wave and test my being-shunned theory, but I was probably just being paranoid anyway. What could I possibly have done to have an entire town ticked at me? The cool breeze sends the scent of cut grass through my open window and I inhale deeply, not even minding the underlying pungent smell of fresh mulch. Perennials planted in beds and hanging pots provide a backdrop of bright color while tall, stately trees lining the street seem to stand guard in front of beautiful old Victorian homes. While Pinewood is surrounded by farmland rapidly being gobbled up by suburbs, the tiny town remains mostly untouched by modern development.

A couple of minutes later I pull into the driveway of Daddy's two-family dwelling, where I'll be living for free since I promised to fix it up a bit for future rentals. While Daddy's main source of income is Dapper Dan's Used Car Emporium, he's recently started to dabble in real estate.

Daddy had warned me that the house was a little rough around the edges but I don't mind. After my itty-bitty city apartment, having a yard will seem like luxury. I pull into the long, rather narrow driveway and head around back to the detached garage, but after I kill the engine I simply sit there for a moment while letting it sink in that I'm back in Pinewood. It's not that I don't love this town, because I do, but I thought my life was going in another direction and now here I am.

Shaking off that sort of sobering thought, I get out of the car and walk over to the back door of the first-floor apartment that's mine for the summer. Not originally a two-family, the old house has a certain charm, making me eager to see the inside. Leaving my knick-knacks stacked in the backseat and trunk for later, I decide to check out the place and get my bearings before calling Mama and Daddy. Sarah should be working at the car lot, which is within walking distance, so I'll meander, not scurry, down there later.

I notice that the sun is quickly warming things up, making me want to shed these jeans and slide into shorts. Luckily, I shipped most of my summer clothing earlier in the week so I should be set. "Hmm," I mutter when the key Mama had promised to leave me beneath the rubber welcome mat isn't there. It's not like her to forget such a detail but when I try the back door, it swings open. I'm not alarmed since we never bother to lock doors here in Pinewood. Maybe Mama meant the front door mat, I'm thinking to myself as I enter a small but cheerful kitchen. After tossing my purse and keys on the oval table, I open the fridge and I'm not at all surprised to find it fully stocked. With a little squeal of delight I grab a Yoo-hoo and start shaking the cold bottle as I head down the short hallway to check out the rest of the place.

"Ohmigod, Sarah!" I shout, surprised but delighted to see my sister sitting on the rather gaudy sofa in the living room. I set the Yoo-hoo down on the coffee table, totally expecting her to jump up and give me a hug but she just sits there, sort of . . . *glaring*. Her lips are puckered and her long legs are crossed with one foot kicking up and down in an agitated manner, so hard that at any moment I expect her sandal to flip off her foot and go flying across the room. "Hey," I try in a cautious but friendly tone, "thought you'd be at the car lot."

Her foot kicks even faster, making me want to duck for cover. "I couldn't bring myself to open the lot today," she says in a tight little voice that cracks at the end.

"Oh my God, Sarah, is it Daddy? Did he take a bad turn?" My heart starts pounding and my knees get so wobbly that I sink down in a weathered wingback chair.

"Daddy's grumpy, Candie, but doin' fine," she assures me in a slightly softer tone.

"Is it Mama then?" I ask in a squeaky voice. My voice gets high-pitched when I get upset.

Sarah flips her golden hair over her shoulder and says, "Mama is a bit stressed but fine too."

"Well then, what's the matter with you?"

Sarah continues to glare at me but her narrowed eyes are rapidly filling with tears. "N-Nick dumped me."

"What? Oh, Sarah, I'm—"

"And it's your damned fault!"

"So, sorry . . . Wait, *what*?"

Her leg keeps kicking, sort of distracting me. "You heard me. I suspected that another woman was the reason he was acting so strange lately but I never thought the *other woman* would be my very own *twin sister*." Her blue eyes, the only identical feature that we share (we're fraternal), shoot watery daggers at me. "My engagement to Nick has ended because of *you!*" she shouts with an emphatic kick that sends the sandal sailing across the room.

I watch the flight of the sandal and then turn my attention back to my sister, who has apparently lost her mind. "Now, just how in the world could I be the other woman, Sarah? I've been gone for two years." I'm doing my best to keep calm, but I'm hanging in there by a thread.

She swallows in a visible effort to stay somewhat calm as well and then says, "He . . . Nick said that"— she pauses and swallows again—"although he loves me that—th-at . . ." Instead of finishing she closes her eyes and inhales a shaky breath.

"What?" I grip the arms of the chair and wait.

Sarah blows out the breath in a huff. "Nick said that he and I don't share that special closeness that he has with *you.*"

"Me?" I squeak so high that I'm afraid dogs might come running. I point to myself so as not to make any mistake.

"Do you have peanut butter in your damned ears?" Sarah asks like Mama used to do, except Mama wouldn't say *damned*. "Yes, you." She points at me and I'm still pointing at myself, so there is really no mistake.

I stick my index finger in my ear and wiggle it—not that I think I have peanut butter in there but I seriously wonder if I'm hearing her right. "Sarah, Nick and I have never been more than friends. We've never even kissed . . . well, except for a little peck beneath the mistletoe this past Christmas and you were right there in the room!"

"Apparently that's when the doubts all started," she spits out, and slaps her leg so hard that she winces. "When you came home for the holidays Nick said that it hit him hard how much he missed you. He said that he wants the same friendship with *me* that he has with *you* and if I can't open up to him in that way then . . . well . . ." She pauses as if she can't finish.

"You're over?"

"Yes," she chokes out. "He went on to explain that he wants the whole package in a wife and when you returned he realized that we didn't have it."

"Did you tell him that we aren't a package deal?" I ask, trying to lighten the mood, but Sarah purses her lips and I wonder if she just might wing the other sandal directly at me.

"Do you have feelings for Nick, Candie? Is that why you ran off to Chicago?"

Her unexpected question immediately sobers me.

"Be honest."

I squirm a little in the wingback chair.

"Please," Sarah quietly pleads, which is much

harder to take than her anger. "I need to understand all of this."

Unsure of how to answer I pluck at a loose string on the arm of the chair. She's asking me to open up about something that I've never divulged to anyone. Mercy, this is not the homecoming I was expecting!

"Candie . . ." Her eyes are no longer shooting daggers and her lips go from a pucker to a tremble.

"You remember how I was growing up, Sarah . . . a strange combo of nerd and jock. Nick was one of the few people who *got* me, you know?"

She nods silently.

I hesitate, not really wanting to get into this discussion but feeling I have no choice. "I valued Nick's friendship so much and when you two started dating it was . . . weird for me. I mean, Nick and I always talked about *everything* but talking about you was . . . awkward."

"Because you had feelings for him?"

"To be honest I wasn't sure if it went deeper than friendship, on my part anyway. But, Sarah, I knew how he felt about you . . . and"—I pause because I get choked up—"you're my *sister*. Rather than try to sort out my feelings for Nick, I decided to leave. Now, of course, there were other reasons. I wanted to spread my wings and see the world and all that stuff." I flip my hand in the air but swallow hard.

"But you didn't want to come between me and Nick?"

I give her a negative shake of my head. "I didn't think I could come between you two, Sarah. Nick loves *you*. It hurt when I lost his friendship that I *so* depended on."

Sarah frowns over at me. "You didn't have to do that. If he still had your friendship, then maybe I wouldn't have to fill that void," Sarah says in a sort of accusatory tone.

"Come on, Sarah, how could I be best friends with my sister's boyfriend?" I put my hands up in the air and give her a look. "Would you really be cool with that?"

"Of course. I trust you!"

"Evidently not!" I remind her. I also want to tell her that *she* should be Nick's best friend, not me, but I don't think she's ready to hear that right now. Besides, if she doesn't already know that, then her relationship truly is in trouble.

"Well, this is just a damned *mess*, now isn't it?"

"It sure . . . ohmigod, *Sarah*! Oh no, you didn't . . ."

"What?" She finally stops kicking her foot in the air.

"Did you tell anyone that I was the cause of your breakup with Nick? Not that I am," I add.

"Um . . . maybe."

"Oh . . . Sarah!"

She uncrosses her legs and leans forward. "I was pissed, okay? You would be too if your fiancé just broke up with you because of a relationship he had with me. Wait a minute. That made sense, right?"

"You told people that I was the other woman! I might as well stamp a scarlet letter on my doggone forehead. Sarah, how could you? Especially when it isn't true!"

"It *is* true, Candie," she says defensively and does her little hair flip.

It's my turn to glare.

"Well, sort of."

My glare intensifies.

"Well, in a roundabout way," she insists and swings her hand in an arc.

"Wow, I get to be the other woman while living more than six hours away."

"I merely mentioned that you were very close friends and came between me and Nick."

"Did you mention that Nick and I are friends *without* benefits?"

"I can't help it if people came to the wrong conclusion!"

"Sarah, I'm being shunned."

"Shunned? Isn't that what those Amish people do or whatever? That's a little overboard, don't ya think?"

"Really?" I grab my sweating Yoo-hoo bottle and start shaking it up harder than necessary. "Well then, how do you explain why no one in this town would wave to me?"

"Pffft." Sarah waves her French manicure in my general direction. "You're mistaken, I'm sure," she says, but looks a bit worried.

"Maybe, but somehow I don't think so. The people in Pinewood love you, Sarah. Have you forgotten that you are the only claim to fame that this town has ever had, Miss Kentucky third runner-up?"

"Oh come on, that was two years ago and I didn't even win. Third runner-up. Big hairy deal."

"In the eyes of the town you should have won—and probably would have . . ." I don't finish since we never mention the unfortunate wardrobe malfunction that cost her the crown. "You are still the little darling of Pinewood. People are goin' to rally around you, especially if they think you've been done wrong."

"It *was* a conspiracy, you know," Sarah says in a low, serious voice, evidently reliving her booby flash to the judges because she closes her eyes and shudders again. "The tape I had personally packed in my kit was *double-sided*."

I nod slowly. "I know." The conspiracy theory was an opinion started by Mama but shared by the town, making Sarah a sympathetic if somewhat fallen beauty queen, which is darned hard to do. Her unfortunate moment occurred during a pivot directly in front of the judge's table, almost as if choreographed . . . stop, turn ... hello boobies! I would have laughed if it hadn't been my very own sister ... oh, but in Pinewood you don't dare joke about the incident unless you duck and run for cover.

After opening her eyes she says, "Why did you have to go and bring that up anyway?"

"I was merely making the point that this town stands behind you, Sarah. We have a business to rebuild together, so not only do we have to get along, which I didn't think was going to be an issue, but we have to present a united front to the community. We have to think of a way to undo the damage, not to mention that we have to work with Nick."

She blinks at me while nibbling on her bottom lip.

"Oh no, what?" I ask, but before she can answer I already have it figured out. "You fired Nick!"

"I had no choice. He dumped me!"

I look down at the sweaty Yoo-hoo, wishing it were something stronger. "Sarah, Anderson Automotive has been detailing our inventory since Daddy opened the dealership."

She juts her chin in the air. "Well, times have changed. Oh, quit looking at me like that. I've already found a replacement."

"Who?"

"Smiley Turner."

"S-Smiley *Turner*?" My voice gets high-pitched again. "That man is older than dirt and smells like my old gym bag."

"It's temporary."

"Yeah, until you hire Nick back!" Sarah's eyes widen at my outburst but come on, I've been pretty doggone understanding about being blamed for her breakup and consequently shunned through no fault of my own, but I'm quickly losing my patience. I don't get angry too often but when I do ... well, run for cover! Well okay, not really, but I *am* getting pretty ticked.

In an effort to keep from losing my cool, I jump up and start pacing the room like the Energizer Bunny. All I need is a big drum but I'd gladly substitute Sarah's head so as to knock some sense into her.

"We need to fix this, don't we?" Sarah asks in a rather timid voice while watching my frantic pacing.

"We?" I stop in my tracks and put my fists on my hips but I feel a little guilty when Sarah looks about ready to burst into noisy tears.

"I'm sorry, Candie. Nick and I have always had this chemistry but I just don't have as much depth as you. I'm just not . . . *enough.*"

"Did Nick say that to you?" Okay, he might be about a foot taller and one hundred pounds of solid muscle heavier but I just might have to kick his butt. Obviously they've got some issues but he didn't have to be mean to my sister.

"Not exactly but it's what he meant."

I drag in a deep breath and blow it out. "Okay, look, you're just going to have to work on your issues together but for now we need to concentrate on the problem at hand. We can't have the town thinking I'm some sort of—of—"

"Slut?" Sarah finishes, but then clasps a hand over her mouth.

"Well, I was thinking more of backstabbing, conniving bitch, but slut works too."

"Oh Candie, people aren't really thinking that about you," she says but doesn't sound at all convinced. "I'm sure you're overreacting about a few lousy people not waving at you."

I flop back down into the chair and take a sip of Yoo-hoo that's gotten too warm to enjoy. "I wish that were true but we both know that gossip in Pinewood travels like wildfire. Lord only knows what's being said and misconstrued as the truth."

"I'll start making some phone calls to set the record straight."

I shake my head. "No, that might not be the best idea. I learned a lot about marketing while working in Chicago. We don't want to throw any fuel on the fire."

"Okay, I see your point."

"Listen, I think I need some time to try and sort things out. Don't tell Mama and Daddy I've arrived just yet, okay?"

Sarah nods. "Candie, I'm sorry . . ."

I put both hands up in the air. "I won't lie. I'm pretty ticked at you but we don't have time to be angry with each other. I'll think on it for a while and you do the same."

Sarah looks surprised for a second but then nods as if pleased that I'm asking for her input. "You know," she says slowly, "it would help defuse the gossip if you had a boyfriend."

"Excuse me while I go pull one out of my hat."

"I was just sayin' . . ."

I sigh. "I know. And it would help if you got back together with Nick. How likely are those two things?"

"At this point not good—getting back together with Nick, that is. You can totally get a boyfriend. I mean, you're like all sophisticated now and everything." She eyes my naturally curly hair, which is now sleek and shiny thanks to a flatiron.

I give her a wry grin. "Thanks, I think."

Sarah stands up to her full five foot ten inches and I stand up to my five foot three. No one would ever guess that we were twins. She comes over and gives me a hug that I dearly need but I keep my emotions in check so we both don't start blubbering. Don't get me wrong. I'm still mad at her but I do love her to pieces.

"It'll all work out," I assure her with more conviction than I'm feeling.

Sarah nods glumly. "I hope so," she says as she heads to the front door. "I'll go up to the car lot and keep an eye on things."

"You want me to come by later?"

She shakes her head. "No, you get settled and unpacked. We'll talk later."

After Sarah leaves I head back to the kitchen and make a beeline for the fridge, hoping that Mama stocked me up on beer. I know it's early to be drinking but this situation calls for a cold one—or two. "Dang!" I mutter when I'm disappointed. Mama isn't much on drinking. There is, however, an abundance of fruit and vegetables, probably in an effort to get me eating healthier. With a sigh I grab an apple but then decide to take a short walk to the corner store and snag a six-pack of beer. I'll only drink *one,* just to calm myself down and get things in perspective.

2

It's Five O'Clock Somewhere . . .

Instead of going to the corner grocery store and risk being seen buying alcohol this early in the day, I decide to duck in a little corner tavern. Normally I wouldn't be so worried about something as innocent as buying a six-pack but I think I need to keep my actions on the down low until I get this whole thing straightened out. After tugging my Chicago Cubs baseball cap lower on my forehead, I enter the bar, figuring anyone drinking this early won't likely remember seeing me even if I do get recognized. That's my excuse and it has nothing to do with spotting in the parking lot what I think might be the pickup truck that the cowboy who tipped his hat at me was driving. Not that I'd approach him anyway. Let's face it, if he's the type of guy who drinks this early in the day, then—oh, wait a minute, *I'm* drinking this early in the day. But then again these are extenuating circumstances. Besides, it's five o'clock somewhere, right?

The smell of stale beer and cigarettes hits me in the face when I enter the bar. Wrinkling my nose I'm thinking about turning right back around when a low, sexy voice dripping with Southern charm stops me in midturn. "Now don't go runnin' off, pretty lady. Come on in and keep me company."

Squinting past dust motes dancing on rays of sunshine streaming through the open door, I realize that the sultry voice belongs to a tall, sexy cowboy standing behind the bar. I know he's a cowboy because I spot his hat hanging on a peg on the wall, which doesn't of course make him authentic, but I choose to give him the benefit of the doubt. I wonder if he really is the guy who tipped his hat at me? Curiosity and thirst make my decision, so I walk over to a stool and take a seat.

The place is deserted except for the cowboy bartender and . . . *ohmigod* I do believe it's Smiley Turner seated—no, make that *slumped*—over a small table at the far end of the room. Breathing in a sigh of beer-scented relief, I'm glad that no one is here who will recognize me—Smiley surely won't remember even if he does place me. Still, I'm suddenly embarrassed to order a beer, so I say in a prim voice, "Diet Coke, please."

"Right . . . ," my sexy cowboy drawls and thumps a cold longneck down in front of me.

"I said Diet Coke," I remind him, but stare longingly at the brown bottle.

"I know." He gives me a killer grin. "But what you really want is a cold beer. Am I right?"

I hesitate a moment but then realize that I'm in a *bar*, for heaven's sake. No one is going to judge me for drinking. "Busted," I admit with a small smile. Damn he's cute, with shaggy blond Keith Urban hair and very blue eyes. I do believe he is my hat-tipping cowboy.

Balancing on his elbows, he leans close to me and says near my ear, "I won't tell." Warm, mint-scented breath makes a tickly little shiver slide down my spine. The spice of his aftershave slices through the stale-beer smell and goes straight to the female wanting-to-kiss-a-cowboy part of my brain. Oh, it might not be documented but it's *there* and would show up on an MRI as a medical mystery.

"It's just kinda early to be drinkin'," I whisper while trying very hard not to stare at his mouth.

"It can be our secret," he whispers back, and I swear I just might slither off the barstool and into a puddle on the floor. "If anyone comes in I'll do a quick switch with a Coke," he says seriously but blue eyes crinkle with amusement.

"Thanks," I tell him, feeling a little foolish but another strong pull of attraction hits me hard when he pats my hand. To distract myself I tip my bottle back and enjoy the cold frothy brew as it slides down my throat and splashes in my stomach—my empty stomach. I make a mental note to keep my limit to *one* since it's likely to go straight to my head unless they have food here.

"Do you serve sandwiches?" I ask while angling my head at his Wrangler-clad butt while he bends over to heft a case of beer up with delicious ease. Biceps the size of baseballs bulge but, hoping I don't have a guilty, I've-been-staring-at-your-butt expression on my face, I quickly avert my gaze when he turns to look at me.

"Usually, but I'm here as a favor to the owner, whose wife just went into labor. I'm just sort of holding down the fort until his little bundle arrives. Sorry, no sandwiches. I might be able to rustle up some pretzels or peanuts."

"Oh, okay." I'm hoping that means he has to bend over again.

"My real job is the new recreational director of Pinewood Parks."

"Oh! I didn't know Pinewood had one of those."

"A park?"

"No, a recreational director," I tell him but blush when he grins and I realize that he's teasing. Unlike Sarah I'm not good at flirting. The only guy I could ever banter with was Nick.

"By the way, I'm Tommy Tucker," he says and offers his hand.

"Candie Montgomery." My hand feels small inside his big, warm handshake that's firm and sure without being overbearing. Another little sizzle of sexual awareness has me removing my hand somewhat quickly, but he doesn't seem to notice.

"Candie Montgomery . . . ," he murmurs thoughtfully while rubbing his chin.

I swallow a sip of beer while wondering what that dark blond stubble would feel like against my skin and then almost choke on my devilish thoughts. Just what in the world is getting into me?

"Oh yeah," he finally says, "you were a volleyball star at Pinewood High and have a sister named Sarah."

"You went to Pinewood?" Wait a minute. Did he just call me a star? I'm liking Tommy Tucker more by the minute.

"This one's on me." He nods as he opens another beer that I shouldn't accept but I do. "Yeah, I moved here when I was a freshman. You were a senior, so our paths didn't cross, but I remember you playing volleyball. You were a defense dynamo. Y'all went all the way to states that year."

"That we did," I tell him with a measure of pride. I still can't remember him but Pinewood High is a pretty big school, drawing in students from across the county. We chat about sports for a while but before you know it I'm on my third beer and soon begin telling him more personal things—my life story, including my daddy's health problems, the struggling used car dealership, and my unfair shunning due to inadvertently breaking my sister's engagement. As it turns out Tommy is friends with Nick and knows Sarah.

"Those two will get back together," he comments and then takes a long pull from a bottle of water. I watch, sort of fascinated by the bobbing of his Adam's apple and the corded muscles in his neck. After tossing the empty bottle toward the trash can at the other end of the bar and making it, I might add, he says, "What you need to throw off the gossip mill is a boyfriend."

"That's what Sarah was sayin'." I feel heat creep into my cheeks. "The problem is I don't have any prospects, you know after being away for two years," I quickly explain even though there weren't any prospects before I left either but he doesn't have to know that.

"How about me?" he asks out of the blue.

This offer is so unexpected that I would have choked on my beer if I hadn't already polished it off. Instead I sit there blinking at him like a dork. "Y-you?"

Tommy reaches up and runs his fingers through his shaggy hair, making it even messier, and gives me a grin that's almost shy. "I'll make you a deal."

"Okay . . . ," I answer skeptically while knowing the answer will most likely be yes.

"Sign up for my sand volleyball team and I'll have the whole town believing I'm head over heels for you."

The three beers are making my brain a little slow. "Okay, let me get this straight. If I play on your volleyball team you'll pose as my boyfriend?"

"It sounded better in my head, but yeah."

I hesitate when I should be jumping all over this deal but I'm a little put out that I have to join his team in order for him to play my boyfriend. It sort of feels like I'd be paying him to spend time with me. "What if

I don't play on your team?" I hear myself ask instead of readily agreeing.

"I'd do it anyway."

Oh good answer, I think to myself while hoping he's attracted to me and not just needing a defense player.

"Plus, I hate gossip," he explains, deflating my ego once more but also making me wonder if he was on the receiving end of some nasty rumors.

"Well, in all fairness the gossip was started by my very own sister."

"But twisted and blown all out of proportion, right?" he says darkly.

Oh, wow. Somebody must have done a number on him. "Pretty much," I admit.

His grin returns, making me forgive him for his ulterior motives. "Then, let's do this thing."

"What makes you think you'd be convincing?" I ask in a surprisingly flirty tone that is the direct result of pouring alcohol into an empty stomach. I feel heat creep up my neck again and I barely resist the urge to clamp my hand over my big mouth.

"Is that a challenge?" Tommy arches one dark blond eyebrow and makes his way around the bar until he's standing directly in front of me.

"Um . . . maybe."

"Well I do believe that I'm up for it." My heart pounds like a jackhammer when he reaches over and gently removes my Cubbies hat. Oh great . . . Hat head, I'm thinking but I don't have time to reach up and fluff my hair because Tommy leans over and presses his mouth to mine.

Oh my . . .

Warm and gentle at first, the kiss heats up when I slide my arms around his neck. The needing-to-kiss-a-cowboy part of my brain goes into high gear and I thread my fingers through his silky hair. His lips are

soft but firm and just slightly moist. When his tongue
tangles with mine I swear my head starts spinning and
it's not from the beer! Well, maybe a little bit but
still . . .

The firm wall of his chest brushes up against my
breasts, making me want to feel the ripple of muscle
over bare skin against my fingertips. My beer buzz is
helping me muster up the nerve to slide my palms beneath his shirt but Smiley Turner interrupts when he
stumbles past us and mumbles for us to "git a danged
room."

Tommy pulls back and chuckles but when he looks
down at me his blue eyes appear thoughtful. I'm hoping this means that he felt something too. "Sorry about
that," he says with a shake of his head.

"Oh . . ." I try not to appear crestfallen even though
it feels like my heart just sank to my toes. "Listen,
about your offer," I begin but then look down at the
floor and swallow. I really should take him up on it as
silly as it seems but—

"You're not gonna turn me down, are you?"

My head snaps up. He actually looks disappointed.

"Wasn't the kiss convincing?" He seems even more
disappointed.

"Well, yes, but then why were you *sorry*?"

He leans one elbow against the bar. "Candie, I was
referring to Smiley's comment about getting a room.
He had no call to say something so crude."

"Oh." Relief washes over me. "Don't worry about
that." I wave a hand in the air.

"I won't let anyone talk smack about my girlfriend," we says with a grin, but there is an underlying
seriousness that I find endearing. Of course I firmly remind myself that he's just a nice guy doing me a
favor—an odd favor at that. I mean I did just tell him
my whole sad story but he's going over and above the
call of duty here.

"You don't really have to do this, Tommy. I shouldn't have dumped my problems on you like that. Geez, you're not even a real bartender and you barely know me."

"I feel like I know you."

"Well, *yeah*, I just told you my life story."

Tommy laughs but then tucks a finger beneath my chin. "Listen, you have a lot on your plate with your daddy's health and the dealership to run. You came home to help your family and you don't need to deal with tongues wagging about something you didn't even do." He shrugs wide shoulders and smiles down at me. "It's not exactly gonna be a hardship to hang out with and cuddle up to a pretty girl."

"But I feel like I dragged you into something that's not your problem. I mean, what if—," I begin but he stops me by moving his fingertip to gently press against my lips.

"Hold on. I offered, remember? Besides, not only will this stop gossip but it will take you out of the picture with Nick in your sister's eyes too."

My eyes widen. "I wanna make it clear that Nick and I were never more than close friends."

"Whoa," he softly protests. "I only meant that it would make things easier on you."

"Oh." My heart pounds a little because he hit a nerve. If I'm honest with myself there have been times when I wondered if we could have been more. "Sarah and I don't always see eye to eye but we would never let a guy come between us." Unexpected tears well up in my eyes. "Look, maybe you really don't want to get involved in this mess," I offer in a husky voice.

"Too late," he says without the grin, "I already am." Then, without warning he lowers his head and gives me a sweet, tender kiss. I melt against his mouth, sink into his embrace, and in that moment I know that I have to be careful because I could probably fall for

Tommy Tucker. The look that he gives me makes me wonder if he's thinking the same thing. Something flickers in his eyes but then he says, "Don't worry so much. Just relax and have some fun with this, okay?"

Relax and have some fun? Now, when was the last time I did that? "I still can't believe you're willing to do this crazy thing for me."

"Hey, it's a tough job but someone has to do it. Might as well be me," he says in a tired voice that has me laughing. "Besides, I am a little bit on the crazy side. Just ask my sisters." He reaches in his pocket and pulls out his cell phone. "Now, give me your number so I can program it into my phone." When I hesitate he crooks one eyebrow. "Candie . . ."

"Oh, okay!" I tell him my number and then slide down from the stool. "I'd better get going." I give him a shy smile.

He nods. "I'll call you later. Oh, and here's my card with my number on it. My home away from home is Pinewood Park, so you can catch me at that number if I don't answer my cell."

I reach out and take the card. "Thank you." Not knowing what else to say I head for the door but then pause and turn around. "Tommy?"

"Yeah?"

"I *will* play on your team, so let me know when you start practice."

"You don't have to," he says but looks happy.

I smile. "I know. I want to." Feeling another stupid blush about to happen I turn and push open the door. Once outside I blink in the bright sunshine and start walking back to my house. It's hard to shake the surreal wow-did-that-just-happen feeling but I have to admit that there's a lightness in my step that wasn't there before.

The rest of my day is spent unpacking after Mama told me that Daddy was sleeping the day away after having had a restless night. I'm dying to see them both but since Mama sounded so tired, I promise to visit as soon as he's up for company. My daddy was always so strong and my mama so energetic that it's hard to swallow that they are getting older.

Later that night I'm sitting on the front porch steps, sipping on some sweet tea with Sarah when my cell phone rings and . . . ohmigod it's *Tommy.*

"Aren't you gonna answer it?" Sarah asks with a frown.

"Oh . . . sure." I flip open the phone. "Hello?" My voice sounds breathless, so I clear my throat and hope he thinks I've been jogging or something.

"Hey, there," Tommy says in his low, sexy voice. My heart starts beating a bit faster, not helping the breathless situation one bit. I can hear noise in the background and I'm guessing he's at the park. "I'm overseeing softball games but I was thinkin' about you and wanted to give you a shout."

"I'm glad that you did," I answer, not really knowing what else to say. I flick a glance at Sarah and of course she's all ears.

"You sound out of breath. It this a bad time?"

"No, I was just, you know, getting settled in. Movin' things around."

"Oh well, let me know if you need any help."

"Why thank you."

"That's one of the perks of having a boyfriend," he teases.

"I can think of several others," I reply, saying out loud what should have been kept silent. I have a bad habit of doing that but he cracks up on the other end and thank the Lord he thinks I was joking.

"Well, I've gotta get back. Talk to you soon."

"Bye." I snap the phone shut and of course Sarah pounces.

"Who was that?"

"A guy I met," I answer. I've decided not to let her know the truth about my arrangement with Tommy. Sarah has a hard time keeping a secret, especially when under the influence of alcohol.

"Who?" she asks just as I knew she would.

"Tommy Tucker."

"Oh . . . ," she says and wiggles her eyebrows. "He's hot. Kinda young though."

"By three years. It doesn't exactly make us like Demi and Ashton."

"Don't go gettin' your feathers ruffled. I was just making a comment. I don't know him real well but he seems like a good guy. A little on the crazy side, but nice."

"Crazy?"

"In a fun way, Candie. Nick and I would occasion- ally see him at Pete's Pub. Are you gonna start seein' him?"

"Yes. Is it so surprising that I have a date?" I ask with a little of the leftover resentment that she always managed to have a date on Saturday night and well . . . I didn't.

"Well yeah, since you've been in town only one day. You have to admit that you're workin' a bit fast. I'm impressed," she adds with a grin. "How did you man- age that? Did you flirt at the grocery store?"

"Um . . . not exactly." I don't really want to admit that I met Tommy in a bar in the middle of the day. "Let's get back to our discussion about the car lot, Sarah."

"Oh no you don't. How'd you meet Tommy? At the park? Were you jogging or somethin'?"

I consider lying but I suck at it so I decide to come clean. "At that little hole-in-the-wall bar down the street."

"Today? Like in the middle of the afternoon?"

It was more like noon, but I nod. "Yes. I was in need of a cold beer after . . . well, our conversation."

Sarah holds her palms up in the air. "I'm not bein' judgmental. Just curious. Well, good for you," she says and gives me a high five as though drinking in the middle of the day is an accomplishment.

"Thanks . . . I guess."

"You work fast."

I take a sip of the tart lemonade and say, "Well, three beers on an empty stomach made me a little flirty."

Sarah shrugs. "Whatever. Tommy seems like a fun guy. You go girl."

I smile but then think to myself that maybe this is more of a joke to Tommy than I realized. I think about how his kiss made me feel and I remind myself not to get serious. Not that it should bother me, because I am leaving once Daddy is on the mend and the car lot is making money again.

"Hey, you okay?"

"Yeah." I force a smile. "Just a bit tired."

Sarah nods. "Me too. I'd better get going," she says but pauses before getting up. "Look, I'm really sorry that I caused people to think poorly of you, Candie. It's not your fault that Nick finds me lacking."

"Sarah—," I begin but she shakes her head.

"Let's not go there. You came home to whip Daddy's dealership back into shape. I don't want to do anything to mess that up."

"We."

She frowns. "What?"

"Not *me*, Sarah. *We* are going to whip the dealership back into shape."

Sarah blinks at me and swallows as if she might be fighting tears. "Yeah," she says softly, "we."

"I'll take your glass in," I offer as she stands up.

"It's so nice out that I'm gonna sit here for a while longer."

"Thanks," she answers. I watch her walk across the lawn to her car. For someone as put together as she seems it hits me that Sarah isn't as confident as everyone thinks she is. She's relied on her looks for so long that I don't think she knows that there could be so much more to her than beauty.

I take in a deep breath of night-scented air that smells so different than the city. I've been here only one day and my world has been turned upside down, making me wonder just what the rest of the summer has in store for me.

3

Working at the Car Lot . . .

"You take him." Sarah nudges me with her elbow as we stare out the window. "Come on, Candie. Paper, rock, scissors?" she asks hopefully.

I shake my head. "No way. Skeeter's your customer."

Sarah widens her blue eyes. "No, he most certainly is *not*."

"I beg to differ, baby sister. He asked for you first. I only waited on him because you were on your doggone cell." I point to the thin silver phone that seems to be permanently attached to her hand. *"Again."*

"I'm not your baby sister."

"Are too."

"By five doggone minutes and that's probably because you pushed me out of the way." She sighs. "Come on! I was talking to Mama about Daddy's condition!" Sarah pulls a pleading face that works on everyone *including* me and she darned well knows it.

"Okay, but the fact remains that Skeeter asked for you, so that makes him yours." Just like most of the guys do but this time I don't mind. It's one of the few occasions when it's more fun not to be the gorgeous

twin and I want to savor it. With a grin I make a shooing motion toward the door of our tiny showroom that
holds one car that right now happens to be a '98 Ford
Taurus. Yes, it's the best we have to offer, so we can't
let even the likes of Skeeter Jones get away. "Scoot."

"He's not going to buy anything."

"You don't know that."

"Candie, he comes by the car lot at least once a
week."

"Still?"

Sarah rolls her eyes. "You might have gone off to
Chicago for two years but here in Pinewood some, no,
make that *most* things never change. The last car
Skeeter bought from Daddy was back in 1977. Yeah,
before we were *born*." She points out the window at a
two-toned blue Caprice Classic that's in mint condition. "He's never gonna trade in that cream puff,
Candie. It's a waste of time."

"You never know."

"Oh, but I do know and while I'm messin' with
Skeeter you'll likely get a real customer who could
have been mine," she protests with a thumb jammed
toward her ample chest. Why did she get those boda-
cious boobies and not me? I mean couldn't we at least
have gotten an equal share?

I shrug. "It's the nature of this business."

"Oh what*ever*." Sarah's Southern drawl is laced
with valley girl lingo, making for an odd speech pat-
tern that I find amusing unless I'm ticked at her, and
then it's just plain annoying. "The last time Skeeter
spit a wad of tobacco on my new shoes. It was totally
gross." Sarah sighs and I get ready for her to stomp her
foot, but she refrains. After one last glare at me she
squares her shoulders and heads out the door.

I have to say that I'm impressed at her resolve when
I fully expected her to argue. Maybe she's matured in
the past two years. I might only be five minutes older

than she but believe me, *she's* the baby sister. Oh and for the record, I didn't push her out of the way but rather paved the way so that she could slide out of the womb pretty as you please—not that I remember or anything but that's how I prefer to see it. Mama says that I was just too antsy to wait for the scheduled cesarean section. As she tells it, I was born kicking and screaming and Sarah slid out pink and smiling, and I suppose that sort of set the stage for things to come. Sarah just has this charm about her that makes people, especially guys, want to do things for her. It made for an easy existence growing up but after I left, Daddy got sick and Nick dumped her. Well, I guess she's recently gotten a harsh taste of reality.

I watch Sarah walk slowly toward Skeeter. She's almost upon him when he suddenly kicks the tire of the old Ford truck with his ratty cowboy boot and then spits out a long, brown stream of tobacco juice onto the blacktop. Sarah's fists clench and she whips around toward the window and sticks her tongue out at me while doing a little head bop. In the past twenty-five years she's done the same thing to me about a million times and it never fails to make me laugh. Of course, when I laugh it never fails to tick her off. Hey, we're sisters. It's my job.

When we were kids Sarah played with dolls and I played sports, and while I don't mind so much anymore that she got Mama's good looks, those long legs would have come in handy on the basketball court. With a grin, I watch Sarah approach Skeeter. Deciding I want to hear the exchange, I push the door open and step into the warm summer evening. Grabbing a nearby broom, I busy myself sweeping up dead leaves while keeping an ear cocked in Sarah's direction.

"Hey there, Skeeter. What's shakin'?"

"Nothin' much. Jes checkin' out this here truck. Whutcha askin' fer it?"

With my head bent I slow down my sweeping and peek over the broom handle at them. The price is clearly marked in bold white letters on the windshield but if Skeeter makes *any* offer we need the money.

"Fifteen hundred," Sarah says, in a lackluster tone while pointing a French-tipped fingernail to the price.

I narrow my eyes at the back of her blond head. *Come on and work it a little. He has some interest or he wouldn't be here!* Of course she stands there with a slight pout as she checks out her manicure. Whoever said that twins have some sort of special mind connection is full of hooey. When she flicks a glance my way I mouth *sell it*, but she rolls her eyes.

"That might be the price on the winder but whadaya take fer the truck?"

A thousand. Tell him a thousand right here, right now, but not tomorrow.

"Maybe twelve hundred." She turns and points to me. "But it's up to Candie. She's the boss while Daddy's laid up."

I stop sweeping and my eyebrows shoot up. When I give her a since-when-am-I-the-boss look she shrugs and gives me an innocent smile that spells trouble.

Skeeter shoots me a tobacco-stained grin that I guess is supposed to sweeten me up. *Ugh.* With a weak little finger wave I smile back while suppressing a shudder.

"Come on over Candie," Sarah urges. "Say hey to Skeeter."

When I hesitate Sarah motions to me with a frown. As I approach she sidesteps quickly so that I'm in the line of tobacco juice fire.

"You remember my twin sister Candie, don't you Skeeter?"

"Sure do." He scratches his grizzly beard. "Y'all don't look nothin' alike."

Thank you, Captain Obvious, I silently sigh but manage

a polite nod. "So we've been told." A million times. I suppose if I were the pretty one I wouldn't have such a stick up my butt about the whole thing because the comment doesn't seem to bother Sarah.

"Don't sound alike either."

"She took off for the city," Sarah says with a solemn nod as if I ran off with the circus or something.

"Oh yeah, Chee-*cog*-o." Skeeter gives me an oh-so-Pinewood-wasn't-good-enough-for-ya look. "Now I recall. Yer pappy told me. Don't worry, yer twang will come back."

"Oh good, I was worried."

Skeeter laughs and slaps his knee, sending a cloud of dust my way. "You got that dry sense of humor like yer pappy."

"So I'm told." I'm surprised that Skeeter got my sarcasm and I have to grin. This, however, was a mistake since Skeeter takes this as me warming up to him.

"So, did ya eat lots of pizza?"

"Excuse me?"

"In Chee-cog-o."

"Oh . . . yes," I admit, and I have the ten extra pounds to show for it, mostly in my butt. Why can't I ever gain weight in my boobs, yet it's the first place I lose weight?

"Crazy, that Chee-cog-o pizza. Turned all upside down with the sauce on the top. And one danged slice weighs 'bout two pounds."

Skeeter pauses and I realize that I'm supposed to comment but I had zoned out for a minute thinking about my pizza-enhanced butt. Okay—*big*, but *enhanced* sounds better. "Um, oh—me too." I nod for emphasis. "So, Skeeter, what brings you over here tonight?" *Other than to chat about pizza.* "Anything special?" *Like buying a beat-up truck perhaps?*

"Naw, jes lookin'."

Sarah gives me a see-I-told-you deadpan stare and I

get it. He has no intention of buying anything. He just wants some company. *Well . . .* With a lift of my chin I crook one eyebrow at Sarah and dig deep for my best used car sales pitch. "This truck's in pretty good shape."

"Not bad." He kicks the tire again. I never did understand why people do that.

"Everybody could use a truck now and then."

"Yup, I s'pose."

Sarah hides what I know is a smile behind her hand. Okay, so that was lame. I'm a little rusty. I narrow my eyes at her and turn back to Skeeter. It is the ultimate challenge to sell someone something when it's obvious that they're just killing time. Daddy always paid me extra when someone uttered those three ugly little words: *I'm just looking.* Of course Skeeter is truly the ultimate challenge since he hasn't bought a car since 1977!

"Think you might be able to use a nice truck like this one?"

Skeeter shrugs, then spits.

Okay, maybe a truck isn't the answer. Shading my eyes from the setting sun I look around the lot and barely suppress a sigh. The meager inventory that we do have looks worn and shabby. It's sad to see so few cars on the lot but Harley Campbell retired and let his fancy-pants son from up east take over Campbell Motors, a huge new car dealership near the edge of town. Harley always sent his lower-end trade-ins over to us but his snooty son Carson feels the need to keep all of the trade-ins for his own lot and it's putting the hurt on us big time. As if that isn't enough, Sarah's refusal to let Nick Anderson service and detail our stock has really hurt business. Smelly old Smiley Turner just plain sucks.

God, we need this sale.

Putting on my game face, I pat the hood of the old

truck hard enough to get Skeeter's full attention. It hurt a little but I hide my grimace. "Skeeter, I think just about everyone could use a truck now and then. Having another vehicle means that you can keep your Caprice Classic in mint condition. Wouldn't that be nice?"

He doesn't answer but he peers at the truck with narrowed eyes while scratching scraggly whiskers that poke out from his cheeks at odd angles. I take his silence as a yes and my heart pumps harder at the prospect of a sale. "I'm prepared to make you an offer you can't refuse."

Both Sarah and Skeeter look at me. "Okay," I begin but pause as if saying the price pains me, "one thousand. Less than what we have *in* the truck. *Waaaay* under book value."

Scratching and spitting, Skeeter mulls this over while slowly walking around the truck. I give Sarah a smug look but she shakes her head, still a nonbeliever. I arch one eyebrow at her and say to Skeeter, "I'll get the keys so you can take her for a spin. She runs like a top." *I hope.* Without waiting for an answer I go inside and grab the keys off the rack.

With a smile I toss the Budweiser key chain at Skeeter and a moment later he's rumbling off the lot, leaving a cloud of dust. I keep my fingers crossed as the truck chugs out into traffic. "I've got him now," I tell Sarah with much more conviction than I'm feeling.

"I'm *so* sure," she retorts with a snort.

"I do," I insist but my smug smile fades when I hear the old truck backfire as loud as a shotgun.

"You're practically giving the truck away, Candie." She flips her blond hair over her shoulder and turns to me with her hands on her hips.

"We need the money."

Sarah's silence tells me that she can't argue with that. I hesitate before asking her my next question but it's a touchy subject that must be addressed. "The lot is looking pretty shabby, Sarah, don't you think?"

"Carson Campbell is keeping all of his old trade-ins. We don't have much to work with," she complains with a pout. "Too bad he's such a jerk because he's totally hot."

"Really?"

Sarah nods. "I know it's hard to picture since his daddy's built like Boss Hog from *The Dukes of Hazard.*"

"Must take after his mama. Wasn't she some sort of beauty queen or somethin'?"

"Yes, and she did some modeling too. Mama said that Harley met her during one of those big new car conventions. You know, where the skimpily clad models, smiling and waving, sit on the hoods of shiny cars while spinning in a slow circle." Sarah mimics the queenly wave but then steps closer. "Got her pregnant," she says in a stage whisper, "married her and then she up and left him! Went back up East right after Carson was born."

"Sad that Harley never got to know his own son."

"Ill-fated from the start, I guess," Sarah says with a slow nod. "Mama says that she broke Harley's heart."

"Harley's always been such a nice guy too." I shade my eyes and look toward the street, wondering where in the world Skeeter drove off to. I hope the old truck didn't break down. "Guess she was after his money."

"I'd bet my bottom dollar on it."

"So, Carson's hot, huh?"

Sarah wrinkles her nose. "Yeah, but he thinks he's all that and a bag of chips."

"So you haven't tried to talk to him about the situation?"

"Daddy did but it got him nowhere. He said that Carson talked down to him. The jerk."

"Well . . . *you* might be a bit more persuasive."

Sarah lets out her breath in a huff. "Why Candie

Montgomery, are you suggesting that I use my womanly charms?"

"Of course not."

"Right . . ."

After a pause I ask, "Think it could work?"

"Doesn't it always?" she asks with a grin.

"Pretty much." I smile while thinking that Sarah should have gotten the cutie-pie name of Candie instead of little old me. I was named after my aunt Candice but of course no one had ever called me that except when I was living in Chicago. Back here I immediately reverted back to Candie. I notice though that Sarah's eyes seem a bit sad. Some of her confidence isn't quite there and I have to wonder if it has something to do with being dumped by Nick. Sarah had always been the dumper, not the dumpee, making what I'm about to say next even harder to spit out. Nibbling on the inside of my cheek I try to think of a way to word it.

"What?" Sarah asks. Maybe she knows me better than what I give her credit for.

"I was wondering where the hell Skeeter drove off to," I lie. I shade my eyes and look toward the street.

"Bull. You want to ask me about Nick."

I raise my eyebrows. Maybe we're finally getting that special twin connection thing. "Have you tried talkin' this out with him?"

"Not really." Pursing her lips Sarah leans up against a red Escort. "But I totally get it that he wants me to be more like you. Like I haven't heard that one before."

"Maybe you were just too high maintenance," I joke to lighten the mood but she doesn't even crack a smile.

"I've thought about that," she surprisingly admits. "Nick is pretty low-key and I can be a royal pain."

"Ya think?" I grin and this time Sarah smiles.

"Shut up!" She chuckles but then sobers. "Nick didn't talk to you about all of this did he?"

"No, I haven't spoken to Nick since Christmas."

"Well, keep it that way. I plan on holding this grudge until the day I die."

"Well . . . I need to talk to you about that."

Sarah pushes away from the Escort. "Oh, don't you dare say it! We are *so* not going to hire him back."

"But Sarah, Smiley sucks. The cars look worn and shabby. We need Nick to fix up our sorry excuse for inventory."

"No *way*!"

"Take a hard look around." I wave my arm in an arc. "If we don't do something soon we might lose this place."

"Oh come on. Daddy owns the dealership. He could sell this corner lot and make a small fortune."

"Is that what you want?"

She sighs and her shoulders slump. "Of course not."

"It would break Daddy's heart and his heart can't take that right now." I put my hands on her shoulders and make her straighten up. "We need to take control of the situation. Daddy always provided for us and now it's up to you and me to whip this dealership back into shape."

"But Candie, I can't talk to Nick!" Her eyes well up with tears.

"You have to."

"No! I'll either burst into tears or slap him. Maybe both. I don't think that will get the job done, do you?"

Dropping my hands from her shoulders, I reluctantly shake my head since I know what she's going to suggest.

"You do it. He always listens to you. Candie, he might even tell you things that could help make sense of the whole thing."

"I won't go there, Sarah. I really *don't* want to talk to Nick, but if I do, it will be strictly business."

"I understand that you must be mad at him for what he did to me too. I know it'll be difficult. The only saving grace in this whole thing is that he's sorta being shunned too. Hasn't helped his business any, that's for sure."

"Oh . . . really?"

With a smug smile Sarah nods.

"That seems a bit harsh."

Her eyes widen. "You're defending him?"

"No, but I don't wish him harm."

"Well, you're *gonna* find out the whole story," she says firmly, "or we're not hiring him back."

"Hmmm, I thought you told Skeeter that I was the boss."

"In an effort to sell the danged truck. Where's the old coot anyway?"

"Good question." We both peer toward the street just in time to see Nick Anderson locking the front door of Anderson Automotive located kitty-corner to our lot. He doesn't even glance our way but I get the feeling that he knows we're standing there.

"Jackass," Sarah mutters and turns her back to him.

"Maybe if you'd just confront him, you could work this out."

"I'll confront him, all right—with my fist."

I barely refrain from rolling my eyes. "Sarah, I can't promise I'll find out any answers for you but I'll talk to Nick about detailing our inventory."

"But you'll try, right? Come on, Candie. You're my sister. My *twin*. We have a special bond. We—"

"Enough!" I raise my hands in surrender. "I get the point. Look, I'll do my best but in return you have to approach Carson Campbell about sending some cars our way, okay?"

"Deal. But *you* have to interface with Nick. I refuse."

"Fair enough," I tell her even though I really don't want to have any close contact with the man who used

me as a lame reason for breaking up with my sister. I'll
do it though, because I love this car lot and I love my
family. Dealing with him will be strictly business and
it won't bother me in the least, I tell myself, even
though deep down I know that my feelings for Nick
are more complicated than that. God, how I've missed
him . . .

"Candie, you okay?"

"Huh? Sure, why do you ask?"

"You suddenly looked so sad. Is everything all
right? Hey, did some dude dump you in Chicago? You
know I'm beginning to think that all guys are jerks.
Every last one of them. Well, except for Daddy. Who
needs 'em, huh?"

"Right, who needs them?" I jump on this band-
wagon to make her feel better but Tommy's handsome
face comes to mind.

She gives me a I-know-how-you're-feeling nod.
"Well, I'm here for you. That's what sisters are for. You
know that you can tell me anything, right?"

I simply nod because I'm too choked up to answer.

"Hey," Sarah says pointing to the street, "here
comes Skeeter."

"You still think I can't sell him that old truck?" I am
glad to change the focus of our conversation.

"Maybe you can with me helping. We'll tag team
him. Skeeter's not walkin' off this lot without the keys
in his grimy hand."

I give Sarah a high five. "That's the spirit we need.
Let's go do this *thang*."

4

Where's the Beef?

I wash down a bite of juicy cheeseburger with a big swallow of Cherry Coke. "You were great, Sarah," I gush, and take another bite of my celebratory sandwich at Biscuits and Burgers, the best little diner in the whole world—well, my world anyway—telling myself that our first sale deserves a few extra calories. Of course if we had missed the sale we would have deserved a few extra calories too. It's just the way my brain works and why I'll never be skinny.

Sarah waves me off but then smiles. "Yeah, we made a pretty good team. Skeeter didn't stand a chance."

Neither of us mentions that we ended up selling him the truck for nine hundred and fifty dollars over the curb meaning tax, title, and everything.

"I can't believe the old coot actually bought something. Daddy will get such a kick out of this."

"I know! That's the best part of this whole thing. The doctors said that Daddy would suffer some depression after the operation. This should put a smile on his face."

Sarah drinks a sip of her water—yeah, *water*—and

then scoops up a dainty spoonful of soup that doesn't even have meat in it.

"Where's the beef?" I ask with a nod toward her cup. A bowl would have been too much to eat.

"I don't eat much meat," she says primly. "Just a little fish and chicken here and there."

"Oh." I notice, though, that she's looking at my onion rings with longing. "Oh, for heaven's sake, have one." I slide my plate across the faded blue Formica. "Sneak a bite of the burger while you're at it. I'll even glance away while you do it."

Sarah looks at me like I just asked her to take a taste of something dead or slimy as on *Fear Factor*. "But they're *deep fried*. I don't do deep fried either."

"One onion ring and a bite of the burger won't hurt."

"Oh . . . okaaaaay." She picks up the juicy burger and sinks her teeth into the soft, buttered bun, closes her eyes, and does this throaty little moan, drawing a look from the table of Red Hat Ladies sitting directly across from us. After licking some mayo from her thumb, she takes another bite, a bigger one this time, and does the moaning thing again, only a tad louder. "God, this is so *good*." By this time all six of the Red Hat Ladies are looking at us from beneath their big brims.

"Sarah," I whisper and give the ladies a small smile. "Get a grip. People are starin'."

"I can't. This is amazing. It's been so long since I've had one. Mmmmm. So thick and juicy . . . even better than I remembered."

The waitress comes over to the Red Hat table and asks, "What'll it be, ladies?"

The one with the big floppy straw hat points to Sarah and says, "Mercy me, I'll have what she's havin'."

"Me *too*," says a little bitty lady next to her and

slaps her knee. The rest of the red hats bob up and down and then they all burst out laughing.

God, how embarrassing. "Sarah, give me my burger back," I hiss, and grab the plate.

"No, I want to keep it. You can have my soup." She keeps a death grip on my plate with one hand and shoves her wimpy cup my way, sloshing a green bean over the edge. "Here."

The soup smells pretty good even minus the meat, so I don't really mind but I put a protective hand around my Cherry Coke, lean forward, and whisper, "Fine, but quit your moaning, will ya? It sounded like you were having a danged *orgasm*. How doggone long has it been anyway?"

"I don't know . . . years, I guess."

"Years? You're kiddin' me."

"Wait, we're talking about the cheeseburger, right?"

"Yes!"

She toys with the saltshaker, examining the yellowed rice in the bottom. "I wish I had more courage like you."

"Courage?" Color me confused. An exceptionally brave person, I'm not.

"Yeah. I would never have had the guts to go off to Chicago and experience the big city life like you did. You've always done what you've wanted and never cared what people thought."

"Did people think poorly of me for leaving Pinewood?"

"'Course not," she says but fiddles with the ketchup bottle instead of looking at me.

"Did Daddy?" I ask softly. Guilt washes over me, hot and strong. Sarah's wrong about me not caring what people think. I always aim to please. "Look at me, Sarah."

She takes a sip of water and then finally gazes across the table at me. "It's no secret that Mama and I always clicked . . . and that you were Daddy's girl, Candie. I won't lie. Daddy missed you but he wanted you to be happy even if that meant living in Chicago. I just don't think he ever quite understood since you loved working at the car lot but he never held it against you."

Of course my eyes well up with tears.

Sarah yanks some paper napkins from the metal container and thrusts them at me. "Now don't you *dare* go thinkin' that his heart problems had anything to do with you. He ate all the wrong things, even though Mama scolded him, and sneaked his cigars when she wasn't around. He didn't get enough exercise and age just caught up with him. He always was a live wire in perpetual motion like you. Daddy needed to slow down and take care of his health but he was stubborn."

I dab at the corners of my eyes. "But if I had been here . . ."

"It wouldn't have made a bit of difference. Look, you're here now and that's all that matters." She reaches over and pats my hand.

I nod slowly, wondering if I should buy what she's selling.

"Oh quit," she says making four syllables out of two.

"Quit what?" God, I realize that I just did the same thing.

"Lookin' all sad and guilty," she says gently but just when it appears as if she's getting all choked up she gives me her sassy little head bop. "Now don't you go thinkin' that the world stopped spinnin' just because you left Pinewood. We got on just fine and dandy without you."

"Did not."

Sarah grins. "Okay, maybe not the dandy part." She picks up an onion ring and shakes it at me. "But we were *fine.* Well, fine until Daddy got sick, I fired Nick, and that jerk Carson blew into town. Now we're not so fine. Candie, what are we gonna do?"

"We're gonna take the bull by the horns." I snag the last onion ring. "Hey, we sold Skeeter a truck. If we can do that we can do anything, right?"

"Right!" Sarah bangs her fists on the table so hard that the silverware jangles and the Red Hat Ladies look our way again. I give them a reassuring smile but they seem unhappy that their cheeseburgers aren't having the same effect on them that they had on Sarah.

"Maybe it was the onion rings," a Red Hatter comments. "We shoulda ordered some of those."

"They make me toot," the little bitty one answers. "Coulda been the condiments that gave her such extreme pleasure."

The one at the far end of the table with the purple flower in the middle of her wide brim says, "Did you say condoms? Lordy Bea, what would you need with a condom? You're way past the birthin' age. Course those glow in the dark ones are a hoot." She claps her hands together. "Mercy, me"

"You mean ole Bert can still stand at attention?" the little bitty one asks and all the red hats turn in her direction. "You lucky dog."

Sarah kicks me under the table and she jerks her head toward the door, but I'm curious in a weird way so I continue to listen.

Bea sighs. "All I can say is that Bob Dole was right. That little blue pill works wonders. Makes Bert's wanker stand right up. Why, one night he took two by mistake because he forgot he swallowed the first one, and by God he—"

"Candie!" Sarah hisses with her eyes wide and her lips twitching, "Pul-ease!"

Understanding, I grab the check and stand up. After

paying we hurry outside, hop in the old Jeep we took from the lot, and then dissolve into a fit of laughter.

"Oh my gawd," Sarah says, laughing so hard that she can't get the key in the ignition. She weakly leans against the battered bucket seat. "I don't know old Bert but I had this picture in my head of his glow in the dark—what did she call it?"

"Wanker," I supply laughing so hard that I snort. I never could control the snort. It just comes out.

"I had to get out of there before I lost it!" Sarah laughs so hard that she wheezes. "Oh, I think I'm gonna pee my pants!"

"They were cute though, weren't they?"

Sarah wipes a tear from the corner of her eye and finally manages to start the engine and flick on the headlights. "Yeah they were. But want to know the sad thing?"

"What?"

"They're having more sex than we are. I haven't seen a wanker, glow in the dark or otherwise, for a while." After looking both ways she eases out into traffic. "Have you?"

"Sarah!"

"Oh come on. Spill. We're sisters. You *have* to share. Did you have a Coyote Ugly night or anything?"

"Yeah right, I would have been hard-pressed to find someone ugly in the fancy martini bars downtown. It was the land of designer clothes and perfect teeth. Truth is I never really fit in."

Sarah gives me a sideways glance but remains silent.

"What?"

"You sure look like you could fit in with your sophisticated hair and polished ways. What the hell happened to your natural curls?"

"I tame them with a flatiron and a little bit of

product." I reach up and touch my pencil-straight, shoulder-length bob. "Don't you like my hair?"

Sarah shrugs. "I always thought your curls were cute. The highlights are pretty, though. And I like how it's stacked in the back and angles toward your face."

"I hear a but."

"Okay, but you're a Southern chick and you should have big hair. You need your accent back too. It's only right."

Sarah says this so seriously that I have to laugh. "My hair will get big on rainy days no matter how flat I iron it and I've already said *y'all* twice today."

"Humph," she grumbles and reaches up to fluff her own big tresses. She suddenly snaps her fingers. "Hey, I know what'll put the redneck back in ya."

"A MoonPie?" I ask hopefully.

"A longneck and a game of pool over at Pete's Pub. Whadaya say? I'll let you choose the first song on the jukebox. Come on, let's blow off a little steam and have some fun."

When she gives me her hopeful pout I can't resist. "Oh okay. *One* beer," I warn holding up my index finger. "I want to get up early tomorrow and visit Daddy before work."

"Sweet!" When we stop for a red light she looks my way. "Say, are you okay livin' in that two-family? If not, you're welcome to move in with me."

"It's a little rough around the edges," I admit, "but I promised Daddy to do some painting and gardening to spiff up the place a bit in exchange for the rent. Plus, it's so close to the car lot that I could walk if I wanted to."

"Well, the offer stands. If you're wondering if I'm still a slob, the answer is no . . . well, not as bad as I used to be anyway. My cooking has improved since I *thought* I was going to be cookin' for Nick. I'm a big Rachael Ray fan."

"Thirty minute quick and easy meals?"

"You're a fan too?"

"Yep. I love the Food Network."

"Cooking is something you and Mama had in common," Sarah comments as she pulls the Jeep into a graveled parking lot shared by Pete's Pub and Gayle's Glamorous Nails. "I still pretty much suck but I'm improving."

"Instead of cookin', I'd like to have the *Take Home Chef* Curtis Stone whip me up a fancy meal," I comment as we pick our way over the lumpy parking lot. I'm wishing that I had on tennis shoes or boots instead of these dressy mules. My khaki slacks and pale blue oxford shirt aren't exactly Pete's Pub attire either but since we're only popping in, I'm not too concerned about how I look. Sarah is a bit more casual in Dockers and a pink golf shirt but in Pete's you really need boots, jeans, and a tight T-shirt to fit into the crowd.

"I'd like that spiky-haired chef to do more than cook for me," Sarah says with a grin. "Like *be* the dessert. Might require a little whipped cream . . ."

"Sarah!"

"Hey, I'm just sayin' . . ."

"His Aussie accent is kind of a turn on," I admit.

"And those eyes!" Sarah gushes as she opens the door to the pub.

"Oh I know!" I reply loudly so as to be heard over the music.

"Are we hard up and horny or what?" Sarah asks just as loudly and as luck would have it the music stops, making her comment heard loud and clear to a couple of guys standing near the door.

"There's a cure for that," none other than Tommy Tucker says, looking yummy in his Wranglers and cowboy hat. Of course I want to die with embarrassment.

"Oh shut up, Tommy," Sarah shoots back. "We're not *that* hard up."

Speak for yourself, I think but thank God refrain from saying it.

Tommy chuckles, flashing white teeth, and then turns to me. "Hey there, *girlfriend.*" He snags me around the waist and pulls me close. "You come in here for a Diet Coke?" Tommy teases before giving me a light peck on the cheek.

"A Coke?" Sarah says. "What's up with that?"

Tommy and I exchange a look and laugh.

This of course doesn't go unnoticed by Sarah. I also suddenly realize that other people in the bar are also looking our way with interest. I had forgotten about the whole shunning thing and there are a few people shooting daggers at me.

Sarah must have noticed it too and gives me an apologetic look. "Sorry some people are givin' you the evil eye," she whispers in my ear. "The fact that we're in here together will help smooth things over. I'll smile at you a lot." Pulling back she gives me a big smile that unfortunately looks totally fake. This seems to make matters worse since more people are looking our way and not one person is waving or smiling in my direction.

Tommy must be feeling the vibe because his arm tightens around me. I kinda like that.

"Sarah," I hiss in her ear, "get the silly smile off your face!"

"Why?" she asks with the clown smile still in place.

"Because it doesn't look real."

"It isn't," she says back in my ear. "I'm suddenly nervous as hell. I'd forgotten that everyone would be lookin' at us. Makes me want to pee my pants."

"Right, easy for you to say," I hiss back. "I'm the evil twin, not you!"

Great. Now it looks like we're fighting.

"Why don't I get you ladies a beer," Tommy offers.

"Okay," we say in unison.

"Bud Lights?" he asks.

"Heineken," I reply and grin when Sarah's eyes widen.

"Just kiddin'. A Bud Light sounds good."

Tommy chuckles and seems to appreciate that I'm trying to lighten the mood. "Coming right up."

"Lord, for a minute there I thought we had lost you to Yuppieville. Don't scare me like that."

"I have found that a martini hits the spot once in a while," I admit.

"Eew, like with olives?"

I wrinkle my nose. "No, the girlie kind like chocolate is my favorite. I look around and acknowledge that except for a couple of flat-screen TVs suspended from the wall, Pete's Pub hasn't changed one bit. Battered round tables with equally worn chairs flank one side of the room with the long wooden bar running the length of the other. There are a couple of ancient pinball machines in one corner and a dartboard in the other. To the rear of the bar is a separate room with three pool tables that always have a wait.

I'm still glancing around but I pause and look through the doorway to the back billiard room when a tall, jean-lad guy bends over to shoot some pool. "My, *my*, that is quite simply the nicest butt I've ever laid eyes on," I mention to Sarah.

"Yeah, well that amazing butt belongs to a big ass."

"Okay, that didn't make an iota of sense." I flick a glance at Sarah before my gaze is drawn back to the butt. Angling my head I suddenly notice that the jeans are sporting a designer label. Guys from around here wear Wranglers or Levi's. "Don't tell me."

"Yep. That's none other than Carson Campbell." Sarah spits his name out as though it's something vile and yet I notice that her eyes are glued to his fine form as well.

Carson straightens up and turns so I can view his profile. "Wow." He's handsome in a Rob Lowe almost too perfect way and although he's dazzling to look at I prefer men who are a little rougher around the edges like Tommy. Someone a bit more . . . "Holy crap." I give Sarah a nudge when Nick Anderson walks into our line of vision. Her eyes narrow and her lips thin, making me more than a bit nervous.

Nick is standing there with one hand casually wrapped around his cue stick while Carson takes his shot. Tall like Carson but more muscular, Nick is definitely no pretty boy. Not that he's not handsome, because he sure is, but in a rugged, should-be-chopping-wood, fixing-a-truck, or tossing-a-football kinda way. I turn to Sarah. The look on her face has me saying, "Let's get outta here."

"Not before I get my beer."

"Forget the beer!"

"I'm thirsty!"

"Well, then chug-a-lug!"

"I can't chug a beer."

"Wuss. Bet I can finish mine before you," I challenge.

Sarah rolls her eyes. "You're just trying to get me outta here without a scene."

"Uh, *yeah*. Unless you think you can stay without creating one."

"Does throwing my drink in Nick's face qualify?"

"Yes, I do believe it falls in that category."

When Tommy comes back we both grab the cold brown bottles. "We're in a bit of a rush," I hastily explain and then say to Sarah, "Okay then. Go!"

Sarah tips her bottle back and starts some pretty impressive chugging. I watch openmouthed for a second before tipping my own bottle up to my lips. I guzzle the icy cold beer, ignoring the brain freeze and the bubble in my tummy that threatens to send the beer back up. I'm an athlete though and while this isn't exactly a sport, except maybe on college campuses, the competitor in me has me winning even though Sarah had a head start. I thump the bottle down on a nearby table while Sarah is still choking her beer down. To her credit she finishes without coming up for air.

"I win!"

"You shoulda told me it was a race," Tommy jokes but he's looking at me as though I'm a bit crazy.

"Now, let's go before they see us," I urge while blinking from the brain freeze coupled with the sudden blast of alcohol to my system. I notice that Sarah is blinking too.

"Give me a minute," she pleads with a discreet little burp behind her hand.

"No! Let's go before we have to deal with a scene!" I turn to Tommy and say, "Sorry."

"Don't worry, I get it." He looks down at me with those blue eyes of his and suddenly I'm reluctant to leave. As if reading my mind he says, "Judging by the look on your sister's face this could get ugly, so you'd better hightail it outta here. I'll be calling you."

I nod and then ease up to my tiptoes to give him an impulsive kiss. "Yes, please do. I think I'm gonna need an ear to bend."

I grab Sarah by the hand and tug but as we sort of wobble out of Pete's Pub I can't resist a look back at Tommy, which is a mistake because at that same moment Nick looks my way. Our gazes lock for just an instant and it hits me hard how much I've missed him.

When we're outside I pause to take a deep breath of warm summer air.

"Hey, are you okay?" Sarah asks with a frown of concern.

"Yeah, I guess. I'm just not used to chugging a beer."

Sarah nods and I'm relieved that she buys my explanation, which is much better than telling her that it was seeing Nick that set my stomach churning. When we reach the Jeep she says, "Thanks for getting me outta there, Candie. I didn't want to cause a scene by dumping my drink on my ex. I've already given this town enough to gossip about."

"It's no biggie."

She looks at me from across the hood of the Jeep. "You know, Candie, I never really did fully understand your need to leave Pinewood but I'm glad that you're back. I'd never be able to save Daddy's car dealership without you."

Pointing my finger at her I say, "Hey, don't go sellin' yourself short. You're much more capable than you realize."

"You think?" She gives me an uncharacteristically shy smile and I think to myself that she isn't nearly as self-assured as I once thought.

"Naw, it's just the beer talkin'," I joke but smile back at her.

"Better than a martini though, huh?"

"You got that right!" I admit as I open the door to the old Jeep. I might have my work cut out for me and it sure is going to be tough approaching Nick, but *damn* it's good to finally be back home.

5

One Way or Another...

The cheerful chirping of birds outside my bedroom window slowly awakens me. Since my alarm clock hasn't yet buzzed I keep my eyes shut and savor the gentle sounds of the countryside instead of horns blaring and sirens wailing. Sunlight tries to tease my eyes open but I resist and snuggle beneath the covers, letting my mind drift between sleeping and wakefulness.

Of course letting my mind wander means that I don't really have any control over the images that filter through my brain. Without warning Tommy's handsome face comes into view and I'm hoping that he'll call today. "Well hells bells, I might as well just get up," I grumble and open my eyes.

For a moment I blink in the sudden brightness, making a mental note to purchase some miniblinds for the bare windows. After tossing back the sheet I swing my legs over the side of the bed and let my feet hit the sun-warmed hardwood floor. Yawning and stretching in my Tweety Bird sleep shirt, I make a beeline for the kitchen to start some coffee.

While the coffee is gurgling and sending a delicious aroma curling through the house, I hop into the shower. Frowning at the wimpy stream of water trickling over me, I add a new showerhead to my growing list of things that I need. As I towel-dry my hair I rehearse in my head what I'm going to say to Nick, knowing that if I don't my brain might fail me when I finally come face-to-face with the man who blamed me for his breakup with my sister. "Just keep your cool," I tell my reflection in the steamed up mirror. "You've known Nick Anderson most of your life and he's your friend. You can surely do this."

"Talkin' to yourself?"

With a little squeal of fright I let go of my towel and whirl around to face Sarah. "You scared the daylights outta me!"

"Sorry!" she says but I can tell by her lips twitching that she's not.

"Sure you are," I grumble. "How'd you get in here anyway?" Locking my doors had become a habit while living in the city.

"I have a key."

"Didn't you think of knockin'?"

"I di-id," she says in a singsong Southern tone, "but you didn't answer. I figured you were in the shower so I let myself in." She holds up a white paper bag and waves it beneath my nose.

"Ohmigod."

"Yep," she says with a smug nod, "I have two cheese Danish from Pat's Bakery. I had her give me the two biggest ones with the most icing."

"She didn't spit on mine, did she?"

"No, I watched real careful," she says in a serious tone but then laughs. "There's already buzz goin' on about you and Tommy Tucker. Just pour us some coffee and enjoy."

I groan. "I used to dream of those and her sugar cookies with the yellow smiley faces painted on them.

Remember Mama would bring them home whenever she went into town to have her hair done?"

Sarah nods. "Yeah, we'd eat the M&M eyes off first. You get dressed and I'll pour the coffee. Oh, and I also came to tell you that Mama called me and said that she's taking Daddy for a checkup this mornin' so you shouldn't drop in until tonight."

"Oh, okay . . ."

"Hey now, don't give me that look. Mama tried to call *you* but you didn't pick up."

My eyes widen because she's reading my mind.

"Duh, we are twins, Candie."

Okay, now she's reading my mind that she's reading my mind! I wag my finger at her. "Don't go thinkin' you can read my thoughts."

She gives me a deadpan look.

"Okay you read *that* one. Lucky guess."

"What*ever*. That coffee sure smells good and strong."

"Is there any other way?"

"Not in my book. Hurry it up."

"You can start eating your Danish without me," I offer while brushing my wet hair away from my face.

"No way. I want to savor them together. Allowing myself a treat like this isn't an everyday thing."

I raise my eyebrows at her in the mirror. "You mean to tell me that you have Pat's Bakery at your disposal and you don't take advantage? That's just not right."

"I don't burn off the calories like I did in high school, Candie."

I sigh while giving my pizza-enhanced butt a pat. "I hear ya. I'm gonna need to start joggin' again. I hated to run in the city. I can't wait to get out into the fresh air. You want to run with me?"

Sarah scrunches up her nose. "You know I never was much into that runnin' stuff but if you keep me eatin' all of this fattening food I might have to start."

"Hey, you're the one who brought the pastries!"

"On account of *you*!"

I shake my head so hard that water droplets spray her way. "You have the strangest way of lookin' at things."

"It's called justification. You're not so bad at it yourself." She gives me that parting shot as she wiggles her annoyingly tiny butt out of the bathroom. I'm not quite sure what she was getting at with that comment but she wasn't far off the mark. Instead of getting dressed I slip on a terrycloth robe, not wanting Sarah to see me taking extra pains with my appearance, which I know I'll do even if I tell myself not to. When a Southern woman goes to meet a man, it's just something you do no matter what.

"Hey, you started without me!"

"I couldn't help myself. You know I don't have much willpower just like with the doggone burger last night. Mercy, they're good."

I plop down into a wooden chair at the little round table in the small but cute kitchen and sink my teeth into the soft pastry, mindful to take a bite big enough to get some of the cream cheese filling. "Mmmmm!" I wiggle my eyebrows since my mouth is too full of heaven to comment. Sarah nods her agreement and I have to smile when she starts eating the outside first, leaving the filling for last just like she did when we were kids. It's nice to know that some things never change.

"What?" Sarah asks when she sees my grin.

"I never did understand why you do that."

"I like to save the best for last."

We both pause for a gulp of coffee and then eat the rest of our breakfast in relative silence. I suspect we're both thinking about the tasks ahead of us. After wiping the crumbs from my mouth with a paper napkin from the bird-shaped holder I ask, "When are you plannin' to pay a visit to Carson Campbell?"

"Later." She flips her hair over her shoulder and avoids my gaze.

"Later . . . *when*?" With most people, later would mean in a little while but with Sarah, later can translate into next week, a month from now, or never. When she fidgets but doesn't reply I narrow my eyes at her.

"What?"

"Don't tell me that you're intimidated by Carson Campbell."

"Of course not," she sputters but then sighs. "Okay . . . maybe a little bit."

"Why?"

Cradling her coffee mug she leans forward. "Candie, he's educated and—and *citified*."

"That doesn't make him better than you."

She gives me a wary look.

"Hey, since when aren't you confident?" I'm sort of teasing but Sarah doesn't smile.

"Since high school I guess, but even then it was more of an act than anything." She gives me a small smile at my obvious surprise. "Unlike you, Candie, I always relied upon my looks."

I'm trying to decide if that was a compliment or not but prompt her to go on.

"After I hung up my pom-poms I was no longer the queen bee. The huge college campus terrified me, which I suppose is why I clung to Nick. He was solid and familiar and still treated me as though I was special when I pretty much felt invisible."

My heart lurches at her unexpected confession. "But you were in a sorority and all that . . ."

Sarah shrugs. "I was one of many. I wish now that I had concentrated on my studies."

"You could always go back, you know."

"It's about time I started moving forward."

"That's not what I meant."

She laughs, lifting the mood. "I suppose I could go to one of those community colleges and take some business courses like you did."

I have to groan. "It was boring as hell."

"But it taught you some skills."

After downing the dregs of my coffee I nod. "True but I would have loved to have experienced campus life."

"I guess we always want what we don't have."

"Yeah, I suppose," I agree.

Sarah sets her coffee mug down. "What? You look . . . wistful or somethin'." How can I tell her that I miss Nick? She lost a fiancé but I lost a friend.

"I do not." Okay, Sarah's insight into my feelings is starting to make me feel uncomfortable, so of course I have to dispute her.

"Do too. Like you're *longing* or whatever."

"What I'm longing for is some new inventory, Sister Sarah."

"Don't call me that! It makes me feel like a nun."

"Now just how would you know what a nun feels like?" I ask as I scoot back from the table.

Sarah gets up too. "Well I ain't gettin' none, that's for sure."

We both laugh and after Sarah sets her mug in the sink she gives me a quick hug. "I know I've already said that I'm glad that you're back but I'm sayin' it again."

"Yeah, yeah, you're just tryin' to butter me up so I'll go to see Nick first, givin' you time to muster up the gumption to visit Carson Campbell."

"You know me too well," she jokes, but I can tell by her expression that she's serious. "I'll open up the car lot while you go over to Nick's shop." She glances down at her watch. "He should be arrivin' in about half an hour."

Frowning, I glance at the digital numbers on the microwave. "It's only seven thirty."

"Yeah well, Nick's been soupin' up some old truck of his. Arrives early and stays late. Sometimes I wonder if he even goes home." She wrinkles her nose and gives me a bitter-ex face. "Not that I care," she grumbles but then holds up one palm. "Nope, I'm not goin' there." But after putting her hand on the kitchen doorknob she turns back to me. "Hey, what should I wear to visit Carson Campbell?"

I raise my eyebrows. "You really want my opinion?"

Sarah rolls her eyes. "Didn't I just ask for it? I'm thinkin' that I want more of a business look instead of the bimbo-boobs-in-his-face approach."

"Good for you, Sarah. Wear a conservative summer suit. Maybe a pale yellow or light blue."

She blinks at me.

"You don't have a conservative suit, do you?"

"Um . . . no." She nibbles on the inside of her lip for a moment and then says, "I'll use my lunch break to go to the mall."

"Good idea. Oh and Sarah? Maybe pull your hair back in a sleek ponytail."

She looks at me as though I've just asked her to shave her head but I ignore her shocked expression and turn around to show her what I mean. With my hand curled around my damp hair that's rapidly curling I say, "About right here. Pulled back tight. It's the new bun—conservative yet a little more modern."

She gives me a disbelieving frown.

"It was the look in Chicago."

"Okaaaay," she finally says with a slow nod but then her shoulders sort of slump. "Maybe you should do this, Candie. I just don't think I can pull it off."

"Oh . . . *horse pucky!*"

Sarah gives me a small smile. "I haven't heard that

one since Daddy's been laid up. Your redneck ways are coming back. Along with your curly hair."

I reach up to touch my hair and encounter a springy curl. "How about this. I'll keep the curls at least for today if you do the sleek ponytail."

"Oh all right," she glumly agrees.

"And understate your makeup."

"You're killin' me."

"You can wear a silk and lace cami beneath your suit. Be sure that some lace peeks out just to keep Carson a little off kilter. This way you'll be businesslike but feminine too."

"Now you're talkin'." She taps her finger against her cheek. "Sort of like a sneak attack."

"Yes, like that," I answer even though I'm not sure what she means.

Sarah arches one neatly plucked and lined eyebrow. "You're much more savvy than I thought. Now *you* go rehire Nick," she tells me but narrows her eyes and continues, "but tell him not to come near me if he knows what's good for him."

"And what's good for him?"

"Damned if I know but I guess it wasn't *me.* Sounded badass though, didn't it?" With that parting comment Sarah swings the door open and leaves. I stand there a minute and have to wonder just what really went wrong between Sarah and Nick and how I figure into it. Was I just an excuse for Nick to break up with Sarah or does he have feelings for me?

"If you're not good for Nick, then just who is?" I whisper.

"You?" a voice rings out in my head but I silence it as I head for the bathroom. There might have been a time when I would have explored having deeper feelings for Nick but not after he declared his love for Sarah. I do, however, miss his friendship something fierce. With a sigh I stare at my curly hair in the medicine cabinet mirror and wish that I hadn't made that deal with Sarah. The curls make my blond hair that almost brushes my shoulders shrink up to nearly chin length. For some reason this seems to make my blue eyes appear bigger and give me a softer, more vulnerable look than I want to present. The next big question of course is what to wear. The white slacks I try on make my butt look too big, so I opt for black ones but then decide that they will be too hot on the car lot later on. Pushing through my closet I spot a summer skirt. Nope, my legs aren't tanned enough and my toenails need polish.

"Okay, *enough*. You're being ridiculous," I grumble under my breath. I remind myself that I'm not trying to attract Nick . . . and then it sort of hits me that maybe I do have some romantic feelings for him. When we were kids growing up our families had been close and although Nick and I had always shared a love of sports and cars, he had always treated me like a buddy . . .

Not that I hadn't daydreamed once or twice about what it might be like to kiss him.

I toss the skirt down on my bed with a sigh. The only time I had ever come close to getting a kiss was this past Christmas when he gave me a light peck beneath the mistletoe. And then *dang*, he had quickly backed away as if I had bad breath or something, which couldn't have been true since I had just eaten a bite of a candy cane, thank the Lord. Still, the incident had left me with the lasting impression that having his lips brush mine had been a distasteful experience for him.

Color me confused but if Nick Anderson thinks he can get away without explaining himself, then he can think again. I would never admit this to Sarah but today I'm going to get some answers. I can be quite intimidating when I want to, I tell myself . . . okay probably not, but I do plan on getting an explanation out of him.

With that in mind I tug on my basic khakis and a white, sleeveless scoop-necked shirt but add a pale blue blazer so I appear more businesslike. I turn to the oval mirror above the pretty cherry dresser that Mama dug up somewhere and give myself the once-over. This leads to wishing I were taller, my butt smaller, and that my lips weren't as puffy. I know that puffy lips are popular but I've always hated mine.

I remind myself that Tommy seemed to find my mouth appealing but I've always thought that my eyes and mouth were too big for my face, so I never played my features up with much makeup and that holds true for today. Reaching up I fluff my curls, totally wishing I had straightened my hair. "Stupid deal," I mutter as I turn away from the mirror. "Sarah better have her hair in a doggone ponytail!"

Stomping around the room in a bit of a tiff I know that I'm being unreasonable and getting all worked up over nothing but it takes my mind off the fact that I'll be face-to-face with Nick in just a little while. Anger feels more powerful than fear . . . well, I'm not really afraid, more like nervous as hell. After taking a deep breath I think of my daddy and what getting Nick working for us again will mean for the car lot and force myself to just suck it up. With that in mind, I grab my purse and head out the door.

6

Old Habits Die Hard

Because Sarah had dropped me off last night I have to walk to Nick's, but I don't mind since it's only around the block and down to the corner of Oak and Main. It's rush hour if you can call it that since hurrying in Pinewood means going slightly faster than slow. Horns honking are pretty much in friendly greeting rather than road rage and I'm happy that I even get a wave or two. Thank you Tommy Tucker, I think to myself and smile softly.

I slow my own pace while silently rehearsing my come-back-to-work-for-us speech. Hefting my purse higher onto my shoulder I take a deep breath and walk up to Anderson Automotive. My heart is already pounding hard when I open the door to his office. The bell over the door jingles but Nick's nowhere in sight. I give it a minute or two and then, while blowing out a sigh of relief, I'm about to turn and leave when I hear a loud clank followed by a muffled curse. The big metal door behind the counter leads to the repair shop and even though I know Nick must be in there I take a step backward.

I know it's stupid, but I'm rapidly losing my nerve.

After staring at the gray door I take another deep breath, march right around the counter, and push open the heavy door. The familiar smells of rubber tires and motor oil make me smile. The place is as neat as a pin and as clean as a garage can be. I notice that not much has changed since I used to bring inventory over for Nick to detail. I still don't see him but my eyes are drawn to a deep blue Ford Ranger with orange flames flicking down the side. Missing a front bumper and side mirrors the truck is obviously a work in progress but very cool nonetheless.

Looking down I see two brown work boots and frayed jeans peeking out from beneath the back of the truck. Why this hits me as sexy I'll never know but I guess it's knowing what's in them. I walk around to the other side of the souped-up truck and see the top of Nick's dark head. My stomach does a nervous flip and I'm thinking that I should just go when I bump into a big red toolbox taller than me and make all kinds of racket.

"Bailey's that you? I need that socket wrench. Will ya hand it to me?" Nick sticks his hand out from beneath the truck.

I glance at the wrench and then over to his outstretched hand and swallow. Walking closer I pick up the tool, kneel down, and place it in his hand.

"Thanks, Bailey. Thought you weren't coming over today."

"Um . . . Nick, it's not Bailey." Whoever that is. "It's Candie."

"What?" He drops the wrench and bangs his head on the truck. "Ouch!"

"You okay?"

"Yeah," he says while rolling the creeper from beneath the truck. While rubbing his forehead he looks up at me. "This is a surprise."

"Good or bad?" I ask, but then wish I hadn't. We always used to tease one another but because of the situation we're in it feels . . . *awkward.*

Nick gives me a measuring look that I can't quite read. "You tell me. Are you here to kick my ass or . . ."

When he fails to finish his thought I automatically prompt, "Or what?" Okay it's probably my imagination but I swear his gaze drops to my mouth. In a panic I wonder if I have some cream cheese on my lips or something. My tongue darts out and I lick my lips just to make sure . . . nope no cream cheese.

Nick's brown eyes widen a fraction and I realize that he must think I'm smacking my lips at him in a predatory kind of way. Of course I'm *not* even though I have to admit that he looks good enough to eat in a white muscle shirt and faded jeans. "Candie . . ."

Suddenly I'm thinking that instead of hovering over him I should stand but as I hastily scramble to my feet my left foot slips forward, kicking his creeper really hard. "Oh, no!" This sends Nick sailing across the smooth garage floor at a surprisingly fast pace. There must be ball bearings in those wheels or something.

"Sorry!" I yell while watching with my hands to my cheek as he bounces off a discarded tire and whacks into a big barrel, sending him in the opposite direction as though he's in a pinball machine. He comes to an abrupt halt as he slams sideways into a wall nailed full of a hubcap collection. The silver discs jingle and I watch wide-eyed as two of them fall. Nick, ever the athlete, rolls to the side just as one hubcap clatters to the concrete floor near where his head would have been. The other one hurries away on its edge as if it's trying to escape captivity.

Nick rolls two more times as I run toward him and comes to a stop faceup at my feet. "Guess that answers my question," he says blinking up at me. "You're here to kick my ass. Nice work."

Normally I would think that Nick is kidding but he gives me a strange look like he isn't sure just what's going on. Well, me neither.

"That—that was an accident."

After coming up to his elbows he says, "Kicking me across the floor was an accident?"

"I slipped . . . *honestly!*" I offer my hand and he gives it a wary look before taking it. His hand feels big and warm but thank the Lord without the tingle that Tommy gave me. I tug a bit harder than needed and he stumbles against me, making me backpedal.

"Whoa there," he says gruffly and slips a steadying arm about my waist. "Shall we dance?" he asks with a grin.

"Dance?" With my heart beating wildly I tilt my head back to look up at him. Then I get it. With his arm about my waist and my hand still clasping his, we are indeed standing there as if we're about to take a spin around the garage floor. "Oh." Feeling silly I let go of his hand.

His smile fades. "Okay . . . you're not here to kick my ass or to dance. So then what brings you here, Candie?" His arm remains around my waist a moment longer while he gazes expectantly at me.

"I'm here to hire you back."

"Ahhh." He removes his hand and takes a step back. For a long moment he stands there rubbing his stubble-darkened chin. "Really? I'm surprised. Sarah was pretty adamant about where I could and couldn't go . . . something like I could go to hell and never step foot on the car lot again."

"I can only imagine."

"Guns and a dog might have been mentioned and . . . ah certain body parts were in jeopardy," he adds with a twist of his lips.

"Can you blame her?" I have to ask even though I suppose it's the wrong thing to say to get him back.

Nick shoves his hands in his jeans pockets and looks down at the floor. "She did go way overboard as only Sarah can do and basically cried foul to anyone who would listen . . . but no, I guess I can't really blame her."

"Sarah says that you never did give a real reason for breaking off the engagement, Nick, unless you count your comment that you wanted the closeness that we once shared. She wants me to find out. She thinks you'll talk to me." His head whips up and his brown eyes look so troubled that I'm sorry I've gone down this path. I take a step closer to him and say, "You *can* talk to me Nick. You know that, right?" I ask softly. "I mean, my loyalty is to my sister, but I always thought that we were friends."

He looks at me for a long moment but then closes his eyes and swallows hard. "I'm sorry about all of this. Sarah is still the town's Miss Kentucky third runner-up and I'm the big bad guy who had the nerve to dump her."

My heart pounds but I have to ask the next question. "Just how in the world did I get dragged into all of this?"

Nick shakes his head. "Sarah should have kept our conversation private," he says tightly.

"Talk to me, Nick. The whole town is ticked at me, so I have a right to know just what in the world is going on here. I'm being blamed for bein' the other woman when I was six doggone hours away from Pinewood!"

"That's not fair," he admits. "I'm sorry."

"Tell me about it!"

"Candie, I just can't talk to you about it, okay?"

No, it's not okay but instead of pressing him, I nod.

"So, you want me to detail your inventory again?"

I know he's changing the subject but I decide to move on, at least for now. "Mercy, yes. Smiley sucks big-time. Of course we don't have much to work with since Carson Campbell hasn't been flipping any cars our way."

"Have you thought about going to any car auctions?"

I shrug. "Those are higher-end cars, Nick. You know that we always carried older but solid inventory."

"You might need to change your way of thinking."

"Maybe. But right now we don't have much money to work with until things pick up. We sure need to do something fast because I don't want this worry on Daddy."

"How is your father? I wanted to visit but I didn't want to upset him."

"I'm sure he realizes that, Nick."

"He's been in my prayers." Again he looks so troubled that I wish I could just hug him.

"I know," I assure him. "So then, will you spruce up what we do have in stock?" When he hesitates I add, "You'll only have to deal with me."

"Let me guess. Sarah refuses." His voice has a bit of a bite but then his expression softens. "Not that I blame her."

"Yes . . . she *is* however going to ask Carson Campbell to consider sending some of his older trade-ins our way as his daddy always did. Sarah says Carson went to some fancy-pants school up east and thinks he knows everything," I snap but then I remember that the two of them were out together the other night. "Oh, I'm sorry! Is Carson your friend?" When Nick leans back against the blue truck and folds his arms across his chest I realize that this conversation isn't going anything like I planned. "I don't really know him, so I suppose I shouldn't be so judgmental."

Nick shrugs, causing a little ripple of muscle that I do my best to ignore. "We're not exactly friends . . . but since Sarah has just about everyone in Pinewood dead set against him too, we sort of hang out together once in a while. I at least have *some* loyal friends but Carson basically has nobody. He's like a fish out of water in this small town. I guess you could say I feel for the guy," he admits but then grins.

"What?

"Nothin'. I'd just love to be a fly on the wall when Sarah confronts Carson. They're both headstrong and used to getting what they want. It'll be interesting to see who comes out on top," he says but then frowns as if forming a picture in his mind that he doesn't like.

Nodding, I make a mental note to tell Sarah to be on her toes. "Hey, by the way your truck is amazing. Is it yours or are you tricking it out for someone?"

"Thanks," Nick says with a pleased smile. "Carson Campbell has one of those sales where he advertised that they would pay top dollar for any trade-in no matter what the condition. Well, this guy takes him up on it and brings this old Ford Ranger in for trade," he explains with a tilt of his head toward the truck. "Carson had no use for it since the engine was blown so I offered to take it off his hands, mostly for the tires and good sound system."

"But you decided to fix her up instead?"

"Yeah, I just couldn't junk her. It felt kinda like taking an old hound to the dog pound. So instead, I swapped out the engine but then added the lift kit and started playing around with the paint job in my spare time, which I've had quite a lot of lately," he says with a pointed look.

His comment brings me back on track. "So Nick, will you work with us again? We don't have much to do right now but hopefully Sarah will convince Carson that turning over his old trade-ins to us for a quick profit is better than having those old cars taking up space on his car lot. Besides, Carson's daddy and my daddy had a gentlemen's agreement. Surely that has to count for somethin'."

Nick shrugs as he steps away from the truck. "I wouldn't be too sure about that. Carson isn't too interested in small-town politics. He does things the way he wants to."

"Well, maybe Mr. Carson Campbell needs to be taken down a notch or two."

Nick inclines his head in agreement. "Your sister just might be the person to do it."

"Nick you've been dancin' around my question. Will you work with us again? I've got an old Ford Escort that needs the paint buffed out."

After hesitating for a heartbeat he nods. "Yeah, sure."

"Thank you!" I feel a warm surge of joy and without really thinking I close the gap between us and give him a hug. He wraps his arms around me and feels so warm, strong, and solid. A lump forms in my throat when I realize how much I've missed him. Embarrassed, I turn away, hoping he doesn't notice. "I'll bring the Escort over later," I tell him as I hurry toward the door.

"Candie," Nick says stopping me in my tracks.

I take a steadying breath and then turn around. His brown eyes look so serious that my heart skips a beat. "Yes?"

"I'm sorry that your daddy's illness brought you back to Pinewood but I'm glad you're home."

Not knowing what to say I simply nod.

"I worried about you in Chicago all by yourself."

"Thanks. It's good to be back." I turn on my heel and give the heavy door a good shove. Once I'm outside I take a deep breath of warm summer air and blink in the glaring sunlight. My eyes tear up and I dig into my purse for my sunglasses but deep down I know that it has nothing to do with the brightness.

Looking across the street I see Sarah attaching balloons to the antennas of the cars and my heart lurches, making me wish that I had gotten more answers out of Nick. There's something beneath the surface that he's up to and by God, I'm eventually going to find out. With a determined sniff I square my shoulders and head across the street to Dapper Dan's Used Car Emporium. My family needs me and I'm going to do everything in my power to make things right.

7

Home Sweet Home

Mama's rockin' on the front porch in her big white wicker chair while sippin' on a big glass of sweet tea when I arrive for my visit with Daddy. I had wanted to wait to stop over until finding out how Sarah's visit went with Carson Campbell but Mama wanted to serve dinner around six o'clock since Daddy goes to bed early these days. In fact, Mama had sounded so frazzled over the phone that I closed up the car lot a good fifteen minutes early—not that we were crawling with customers anyway.

I smile as I pass the old tire swing dangling from the huge oak tree in the side yard. Daddy hung it there the year Sarah and I turned five and it's been there ever since. Mama keeps hinting that she's waiting for grandkids to swing in the old tire but at the rate Sarah and I are going that's not likely to happen anytime soon. Big baskets of Boston ferns suspended from ceiling hooks sway in the soft summer breeze that sends the scent of supper cookin' my way. I note with a sense of satisfaction that except for a freshly painted trim of hunter green, the rambling farmhouse looks the same as always. Set back from the street on fifteen rolling acres, *this* will always be home no matter how far I go away. Except for Mama's big garden it's not really a working farm but from fishing and swimming in the stocked lake to four-wheeling through the woods we were never at a loss for something fun to do. Daddy always worked hard but he played hard as well.

Guessing by the tired lines bracketing Mama's mouth, I imagine that he's been a tough patient to keep sitting still. "Thank goodness you're here," Mama says with a weary shake of her head. "Your daddy's about to drive me insane."

After leaning over to give her a kiss on the cheek I offer, "Want me to go on inside and talk to him while you rest a bit?"

"No, he's dozed off in his recliner," Mama replies and gestures toward the other big rocker. "Have a seat. I poured you a glass of tea with a refreshing sprig of mint in it. Supper's warmin' in the oven, so just sit with me a spell and let me vent."

"So, has Daddy been givin' you a hard time?" I ask as I ease into the big chair.

"Does a bear shit in the woods?"

I laugh at Mama's unexpected candor.

"Forgive me for bein' so vulgar but I'm in a bit of a snit." After taking a sip of tea she explains, "I know that bein' laid up has your daddy goin' stir-crazy and I'm tryin' real hard to be sympathetic, but *Candie*, that man has been following me around like a lost puppy. I wouldn't have so much of a problem with that either, except he thinks he has to tell me how to do everything from how to drive the car to weedin' my garden!"

"Oh Mama . . . what can I do?"

"Don't worry about it." She shoos me with her hand. "Uncle Theo is takin' him down to the lake to fish a bit tomorrow, thank the Lord, so I can tend my garden in peace." She sighs. "I don't mean to sound so harsh. I love your daddy to pieces but, child, I can take only so much."

"I understand. He's been following doctor's orders though, hasn't he?"

"Reluctantly so, but yes."

"Then he'll mend quickly. I do have some news that will cheer him up if it's okay to talk business with him."

"Mercy yes! He's dying for some shoptalk." She picks up her glass. "I'll get supper on the table. Go wake up your father and have a chat."

"I hate to wake him."

Mama shrugs. "It's fine. He'll sleep better tonight if you do."

With that in mind I follow Mama into the house. He wakes when I turn off ESPN golf.

"Hey, I was watchin' that, Marilee," he grumbles but then smiles when he sees that it's me. "Hey there, little girlie. Come give your daddy a kiss."

Trying not to tear up with seeing him looking tired and pale in the big chair, I hurry over and kiss him on his whiskery cheeks. "So you've got the sexy non-shaven look goin', huh Daddy?"

"Sexy, huh?" He snorts. "Tell your mother that. She keeps harpin' on me to shave."

"Mama!" I yell in the direction of the kitchen. "I think Daddy's whiskers are sexy."

"He looks like a bum!" she shouts back.

"See? Harps on me all the time," he says loudly but then drops to a low voice that Mama can't hear. "She's been real good to me. Waits on me hand and foot. I'm gonna make it up to her when I'm up and about again. I know I've been drivin' her plumb crazy but I just can't help myself."

After sitting down on the overstuffed sofa, I give him a smile. "I have some good news."

"Sarah told me. You sold old Skeeter a truck!" He slaps his knee. "Wish I'd been there for that!"

"We double-teamed him."

"Good for you."

I scoot forward on the sofa. "I have better news than that. Nick is going to start detailing our inventory again. I talked to him today."

Daddy nods. "That *is* good news. I don't know what happened between him and your sister but I always liked Nick. I would have been thrilled to have him for a son-in-law but I guess that's out of the question now."

"Looks that way," I answer trying not to let the familiar sadness where that's concerned settle like a rock in my tummy. "Sarah's going to work on Carson Campbell to start flipping some cars our way," I tell him, trying to change the subject.

"Hope she can pull it off. That Campbell boy is stubborn."

"Well, Sarah can be persuasive when she sets her mind to somethin'."

"True enough," Daddy admits, and then slowly pushes up to his feet when Mama calls that dinner is served. It pains me to watch him shuffle so slowly to the dining room but I know him well enough not to offer help.

"Have a seat and get it while it's hot," Mama says with a smile. I notice the absence of the saltshaker and butter on the table as I sit down. I'll miss both but I make a mental note not to ask for either.

"Mama, this smells so delicious," I tell her, and she beams a smile at me.

"The mashed potatoes are made with low-fat milk and just a hint of butter. I've been trying to trim the fat from my recipes."

"The chicken is roasted to a juicy perfection and the

vegetables are steamed just right. I've missed your cookin'."

"You're quite a good cook yourself."

"She learned from the best," Daddy chimes in.

"I should have trimmed the fat from my food a long time ago." Mama's eyes tear up. She and Sarah can cry at the drop of a hat.

"Oh now, Marilee, don't go blamin' my heart troubles on your cookin'. You tried to get me to mend my ways a long time ago."

She sniffs and reaches over to pat his hand. My throat closes up at their easy affection. They might bicker but the love they have for each other is as strong as ever. I can only hope to one day be blessed with such a union.

After dinner I decline dessert since I'm dying to hear how Sarah's meeting with Carson went. She texted me, saying that she'd be over to my house later. I'd hidden my phone in my pocket during dinner. After kissing Daddy good-bye, I follow Mama into the kitchen where she wraps up a piece of low-fat apple cake for me.

"Oh, let me wrap up a piece for Sarah too. Will you be seeing her later?"

I nod. "She's stopping over."

"Are you getting settled in over in that two-family? I wish I could be more help."

I give her a hug. "You have your hands full. The place is shaping up."

"I'm so glad that you're back from that big cold city," she says with an extra squeeze and then presses the foil-wrapped cake into my hands. "I know that you and Sarah are busy with the car lot but stop by whenever you get the chance, you hear?"

I nod and for some reason feel like bursting into tears. I give Mama a quick peck on the cheek and hurry out the back door before I do just that because I just know she would start blubbering too and then Daddy would get all upset over nothing. I do have to grin when I think of how hard it must have been for him sometimes living with a household of emotional women. No wonder he was wishing for a son-in-law.

As I slide into the driver's side of the used Chevy Blazer my thoughts turn to Nick. While I'm glad he's agreed to work with us, the meeting with him was . . . weird. I feel like he was holding something back but I can't put my finger on it. His comments about his failed engagement with Sarah were cryptic and rather confusing. Hopefully one day the truth will come out. I'm thinking about all of this stuff as I enter my house, which is why I suppose I didn't immediately see Sarah sitting at my kitchen table. "Oh Lord, have mercy!" I yell, putting my hand over my heart. "How did you get in here?"

"I told you I have a key," she says sullenly. Uh-oh . . . *not* a good sign.

"I didn't notice your car."

"I'm driving that cruddy old Jeep. It's right out front, Candie."

"I guess my mind was elsewhere."

"You got anything to drink?"

I turn and open the fridge. "Um . . . Diet Coke, bottled water, or orange juice."

"No, I mean something to *drink*."

"Oh you mean like a beer?"

"Yeah or whiskey . . . vodka. *Whatever*."

I wince. "Sorry, no." After plopping down in the chair across from her I ask, "It went that badly?"

Sarah puts her palms on the kitchen table and leans forward. "The man is a jerk. Wait a minute—that isn't nasty enough. He's a—a—*prick*!"

"Ew . . . Sarah . . ." I wrinkle my nose.

"I call 'em like I see 'em."

"Have you already been drinkin'?"

"No! But I'm fixin' to. Wanna join me?"

"First tell me what happened."

"Well"—she points to her sleek ponytail and subtle . . . well, subtle for Sarah . . . makeup—"the whole businesswoman thing didn't work. *At all.* Carson Campbell treated me like a—a redneck. No, a bimbo. No wait—a redneck bimbo."

"A redneck bimbo?" I want to smile but Sarah is clearly distraught.

"Yes. Allow me to explain."

"Do."

"Don't mock me, Candie. It was awful. If I didn't hate Nick I'd call him and tell him to kick Carson's ass."

"They're kinda friends."

Sarah swings her hands up in the air. "Oh right, isn't that just rich!"

I realize that I'm making matters worse so I shut up and let her talk.

"Well, first, the secretary, *Missy Palmer*, of all people . . ."

"Wait, who is Missy Palmer?"

Sarah shakes her head. "Long story for another time. Anyway, she tells me that I have to make an appointment to see Carson. Yeah, like he's a doctor or somethin'. An appointment, my sweet ass."

"You didn't say that, did you?"

"No. I was being Miss Sleek Ponytail business bitch."

"Sarah . . ."

"Stop goin' all Mama on me, Candie, and let me finish!"

"Okay."

"I sat down all polite and whatever and sweetly informed *Missy Palmer* that I'd wait until Carson had a spare moment."

"So, you just sat there?"

"Yes, all prim and everything in my Ann Taylor suit for thirty-seven minutes. I even picked up a *Newsweek* and pretended to read it when I really wanted to page through *People.*" Her ponytail slips over her shoulder and she gives it an annoying flip. "Finally, Mr. High-and-Mighty comes out of his office."

"So you approached him?"

"Well, *yes.* I stood up and introduced myself and asked for a moment of his time. I offered my hand and he shook it but lingered a bit too long and gave me the once-over." She narrows her eyes.

"You like it when guys give you the once-over," I joke since she's getting all fired up and Sarah all fired up can be a dangerous thing.

"I wanted him to take me seriously. That was the plan, remember? You wouldn't understand because people take *you* seriously."

When her voice cracks my smile fades. "So, what happened next?"

"Well, he holds his office door open for me even though Missy Palmer is sputtering her protests that I didn't have an appointment. I give her a smug look and for a moment there I'm feeling better about the situation until he shuts the door."

I gasp. "Did he make a move on you?" I'm starting to get fired up too.

"Well," she says in a clipped tone, "he leans back against his huge desk, lookin' all GQ in his dark blue suit and intense blue eyes, and tells me that I have one minute! He even holds up his finger like this!" With her lips pursed she demonstrates.

"Oh." I was expecting something far worse.

"I'm getting sort of frustrated since I needed more than a danged minute but I tell him that I'm from Dapper Dan's Used Car Emporium and he says 'Oh that little used car lot.' *Little!* But I keep my cool and I explain that we would like to take his older trade-ins off his hands for a quick profit. I remind him that his daddy, Harley Campbell, and our daddy, Dan Montgomery, had an agreement of sorts and do you know what he says?"

I shake my head.

"He says that *he's* in charge now. Then he glances at his fancy gold watch and tells me that my time is up. Just like that." Sarah snaps her fingers.

"I'm guessing that this is where it goes downhill like a bike without brakes."

"Pretty much. I walked right over to Mr. Carson Campbell, poked my fingertip in the middle of his starched shirt, and proceeded to tell him that if he wanted to succeed in a small town, he had better learn our ways."

"What did he say to that?"

"He smugly informed me that business was booming and that the older used cars were flying off the lot. He said that good-ole-boy ways are a thing of the past."

"Oh . . ."

"Yeah, not good. He said not to take it personal but that business was business."

Gripping the wooden arms of the chair I ask, "So what did you say?"

Sarah rests her head in her hands and wails, "I said that I'd rather be a good ole boy than a jackass."

"Good for you."

"I'm so sorry, Candie. I just lost my . . . Wait a minute . . . What did you say?" Her head comes up and she frowns across the table at me.

"I said, 'good for you.' "

"Really?"

I reach over and pat her hand. "Might not have been the most tactful way to put it but he deserved to be told a thing or two."

"Well," she admits in a small voice, "that's not all . . ."

I pull my hand from her and wait for the other shoe to drop. "What did you do, Sarah? My God, you didn't hit him did you?"

"Can-deee!" She gives me an I'm-appalled-that-you-would-suggest-that look. "Okay, I'll admit that it crossed my mind but I was bein' Business Barbie, remember?"

"As I recall, you had your finger pokin' in his chest and called him a jackass."

"Well, I didn't smack him. I might have given him a little hard shove with my finger. But that was all."

"Thank God."

"At that point anyway."

I swallow a groan.

"I turn around and I'm about to leave his office when he asks me out to dinner. At first I was pleased since I had a whole bunch of information, you know, charts and spreadsheets that I wanted to show him, for instance how many cars Daddy has bought from Harley over the years."

"Wow, Sarah, I'm impressed."

"Thank you. I *did* take some business courses in college, you know. I even went to class once in a while. Anyway, I also wanted to point out that Daddy would sometimes go strong on his appraisals just to get Harley the deal. I had worked all day on my proposal and I was itching to present it to him even if it meant over dinner."

"I hear a but . . ."

"But when I mentioned my proposal he made it clear that his invitation had nothing to do with *business*," she says with a head bop. But then her anger fades and she continues softly, "You know, Candie, even though I complained it really felt good to be in a business suit. I worked hard on that proposal! For once

I wanted to get the job based on merit." She sighs. "I know I used my looks to get what I wanted most of my life. It was always the easy way out especially since you were a tough act to follow academically and you know, that never gettin' in trouble nonsense. But after Nick dumped me I got to thinkin' that there needs to be more substance to me."

I reach over and grab both of her hands this time. "You're a Montgomery, Sarah. There is plenty of substance to you. You just need to use it."

"Yeah well, the bottom line here is that you got the job done and I didn't. Oh, you want to know what else Carson said? He said that the only business proposition he would entertain is buying the car lot *from* us. Yeah, he's thinking of expanding and that he might entertain the notion of taking our little car lot off our hands."

"Oh *really.*" Okay, now I'm ticked. I'm trying to hold back because I don't want to get Sarah all fired up again but I just can't contain myself. "Well, you know *what*? He can have his doggone cars."

"Yeah!" Sarah chimes in. "He can stick them where the sun never shines!"

"Yeah! Buy us out! Just who does he think he is anyway? Who needs him! Arrogant *jerk.*"

Sarah gives me a high five. "Hey, let's go egg his car. He's got a red Beemer convertible."

"What? You're crazy! We can't go eggin' his car."

"Sure we can. Mama might not have stocked you up with beer but you have a dozen eggs in the fridge. I scrambled two for my dinner but that leaves ten to throw at his car."

"We can't," I say firmly. "My God that is so high school, Sarah!"

"I know." She rubs her hands together. "It's perfect. No one will suspect us."

"But—but what if we get caught?"

Sarah wiggles her eyebrows. "That's what makes it excitin'. We'll wait 'til it's dark and wear all black. Carson's livin' in Harley's big tudor over on Maple Lane so we can sneak over through the woods."

"You are totally insane," I tell her but feel a little shiver of excitement.

"You want to."

"I most certainly do *not*."

"Liar. I bet you never even egged a car before, have you, Miss Goody Two-shoes."

"No! And I'm not about to start tonight. To think I was buying your speech about wanting to be respected."

"Candie, no one will know," she whispers.

I can't resist when her eyes dance and even though I know it's silly and adolescent I nod my head. "Okay, but you can bring two eggs . . . one in each pocket."

"Two? I was thinking all ten."

I hold up my index and middle fingers. "Two. We sneak over there, you wing them at his car, and we run like hell."

Sarah gives me a pout but nods. "Okay."

I give her a knuckle bump. "Cool. Now, let's get our egg throwin' outfits ready." I need a good run and I'm not really worried about Sarah egging Carson's BMW since she couldn't hit the broad side of a barn. My clothes are still in suitcases and boxes so it takes us a while to sort through my stuff.

"You seriously need Stacy and Clinton to clean out your closet," Sarah says while holding up my prized Jimmy Buffet Margaritaville T-shirt and tosses it at me. Do you actually wear this stuff?"

"Hey, I'm a parrot-head and proud of it," I tell her, referring to what huge Jimmy Buffet fans are called, me being one of them. Who are Stacy and Clinton?"

Sarah gasps. "Why, the hosts of *What Not to Wear!*" She holds up an ancient UK Wildcats T-shirt and shakes her head. "Stacy would have a field day with you."

"Look who's talkin' Miss I-Don't-Own-a-Business-Suit."

"I have one now," she says sticking out her tongue. She does however help me get my stuff unpacked but finding her something of mine that fits her is next to impossible.

"Maybe you should go home and get something black that actually fits," I comment when she tugs on a pair of my sweatpants that fit her like capris. A black T-shirt stretches across her chest like a second skin while exposing a couple of inches of her torso.

"No one is gonna see us, so what's the point?" After glancing out of the window she smiles. "It's finally dark. Let's pocket the eggs and go!"

"Not yet. We need to cover our blond hair or we'll glow in the dark."

"Do you have anything to do that?"

After tapping my finger on my cheek I finally remember that I have a couple of black baseball caps from a company softball team I was on in Chicago. After digging them out of a box I toss her one.

"Okay, now we're ready," she says, donning the hat.

After slipping on my own hat I suddenly feel a surge of uncertainty now that we're no longer in the heat of the hating Carson moment. While adjusting the bill of my cap I nibble on the inside of my cheek.

"Oh come on, Candie, don't chicken out on me now."

I nibble a moment longer and remind myself that Sarah can't throw worth a darn so I might as well humor her. Plus we're bonding and that's a good thing, right?

Sarah reaches over and tugs on my hand, making me stumble forward. "We're not gonna get caught. Trust me . . ."

8

Famous Last Words

The path through the woods begins at the far edge of my backyard. The silvery glow from the full moon and lights from nearby homes help us find our way but it's still creepy when we enter the cover of tall trees. Luckily the path is wide and well-worn from kids taking a shortcut to the city park that butts up to the other side. Still, it's dark and shadowy, making me shiver.

"Come on," Sarah urges with an impatient wave of her hand. I'm trailing behind since I'm looking this way and that for beady little eyes or other such things that go bump in the night. I know I'm a farm girl but I prefer nature in the daylight, thank you very much.

"I'm comin'," I hiss back and pick up my pace when something scurries across my path. Oh, why did I ever agree to this insanity? A few minutes later we reach the city park and wind our way past picnic tables and swing sets. All too soon we're crouched down behind a row of bushes at the edge of Carson Campbell's front property.

"There's his car," Sarah whispers while pointing to the top of the long driveway winding alongside the sloped front lawn.

"Good. Toss your eggs and let's get outta here."

"We have to get closer!"

"The bushes don't go that far and it's your only cover. Throw the doggone things."

"That big-ass tree is in the way."

"Aim to the left."

She hands me the egg. "You do it."

I shake my head. "Oh no you don't."

"Then we have to get *closer*. At least to the end of the row of bushes."

"Okay," I whisper. We creep up the yard in a stooped position hidden from the house by the bushes . . . but then a thought hits me and I reach up to tug on Sarah's shirt.

"What?" she hisses over her shoulder.

I point to the huge house. "He can see us if he's lookin' out the upstairs window!"

"The house is dark. He must be sleepin'."

I glance at my watch. "At ten thirty?"

"Maybe bein' such a jerk is tiring. I don't know!"

"No, look!" I point to a small window in the center of the upstairs. "I bet that's a bathroom. He must be in the shower or somethin'. Toss the egg. You're close enough."

Sarah peeks her head above the bush. "The damned tree is still in the way. Just a bit closer . . ."

"No!"

"Oh, okay!" She reaches in her pocket and comes out with an egg. With a grin she stands up and wings it in the direction of the red Beemer but it splats against the tree trunk; then she throws and misses again.

"Damn!" Sarah groans when the second egg misses the tree but splats harmlessly in the driveway.

"Too bad," I whisper in a sad voice. "Now let's hightail it outta here!"

"No, wait." She produces another egg.

"Hey," I hiss, "I told you only two eggs!"

"You're not the boss of me."

"Wanna bet!" I grab at her tight shirt but miss.

"Where were you hidin' those?"

"In my hands. I was carrying them."

"How many more do you have?"

She holds an egg up for me to see. "This is it. I'm gonna get close enough this time not to miss."

"No! Give me the damned thing!"

With a grin she hands me the egg. I was a southpaw first baseman in fast-pitch softball since sixth grade and made the varsity team as a freshman. "I'm not gonna miss, so be prepared to run for the woods."

With a sharp nod Sarah comes up to her haunches. "I'm ready to roll," she says like we're part of a covert operation.

My heart starts hammering in my chest and I'm wondering why in the hell I'm doing this, but I stand up and wing the egg at the red car parked innocently in the driveway. It hits with a crunchy thwap but then, *holy crap*, the car alarm starts sending loud *whop-whop*s into the silence. Why didn't I think of that?

Sarah's eyes widen and her mouth forms a big O.

"Keep low and run!" I tell Sarah, not really knowing why I said the keep low part because it will make it harder to run. "Head for the woods!" I add and take off like a bat outta hell. My legs are short but I'm fast and going downhill helps me pick up speed.

"Hey! Who's out there?" I hear Carson bellow. Unable to help myself I look over my shoulder and see him standing at the top of the driveway, shirtless and in his boxers. My eyes widen when he spots Sarah, who is also looking over her shoulder.

"Come back here!" Carson shouts. Then he starts chasing after Sarah! I watch with growing horror as he quickly closes the gap between them. Sarah attempts to zigzag across the front lawn in an effort I suppose to throw him off as if she's heading for the end zone for a touchdown, but Carson reaches out with one long arm, snags her around the waist, and tackles her. Sarah screams and I watch them hit the ground and roll over several times, which is when I realize that running forward downhill at top speed while looking backward is not a good idea . . .

My feet snag on a tree root, making me go airborne before crashing to the ground with a painful thud. The air leaves my lungs with a whoosh and my hat goes flying. For a moment I'm stunned and wheezing.

"Get off of meeee!" I hear Sarah screech.

"What the hell?" Carson bellows. *"Sarah?"*

Spitting grass from my mouth I push up to my knees and spot Sarah with Carson straddling her in his underwear while holding her arms trapped above her head.

"Let me go!"

Since I'm near the end of the lawn I strain to see them in the darkness but it looks like her shoulders wiggle back and forth but other than that she's trapped.

"Did you just egg my car?" he shouts, making no attempt to slide off her.

"No!" she shouts back, lifting her head and shoulders off the ground. I can only imagine that in my too-small-for-her-boobs T-shirt she is quite a sight.

"Then what the hell are you doing here?"

"I was . . . *jogging,*" she says, which I suppose is technically the truth. Jogging away from the scene of the crime, that is. Then it hits me. I threw the egg and in a moment Carson is going to spot me wheezing and kneeling on his front lawn. In the background his car alarm is still sounding until he releases one of Sarah's arms and points a remote at his car. I wince when she takes a swing at him with her free arm and thumps him a good one on the back.

"Ouch!" he grumbles while dodging her uppercut to his jaw. "Settle down!"

Her answer is to buck and twist like a crazy person.

Thank God, the alarm has stopped even though I doubt that God is helping us out on this one. Hoping that Sarah will convince Carson of her innocence instead of trying to beat him up I scramble behind the big Oak tree and hide.

"So if *you* didn't egg my car," he asks in a voice dripping with suspicion, "then who did?"

"Now just how would I know? An unsatisfied customer, perhaps?" she asks sweetly. "Are you gonna let me go now? You're heavy, not to mention practically naked!"

"Oh, so you noticed?"

"It's kinda hard not to since you're sittin' on top of me! Let me go!"

"Not until you explain why you were *jogging* across my front lawn."

Think fast, Sarah, I silently plead as I peek around the fat tree trunk. Wow, Carson is built. Wide shoulders, narrow waist, and sculpted abs. Too bad he's such a jerk. He leans in closer to Sarah's face and says softly, "You had better come up with something plausible or I'll call the police."

"Maybe while I was jogging by I heard the car alarm and wanted to warn you that one of your many enemies was vandalizing your car."

"Or maybe *you* were vandalizing my car."

"Yeah, and maybe your trouser monster is hanging out."

"What?"

Sarah! I put my hand over my mouth to keep from laughing and blowing my cover.

"Do you really think I would stoop to such a childish prank? I have better things to do, I'll have you know."

"So you didn't throw the egg at my car?"

"I most certainly did *not*. Oh, and by the way, when you call the police I want you to explain why you tackled an innocent jogger and showed me your trouser monster."

"I didn't show you my . . . *trouser monster*," he growls.

"So you're innocent, huh? You might want to explain to the police why you jog at night dressed in all black."

"*You* might want to explain why you broke the wrist of an innocent person!"

"What?" He scrambles off Sarah. "Let me see."

I peek around the tree, wondering if this is a ploy or if Sarah is really hurt. She sits up and Carson bends his head to examine her hand.

"Ouch!" Sarah says and I breathe a sigh of relief. I know her real moan of pain and although she might be banged up a bit I doubt if her wrist is broken.

"Sorry," Carson says gruffly and I smile. He's buying her bull. "Your knuckles are scraped and your wrist looks a bit swollen but I don't think it's broken."

"Would you mind getting me a bag of ice to hold on it while I jog back home?" Sarah says loud enough to make her point clear to me: Get the hell outta there.

"Sure," he says with surprising gentleness. "Come on inside." He helps to tug her to her feet with her good hand.

"Okay but only for a minute." Sarah makes a shooing motion at me behind her back and I have to grin until she takes her first step and gives a little cry of pain. When she stumbles, Carson's arm slips around her waist.

"Sarah, are you okay?"

"I might have twisted my ankle," she answers with a little whimper and I lean back against the tree trunk, wondering just how much of this she's faking. Carson is a big guy and she did go down pretty hard.

"Hey," Sarah yelps, "what do you think you're doing?"

I poke my head from behind the tree and swallow a gasp when I see that Carson has scooped Sarah up in his arms.

"Put me down!"

"I will as soon as I get you settled on the sofa and ice your ankle and wrist. You might as well quit your squirming. I'm not putting you down, so wrap your arms around my neck."

"I'm perfectly fine!"

"That you are."

"Are you flirting with me? Because it's sort of futile to flirt with someone you just body-slammed."

"Oh, *body-slammed*. I like the sound of that."

"That's it. Put me down!"

They continue to bicker as they head for the house, reminding me a little of Mama and Daddy and I have to wonder if there might be something starting to simmer between those two. "Now wouldn't that just beat all?" I mutter under my breath. I sit there in the cool grass a moment longer until I hear the front door close and then make a beeline for the woods.

An adrenaline buzz has my feet flying, plus I really don't like the woods at night. I'm back home in almost no time and after snagging a bottle of water I grab my cell phone and wait with bated breath for Sarah to call.

"Call already!" I say to the little silver phone. Finally I get a text message that says that nothing is broken and that Carson is driving her home later. I wait for another message or call but get nothing, making me wonder just what the hell is keeping her occupied. Finally, I give up and get ready for bed.

"Sarah, you're killin' me," I say out loud as I place the phone on my nightstand. After living by myself for the past two years I've developed the habit of talking to the television, my computer, and myself. Even as a kid growing up I'd always been somewhat of a loner. Mama always had her clubs, Daddy always seemed to be working, and Sarah had a full social life, leaving me to myself on many an evening. It wasn't as though I was unpopular and I played on several sports teams, but I was far from being a social butterfly.

With an exasperated sigh I tug the quilt up to my chin and roll over onto my side. I groan while determinedly trying to chase away my insecurities. I have to admit that I'm also a little disappointed that I haven't heard more from Tommy lately. Maybe he's having second thoughts about pretending to be my boyfriend. His handsome face and sweet smile drift into my brain but I determinedly try to chase him away. Since he hasn't called he doesn't deserve my attention! *Think of someone else,* I tell myself. Okay, but who? George Clooney . . . nah. Brad Pitt . . . nope. Alex Rodriguez? Hmmm, now we're talkin' but somehow Tommy weaves his way back into my brain, beating out the image of A-Rod, for goodness sake. Is there no hope for me? I grab the second pillow and tuck the softness between my arms, wondering if I'll ever have a warm body to hug instead.

"Oh stop," I tell myself but my voice, sounds hollow in the dark, silent room. Hugging the pillow tighter I close my eyes and hope that fatigue from my rather adventurous day will send me into la-la land . . .

I'm drifting off and slipping into a delicious dream where Derek Jeter and A-Rod are fighting over my affections when the sound of my phone ringing startles me into a sitting position. I'm disoriented for a second, thinking I'm back in my Chicago apartment, and then I remember that I'm in Pinewood in Daddy's two-family. Pushing my tangled curls from my eyes I slap my hand toward the nightstand and locate my ringing, blinking, and vibrating phone.

Thinking it's finally Sarah I flip it open and sort of growl, "Hello!"

"Hey," says a husky male voice that slides over me like honey on a biscuit, "I'm sorry, did I wake ya?"

Ohmigod, it's Tommy. "Oh . . . no," I lie in a softer tone wondering why I always fib when someone wakes me.

"Sorry, Candie. I was doin' paperwork and didn't realize that it's pushin' midnight. I'm sorry. Do you want me to call back tomorrow?"

"No!" I quickly protest but then realize that I sounded a little desperate. "I mean, unless you'd rather."

"Not at all. Just hearing your pretty little voice is calming me down. I've been stressed to the max with this softball tournament. It's become a real pain. Two teams dropped out and I had to redo the whole schedule."

"I'm sorry to hear that." I scoot up and lean against the headboard.

"So, how are things? It sucked that we didn't get to spend time together at the pub but you were right to go. Sarah looked ready to take a bite outta Nick. They have some issues, that's for sure, but I don't think Sarah would have been so pissed if there weren't still some strong feelings," he says seriously but then chuckles. "Damn I sound like . . . what's that big dude's name? On TV?"

"Um, you mean Dr. Phil?"

"Yeah, him. Except I don't know what I'm talking about."

"Well, you are a bartender," I tease, "so you do have some therapy skills."

"Naw, I was just fillin' in. And speakin' of that, when do I get to be your boyfriend again?"

My heart does a funny little lurch when I remind myself that this is just pretend and not the real deal. I wonder again if this is a mistake.

"Hey, you there?"

"Yeah."

"Good. For a minute there I thought you'd fallen asleep on me. Not good for my ego."

While twirling a bed-head curl around my finger I say, "Something tells me you don't have a problem in that area."

"In bed or my ego?"

"Your ego!" I quickly respond, glad that he can't see my flaming face but the thought runs through my brain that he *would* be amazing in bed.

"You're blushing, aren't you?" he asks with a low sexy laugh that makes me grip the tiny phone tighter.

"Of course not!" I protest a bit too much. I don't want him to think that I'm you know . . . not cool and so I say the first thing that comes to mind probably because it's *on* my mind: "I think you'd be great in bed." Oh God! "Um, not that I'm thinking about that or anything!" I try for a quick save. "You know I'm just sayin' that since you're an athlete and everything you'd be, you know . . ."

"Athletic?"

"Yeah," I finish in a small voice and then squeeze my eyes shut. "Okay, I think I'll hang up now."

"Don't you dare. That was my fault for leading you on that way," he tries to say seriously but I detect barely suppressed mirth in his voice.

"I'm such a dork. Go ahead and laugh."

"You're *not* a dork," he insists, but then can't hold back and bursts into infectious laughter. "God, I needed that."

"Glad to be of service," I answer, amazed that he's able to put me at ease even when I'm embarrassed.

"Wow, now just how am I gonna get to sleep?"

"Sorry to make you laugh so hard. It wasn't my intention," I admit leaning back against the pillow.

"It's not that . . . ," he says a bit hesitantly.

My heart kicks it up a notch, "What then?"

"I'm thinkin' about you sittin' there in bed lookin' cute and cuddly as hell."

"Oh, yeah right. I'm real sexy in my Tweety Bird sleep shirt." I try to joke but it comes out a bit breathless.

"You know," he begins and I can hear the smile in his voice, "that just fits you to a T and believe me when I say it is *sexy as hell*. And hey, if it makes you feel any better I'm sittin' here in blue boxers with red-hot chili peppers all over them."

"Yeah, a little, but . . . ," I begin but don't have the nerve to finish my thought.

"But what?"

"Nothing," I tell him and start twirling my hair.

"Oh no you don't. Spill."

I can't tell him that I'm picturing him in his boxers, so I remain silent while trying to think of something clever to say. Of course nothing comes to mind *now* but will later when I'm lying here awake, reliving this conversation.

"Okay, I'll make a confession instead."

I swallow and wait, and for some reason feel the need to hold my breath.

"I'm dying to kiss you."

Wow . . . Oh, I know it's my turn to say something flirty back but my heart is pounding and I'm imagining him shirtless in red-hot chili pepper boxers with his shaggy blond hair needing my fingers in it and my brain is too overloaded to function. So I just sit there like a toad.

Tommy clears his throat. "Okay, am I coming on too strong?"

"No," I readily assure him.

"Hey, would you like to go for some hot wings and watch a baseball game tomorrow night? My sister owns a new wings joint. The food's pretty good."

"That sounds lovely." Lovely? Who says lovely? I shake my head.

"Awesome. I'll call you tomorrow. Night, Candie."

"G'night," I manage but sit there blinking until the annoying recorded message "If you'd like to make a call, please hang up" comes on, and I finally flip the phone shut. I sit there for a while longer with a silly grin on my face.

He might be a flirt and full of bull but for right now Tommy Tucker is just what the doctor ordered.

9

Let the Games Begin

"Well, it's about time," I comment when Sarah comes pushing through the office door at nearly ten o'clock. I soften a bit when I see that she's limping slightly.

"I called but the line was busy. I also left a message on your cell."

"Really?" When Sarah nods I glance down at my phone and sure enough there's a missed call indicated on the small screen. "Sorry. I've been busy with the books."

"How bad is it?" Sarah asks as she gingerly sits down in the old chair across from the equally old metal desk. I notice that her knuckles on her left hand are scraped but her wrist seems to be okay.

"Bad, unless you convinced Carson to send some cars our way. What time did you get home last night anyway?"

"Umm . . . I didn't go home."

"Sarah!"

"Oh stop giving me that look like I'm some sort of hussy. I fell asleep on Carson's sofa. Not that I wouldn't have been willing to take one for the team . . . Damn, that man is built."

"You're kiddin', right?"

"Yeah, about the sleeping with him part but he *is* hot. You have to admit that, Candie. Didn't you notice when he was standing there in his boxers?"

"Maybe." I think of Tommy in his red-hot chili pepper boxers and grin. "Okay, I did. So he didn't offer to sell us any cars?"

"When I approached the subject he was clear that business is business and they're making money keeping the older inventory on hand. If I could have shown him my charts, then maybe he would have come around to my way of thinkin' but he wouldn't even entertain the idea."

"That doesn't seem fair or good business practice not to listen. He'll learn the hard way that small-town businesses need to stick together."

"I'd already been down that line of reasoning, Candie, and I wasn't about to go there again."

I shrug. "We'll think of something else. Screw him."

"Okay." Sarah grins and then gets up to pour herself a cup of coffee from the pot on the shelf behind her.

"I didn't mean that literally, you know."

After stirring in a pack of sweetener she turns around. "I *know*." She takes a sip of coffee and then says, "Look, I realize that Carson is an arrogant jerk but he was really nice to me last night."

After taking a guzzle of my own caffeine in a can, better known as Mountain Dew, I sputter, "Well I guess. He tackled you for heaven's sake! You're still limpin'. Carson was probably worried about a lawsuit."

"Candie, he thought I was vandalizing his car."

"Thought?" I raise my eyebrows.

"Technically it was you."

I narrow my eyes at her.

"Just kiddin'! Man, who pooped in your Cheerios?"

"Gross!"

"I'm just sayin'," she comments as she sits back down, "that you're sure in a bad mood."

"And you're sure in a good mood," I observe and give her a suspicious arch of one eyebrow.

"What?" she asks but lowers her gaze to her mug.

I gasp. "You *kissed* him, didn't you?"

Sarah thumps her coffee mug down. "My resolve was weakened by a warm snifter of brandy. It went straight to my head and I wasn't thinking clearly. He was bending over me all shirtless and smelling fresh-out-of-the-shower good and suddenly my tongue was in his mouth."

"So *you* kissed *him*?"

With a little bop of her head she replies, "I do believe that I explained that I wasn't thinkin' clearly. It was the booze and the painkillers, I tell ya!"

"He gave you pills?" I squeeze the Mountain Dew can so hard I put a dent in it.

"Calm down. It was Advil, to keep the swellin' down."

"Did he kiss you back?"

"Of course. I'm a very good kisser."

"And then what?"

"What makes you think there's more?"

"The guilty look on you face." Which tells me she was thinking of Nick the whole doggone time but I don't point that out to her.

Sarah shifts in her seat and takes another sip of coffee while I drum my fingernails on the desk. Finally she says, "I might have agreed to play on his sand volleyball team."

I place the palms of my hands on the desk blotter and lean forward. "You what?"

"He blackmailed me, Candie. He said that if I played on his volleyball team that he would forget all about the egg thowin' incident."

"So he didn't believe that you were simply jogging?" I ask in a small voice.

"Not so much . . ."

While leaning back in the creaky old chair I groan. "We should never have done such a crazy thing. *Egging his car.* What was I thinkin'?"

"Our emotions were runnin' high."

"That's no excuse."

"Oh, come on. It was fun. Admit it."

"I will admit to no such thing!"

"Admit it."

I give her a deadpan stare.

"Okay maybe fun was the wrong word . . . exciting then."

"How about stupid!" I suggest but have to grin.

"Ahhh, see." She wags a finger at me. "You should have run with me in high school instead of doin' all that useless studyin'," she jokes.

But then I remember something. "Oh no."

"That didn't sound good."

"I'm playing on a volleyball team too," I admit with a wince. "On Tommy Tucker's team."

"Who just happens to be sponsored by Anderson Automotive, *Nick's team!*"

Heat rises to my cheeks.

"Now who's sleepin' with the enemy!"

"I'm not sleepin' with anyone." Unfortunately. "When Tommy Tucker asked me to play I said yes as a favor without even knowing it was also Nick's team. I have a hard time thinkin' of him as the enemy anyway."

"Wait . . . *Tommy* asked you?"

"Yes, and he wanted you on our team too."

"Like I could play for Nick?" she says with a scowl.

"I wasn't thinkin', okay? And Tommy was goin' on about how great an athlete I was and I caved."

"So did he ask you *out*?"

"It happens once in a while," I answer dryly.

"What did you say?"

I shrug. "I said yes."

"Wow. Tommy Tucker," she drawls slowly.

"What?"

"Nothin'," she says, and takes a sip of coffee.

"Oh no you don't. What?"

"He's cute and all in a cowboy kinda way but I just can't see the two of you together."

"And why not?"

"He's a bit of a walk on the wild side for you, Candie, and a little young if you ask me."

I toss my Mountain Dew can in the trash. "Well, I'm not askin' you."

"Well *la-de-da*."

"You really think he's too young?"

"I'm just givin' you a hard time. Tommy is cute and fun to be around. Have a good time and don't worry."

"You think?"

Sarah nods as she pushes up to her feet and gingerly puts her weight on her tender ankle.

I sigh with relief.

"Besides, who cares what people think?"

Great. Her comment takes the wind right out of my sails.

"Oh, stop with the long face. Nobody cares if you date Tommy Tucker." She hesitates and then says, "Well, except maybe Mama."

"Mama? Why?" I ask, but then see the smirk on Sarah's face. "Would you quit messin' with me?"

"Why? It's so much fun."

"You'd better be careful," I warn her. "You might have those long legs but I can run you down with that gimp." Reaching in the bottom drawer I pull out two white shoe polish tubes. "Here, put that imagination to better use than harassing me. Let's go write some stuff on the windshields of our sorry inventory."

"Like what kinda stuff?" Sarah asks.

"Low miles, one owner, great buy . . . you know . . . the usual."

"Think it will help?"

"No, but it gives us somethin' to do. Nick is starting to detail that old Escort," I tell her as we head outside into the bright, warm sunshine. "He's going to buff up the paint and add pinstriping."

"Sounds good."

"You know if we move this old stuff then we might have to go to the auto auction for some inventory."

Sarah scrunches up her nose. "I hate goin' to those things."

"We might not have a choice." I point to the left. "I'll take that side and you take the other, okay?"

Sarah nods and we get to work. After making my way down the front row of cars I'm running out of catchy things to write on the windshields. With a sigh I gaze at the old red Chevy S10 pickup truck. Nothing flattering comes to mind as I check out the high miles, a dent in the tailgate, and rust over the wheel wells. *Piece of junk* is what it should say in bold letters . . . but then a sudden lightbulb moment of inspiration hits me!

Nick could take this piece of junk and trick it out to look like a million bucks. Well maybe not a million bucks but *way* better.

My pulse starts racing with the notion that I could really be on to something. Glancing around I see that we have another crappy truck that could be transformed into a work of art that would sell in a heartbeat. Nick has the time, the talent, and the facility. Sure, this would take a while to get rolling but it could be the answer we've been waiting for.

Hot damn.

"Are you daydreaming about your date with Tommy?"

"Eeek!" I jump about a foot into the air at the sound of Sarah's voice. Pointing my shoe polish stick at her I grumble, "Do you have to go sneaking up on a person?"

"Candie, I said your name about three times but you were in la-la land . . . or maybe *Tuckerville.*"

"I was in we-need-some-business land."

"Good luck with that one," she comments but then pushes her sunglasses up and peers at me more closely. "Hey, you look like your wheels are spinnin'. Puh-lease tell me you have an idea."

"I have an idea."

"Don't toy with me, Candie. It wouldn't be right."

"Well . . ." I hesitate and wonder if I should wait to see if Nick is interested in my sudden idea to turn our lot into customized truck heaven . . . Hey that might make a good slogan, I think with a smile. Maybe my two years working at an ad agency will finally pay off.

"What!"

I jump and then put my hands on my hips. "You don't have to yell."

"You were in la-la land again. Come on, Candie, lay it on me."

"Promise to keep your cool and hear me out."

"Okay," she begins impatiently but then her eyes widen. "This plan of yours is gonna involve Nick, isn't it?"

"Just hear me out, Sarah!"

"Oh my God it is!" She stomps her foot but then visibly tries to calm herself down. After a deep breath and a flip of her hair she says, "Spill."

"Okay, here goes. The truck he's customizing is amazing. He could sell it in a heartbeat."

"So?"

"We have two old trucks on the lot that Nick could trick out. He has the facility and the know-how. We have the car lot and the inventory. Together we could start a custom truck business."

Sarah frowns. "Yeah but that takes time, and money. We have the time, but the money? Not so much."

"I know. We would have to start off small."

"We could go to Daddy."

"No, I don't want any extra stress on him right now."

"True. Do you think he'll do it?"

I shrug. "I don't see why not. He indicated that it was pretty much a hobby at this point. But Sarah, the truck really rocks." I take a deep breath and then ask, "What do you think? Is it worth a shot?"

Sarah purses her lips for a long moment and then says, "I think it's genius but I have to tell you that I really don't relish working with him. If Nick were interested you would have to deal with him. I know that someday I'll get over him dumping me but that day hasn't arrived."

"I understand. So are you okay with me approaching him about this?"

"Sure."

"Great! Oh, but Sarah, I want to keep this on the down low. Don't tell anyone."

"Why do we have to be so secretive?"

"I learned a thing or two while working for the ad agency in Chicago. Marketing is everything. We don't want the word out so we can make a big splash when we have some trucks to display."

"Okay. Mum's the word." She makes a show of locking her lips and throwing away the key.

"I guess I'm puttin' the cart before the horse. First, I have to go and see if Nick is interested before getting all worked up about this."

"Well then, I suggest you go over and talk to the *horse's ass* to see."

"Sarah!"

"I'm just sayin'." She takes my shoe polish from me and shoos me away. "Go."

"Can you hold the fort down here?"

"I think I can manage all of the customers myself," she answers dryly.

"Point taken," I reply with a grin. A nervous little flutter ripples through my stomach when I look across the street to Nick's shop but I start walking in that direction anyway. Once I'm to the sidewalk I glance back to see if Sarah is watching but she's busy writing on the windshield of a Chevy Cavalier. What? I shake my head and chuckle when I see that she's painting SEXY BEAST in big bold letters. As if knowing I'm watching, Sarah looks my way.

"What?" she shouts. "Don't ya think it fits?" I give her a thumbs-up and she laughs.

Then, squaring my shoulders I look both ways and cross the street while muttering a prayer beneath my breath that Nick will think this is a great idea.

10

The Best of Times . . . the Worst of Times

The front door to Anderson Automotive is open and although the little bell jingles over the door as I walk inside, Nick is once again nowhere in sight. A moment later I spot a note saying that he's back in the shop working. As I push the door open I'm feeling a little nervous since I don't have anything prepared. I guess I'll just have to plunge right in and see what he has to say.

Nick is putting the finishing touches on some pin-striping down the side of the Ford Escort that he's de-tailing for us. Dressed in his usual work attire of jeans and a white muscle shirt, he takes a step back and an-gles his head as if checking out his work. I'm doing my very best not to admire his butt, really I am . . .

"What the . . . ," I whisper and my mouth drops open when Nick's hips start to sway side to side. His shoulders move in the opposite direction of his butt, slowly at first, and then with more enthusiasm. His head dips and comes back up to dip again and I'm thinking he's having a seizure or something. My mouth clamps shut and I'm trying to recall how to do the Heimlich or CPR or whatever needed when he starts twitching.

Nick!" I call out, but he ignores me. Really concerned now, I take a step toward him and see the cause of his twitching and swaying. Earphone wires dangle from his head and a silver iPod is clipped to his jeans.

Nick is dancing . . . if you can call it that. His moves would make Elaine on *Seinfeld* look smooth. Trying to suppress my mirth I put my hand over my mouth and entertain myself watching. I'm able to keep my laughter under control until, *oh God*, he starts singing.

"*Born* . . . in the U.S.-A. I was *born* . . . in the U.S.-A." Dancing becomes a full-blown air guitar performance. He's so dorky that it's endearing.

"*Born* . . . in the U.S . . ." He does a wobbly spin and slide move but trails off when he's suddenly facing me. Our eyes meet and instead of appearing embarrassed he gives a boyish grin before reaching up and tugging the earphones from his ears. "Springsteen. You gotta sing with the Boss."

"You were amazing."

"You mean that in a good way, right?"

"Absolutely." Wide-eyed and nodding I manage not to laugh.

"You lie," he teases just like he always used to do so effortlessly with me. His grin widens to a smile and the warmth of his friendship wraps around me like a treasured quilt.

"No, seriously . . . you were, hmmm, how should I put this? A sight to behold."

"I'll choose to take that as a compliment," he says with one of the old Nick grins that I've missed so doggone much. A sense of that lost friendship hangs in the air between us and he clears his throat. "Um, I'm not done with the Escort. Thought she needed a pinstripe."

My gaze flicks over to the car. "Looks good, Nick."

"Yeah," he says in that low and raspy voice that's uniquely his. "Sure does." Something in his tone has my head whipping back to look at him but he's suddenly preoccupied with his iPod.

"That's not why I'm here."

Nick's green eyes are immediately gazing back at me. "Oh," he says slowly, "why then?"

"I have a proposition for you."

His dark eyebrows arch up. "I'm all ears," he teases.

"A *business* proposition," I tell him firmly, and I'm sure my cheeks are flaming. "It sounded better in my head."

"So you still blush at the drop of a hat. I was only teasing, Candie Land."

"I'm not a kid. Candie jokes don't bother me anymore," I assure him with a lift of my chin.

"Okay, Candie Cane."

I narrow my eyes but I say calmly, "Nope, nothin'."

He purses his lips and then nods. "I hear ya, Candie Corn."

"Okay, stop!"

"Make me, Candie Apple."

"I can still beat you up, you know."

"Hey, that one time in second grade was a fluke." He rubs his chin as if remembering the incident when he called me Candie Corn and I took a wild swing at him connecting with his chin. I felt horrid afterward. "You did pack quite a wallop for such a tiny thing."

"So you're willing to take that risk?"

He folds his arms across his chest, making his biceps bulge and making me think that Sarah is crazy for not hanging on to him. He still has that devilish twinkle in his green eyes that always made me wonder what he was going to do next. But just when I think that he's going to tease me with another candy-related name he goes all serious on me. "I've missed you, Candie."

"Same here," I admit, thinking that there's no reason not to own up to our friendship that goes back to playing in the sandbox together.

"Even after I went away to college we used to call each other all the time. I had your number on speed dial. What happened?"

"You got engaged to my sister."

"But what did that have to do with our friendship?" he persists.

I would have tried to come up with a joke or simply looked away but he has me pinned with an intense gaze that leaves no room for waffling. "It just didn't seem right."

"And just why is that?" As if the question isn't unnerving enough Nick takes a step closer, invading my space and flustering the heck out of me. Just what's going on here?

"I'm—I'm not sure." Feeling cornered I take a step backward and trip over the thick, orange extension cord. Luckily, Nick's hands shoot out and grab my upper arms, keeping me from taking a tumble.

"Maybe this will help," he says in a low, emotional tone that takes me by surprise.

"What do you—" The rest of my question is silenced when Nick dips his head and captures my mouth with his. His mouth is warm, his lips firm and yet pliant, tasting faintly of spearmint. The sensation is pleasant, nice even but without the fireworks that I felt with Tommy—thank God. I don't need more complications in my love life right now.

Hey wait a minute. I have a love life! I'm smiling on the inside at the thought but then glare up at Nick. "Just what the hell do you think you're doin'?"

"Sorry, I had to do that."

"Right, like there was a gun to your head! Explain

your sorry self before I connect with your chin—and this time I won't feel bad afterward!"

He runs a hand down his face, leaving a smear of grease on his cheek. "I needed to find out something for sure."

I blink up at him and it slowly dawns on me. "No!"

"Candie . . ."

"You . . . I'm . . ." I shake my head while backing up but because my hands are still hanging on to his shirt, he stumbles forward with me. Realizing my mistake I let go and put some distance between us. "Nick, are you trying to say that you have feelings other than friendship with me? My God, I really am . . . *the other woman!*" I squeak.

"I wouldn't put it that way," he says with hesitation in his voice. Shoving his fingers through his hair he continues, "But, in a way . . . *yes.*"

My heart starts to race. "But . . . why . . . ? How . . . ? I mean, I don't understand. Where did this suddenly come from?"

"It's complicated. And come on, Candie, didn't you ever wonder what it would be like to kiss me?"

I dig deep for a no-nonsense tone. "Of course not!"

"Really?"

I fidget a little. I'm really bad at lying, especially to him. "Well . . . *yeah,* I mean you were always so special in my life that I confess that it crossed my mind. But Nick, you might have been close to me but it was Sarah who turned your head."

Nick closes his eyes for a moment and then blows out a long breath. "I know, but when you came home for Christmas I realized how damned much I missed you. We talked about everything and I do love Sarah, but she . . . holds back." He scrapes the steel toe of his boot across the floor and then pins me with a level look. "I thought maybe I had—"

"No! Don't!" I shake my head slowly and feel my

eyes fill with tears. "I thought the issue is that you wanted Sarah to be your *friend* . . . not me to be your *lover!*" My face heats up at the statement but I had to say it.

"It started me thinking that I was mistaking physical attraction for something more."

"So you asked Sarah to marry you because she was *pretty?*" I choke out.

"No . . . *no.* Hear me out, please."

I nod. "Okay but just be warned that I'm feeling the urge to smack you silly."

"When Sarah and I went to college Sarah had a hard time adjusting from small-town Pinewood to a big university campus. She was the queen bee at Pinewood High School, remember?"

"Oh, yeah." How can I forget?

"On a huge campus she was intimidated and not at all her usual confident self. She was like my shadow for a while and I guess I felt protective of her. This vulnerable side of Sarah got to me and instead of just flirting she and I took it a step further. We started dating and as she settled into campus life her confidence returned. We seemed like the perfect couple. We rarely argued and had fun but recently I began to fear that there wasn't much beneath the surface of our relationship." He pauses and takes a deep breath. "What she and I had just wasn't enough anymore. When she gets past her anger I think she will admit to that. I do think she has more to give, Candie, but she won't give it."

Angling my head I say, "So the kiss was to see if there was a spark between us? Then you could have the whole package?"

He gives me a sheepish look. "Yeah. For a minute there it seemed like a good idea."

"So how was it?" I ask even though I already know the answer. He shifts his weight from one boot to the other.

"Let me answer for you. Nice but no fireworks, right?"

Nick looks so relieved that I *almost* laugh. "That pretty much sums it up." His eyebrows rise. "Thank God. Sarah would kick both our butts."

"Nick! How could you even think to put me in that position?"

"Sorry. It was . . ."

"Selfish, stupid . . . wrong?"

"Yeah. Damnit, Candie, I'm just so confused."

"So, now what are you going to do about Sarah?" I ask quietly. I'm torn between giving him the hug that he looks like he needs and kicking his ass for his little experiment, but in truth I needed to know too, not that I'd *ever* in this lifetime admit to it even if Jack Bauer was involved. Well, yeah, I probably would as soon as something sharp was wiggled beneath my nose.

"Damned if I know."

"You deserve to have it all, Nick, but Sarah's hurt."

After inhaling a deep breath he says, "Don't you think I know that?"

"Talk to her!"

"Candie, I've tried. She just doesn't understand what I need from her. The part that really gets me right here," he says, and jams his thumb to his chest, "is that she has so much more to give to me and just won't. I've seen bits and pieces and it kills me."

"What can I do?"

"Maybe talk to her? I want to be more than just a cute couple. I really want her to be my lover and my best friend all rolled up into one." He shakes his head sadly. "Am I wrong?"

"No." I put a hand on his cheek and rub away the grease. "But don't give up on Sarah yet. I've seen changes in her already. I think she needed this to shake herself up and to realize that she should be a giver and not just a taker."

He closes his eyes and swallows.

"Hey, are you okay?"

He laughs without humor. "You're the first person to ask that. Everyone pretty much hates me for dumping her."

"Tell me about it. I'm gettin' the cold shoulder too."

He swallows hard. "Candie, if you hate me too . . ." He growls but then inhales a shaky breath. I've never seen Nick this emotional and it claws at my heart. But of course he's a guy, so he holds it together. "Losing you was tough, you know."

"I know."

"Ah, Candie," Nick says gruffly. He reaches over and wipes my own tears away with the pad of his thumb and then draws me into his arms. Unable to resist the comfort I rest my cheek on his chest for a few moments. We stand there silent and sad, each of us lost in our own thoughts. "When did life get so damned complicated?"

"When we grew up. It would be fun to go back to shooting hoops and swimming all summer long but we have to get down to business."

Nick sighs. "Yeah, guess you're right." He pulls back and says, "Hey, what's this I hear about you and Tommy Tucker?"

After all we've talked about, his question takes me by surprise, "We're sort of seeing each other." I leave out the part that it's just a favor on Tommy's part.

"Well, tell him to keep in line or I'll have to kick his ass."

I laugh and give Nick another quick hug. It feels so good to be back to our old friendship.

"Seriously, I know this thing with Sarah and me makes things awkward but you know you can come to me with anything, right?"

"Yes, Nick, I do."

"Good," he says and looks relieved. "Sorry about

the kiss. I've been so damned depressed and confused, but that was way out of line."

"Don't worry. I'm not going to go runnin' my mouth off about it. No one needs to know."

"Thanks . . . no more drama, please!" he jokes, but the words have such an edge of sadness that it breaks my heart. "Okay now, just what is this proposition of yours?"

11

False Alarm

"Okay, here goes. Your truck is a work of art, Nick."

My statement seems to surprise but please him. He glances at the truck and then looks at me with a sort of shy pride. "Thanks."

"How long did it take you to trick it out like that?"

Nick shrugs. "Been working on it for about six months but only in my spare time. Where are you goin' with this?"

"I'm not entirely sure but I know that I could sell custom trucks like that on the lot. If I could provide you with the inventory and you do the custom work, maybe we could split the profits? I know your cousin Bailey owns the junkyard just outside of town so you have an in for parts." I sweep my hand in an arc. "You have the equipment here so we have that covered. It would take some doin' but we just might make it work."

"Maybe." Nick rocks back on his heels as if pondering the whole thing but shows enough interest to give me hope.

"I already have a couple of old trucks that you could get working on right away. I would love to start with the one you're almost finished with but if you don't want to sell it I understand. We at least need to have a front row of custom trucks before showing them to the public so we could make a splash . . . maybe even get some media coverage and have a grand opening of sorts."

Nick's eyebrows rise and he gives me another look of surprise.

"I worked for an ad agency in Chicago," I remind him.

"Sounds like you learned a few things."

"A few. Look, I know I don't exactly have a business plan here so I'm winging it but I think we could figure something out. What're your initial thoughts?"

He rubs the stubble on his chin. "The trucks would definitely sell. I've had people beggin' me to sell this one," he says, and gestures to his truck, "but I don't know if I'm ready to give her up. Quite honestly your biggest problem would be finding the trucks to trick out and then keeping inventory ready to go. I work pretty fast but it's still time-consuming."

My heart starts to pound at the prospect that he's on board. "Could you hire some part-timers?"

"Yeah. Bailey could help. But the sooner we can get this truck thing goin' the better."

I feel a little surge of joy. "So you're on board with it?"

"Yeah," he says with a slow smile. "I am. As soon as I get this Escort done I'll want those trucks you told me about. Then you and Sarah need to work on getting me more inventory. You might need to hit the back roads. If you find trucks that don't run, I can get them towed here."

"Okay. Oh, but remember to keep this quiet. We want this to be a surprise to the community to have the most impact. Of course Tommy and Bailey will have to know not to breathe a word."

"That won't be a problem. We both know who we need to worry about."

"Sarah."

Nick nods. "She has a tough time keeping a secret."

"Yeah, but I think she will respect the importance of this. I especially don't want her telling Carson Campbell."

"Is she seeing him?" He asks casually but I can tell it really bothers him.

"I don't know if you could call it *that*," I say carefully but I can't help but try to make him a bit jealous. Sisters do that sort of thing. "Sparks though are definitely flying. Do you know that she's playin' on his volleyball team? Her excuse is that she's tryin' to get on his good side so that he sends cars our way."

"Sounds like you don't care for him."

"Well, he's self-centered and arrogant. Not much to like, if you ask me. Sarah should watch herself," I tell him and widen my eyes for good measure. "I mean, I know you two are sort of friends but still . . ."

"Well, he's had a bit of a tough time adjusting to small-town life. He's like a fish out of water here in Pinewood. I was just bein' you know . . . ," he says, and shrugs, "friendly."

"You're a nice guy, Nick."

"Yeah, isn't there a sayin' about nice guys finishing last?" He chuckles but there's a sad edge to his laughter making the urge to draw him into my arms almost unbearable.

"Things are gonna work out for you and Sarah. I just know it."

"I wish I had your confidence," he says, and it's hard for me not to be angry with Sarah for doing this to him. God, I just want to knock their damned heads together!

"Well, I'd better get back to work."

Nick nods and looks like he wants to say something but stays quiet. "I'll get busy."

With a smile I head out the door but as soon as I get outside my emotions get a bit wacky as I cross the street. Trying to get my act together before entering the office I quickly go to the bathroom since I'm feeling close to tears.

"Hey, you okay?" Sarah calls out.

"Yes, I'll be out in a minute." After dampening the towel I put it to my forehead, hoping that the cool sensation will help to calm me down. A nice shot of smooth Kentucky bourbon would hit the spot, but although I know where Daddy keeps his emergency stash, I think it's a bit early in the day to start drinkin'. I shake my head at my wide-eyed reflection in the weathered mirror above the tiny sink and reconsider. "Maybe it's not too early."

"Get it to*gether*," I tell myself, and continue blotting. Finally, with a little shiver I toss the towel into the trash and determinedly sniff back the threat of tears.

"Hey, you okay in there?" Sarah asks and knocks on the door.

"Yeah, I'll be out in a minute." I give myself long enough to when I know Sarah is likely to knock again and then open the door.

"Better?" Sarah asks with a genuine look of concern that makes me feel guilty but how can I explain that her ex-fiancé just kissed me to make sure he didn't have feelings for me? I feel like I'm keeping a secret but what good would it do for her to know?

"Yeah, a little bit." I make a show of putting my palm to my tummy. "Thanks."

"So tell me what happened with Nick. You were over there a pretty long time."

I will my cheeks not to blush but of course it doesn't do any good. I feel as if my face is on fire.

"You sure you're okay? You look flushed like you

could be comin' down with somethin'. You didn't go eatin' breakfast at Spooner's, did ya? I meant to tell ya that when Charlie Spooner died his son took over that joint and Freddie has already gotten written up by the board of health twice now."

"No, I didn't, but thanks for the heads-up. Sarah, understand that it wasn't an easy endeavor to approach Nick." I make a show of fanning my cheeks. "Forgive me if I'm a little bit shaken!" Okay, the understatement of the year award officially goes to me . . . and maybe an Oscar too. "Okay just *why* are you givin' me that silly grin?"

"Your accent!" she joyfully proclaims. "Unnecessary words, extra syllables . . . talkin' with your hands. All of that citified mumbo jumbo has been purged!"

"Must have been the MoonPie," I tell her with a chuckle. "I was craving one last night and Mama stocked me up with several flavors. One bite and I turned right back into a redneck."

"Well, it's about time." She puts her hands up for a double high five. "Praise the Lord!"

With a laugh I high-five her back.

"Ouch!" Sarah says with a grimace.

"Oh sorry! Your wrist still tender?"

"A little. I'll have to tape it for volleyball. We're gonna win, you know. I plan on crammin' the ball right down Nick's throat," she mutters darkly as she flexes her wrist.

"Are you still in love with him, Sarah?" I quietly ask, surprising myself, and judging by her startled expression, her too.

Sarah hesitates a moment too long and then says, "Of course . . . *not*." She is completely unconvincing. "I mean, I still care about his well-being and all, but you know, after what he did, I would have to dig deep for those feelings," she stutters, but then purses her lips, seeming to consider the question further, but then her blue eyes widen. "Why? Did y'all talk about me?"

"A little," I admit while guilt uses me for a punching bag.

"Did . . . did Nick tell you why he dumped me?"

Good God, yes. Why did I just go down this slippery slope? *Why?* What should I do? I can't tell her everything but I don't want to lie either.

"Is there someone else?" Sarah demands with a gasp. "Was that whole *he needs the closeness that you and he shared* a bunch of bullshit? Did Nick finally come clean?"

Well, sort of, but it was a false alarm, I want to say but can't. My stomach becomes a nervous ball of ice while I consider how to answer.

"Oh my God! There was!" She slaps her hands down on the desk and winces. "I knew it! That two-timin', cheatin', low-life, yellow-bellied . . . wait, what's yellow-bellied mean? "

"A coward."

"Okay, yellow-bellied, no-count—"

"No! Sarah . . . *no*. Nick wasn't cheatin' on you." There, that *is* the truth.

"Oh." She looks relieved but confused as she twirls her finger in a lock of blond hair. "Cold feet then? That's what Mama thinks." Sarah looks at me expectantly and I try not to squirm.

"I guess you could call it that," I tell her with hesitation. "But Sarah, I have to ask . . . if it was a bad case of cold feet, would you want Nick back?"

"I . . ." Her mouth opens and then snaps shut. "I don't know. I mean, he *humiliated* me even more than my booby flash and that was hard to do. I'm still angry. He would have to get down on his knees and all that."

"And then would you?"

Her eyes widen. "Did he ask you that?"

"Sarah, you're dodging the question. Are you more angry than hurt?"

"Are you seriously takin' his side?"

"I'm tryin' to help you analyze the situation minus the anger."

"And humilation."

"Okay and that."

"Well, *that* might take a while," she says with a huff but suddenly looks uncomfortable. "To hell with him," she continues with a flip of her hand but swallows hard. "Now tell me about the custom truck business. Is he on board with it or not?"

I'm somewhat relieved by getting off the hook but I really wanted to know how Sarah truly feels about Nick. Judging by the look on her face this is not the time to push the question, so I give her a brisk nod. "We haven't worked out all of the details but Nick thinks it's a great idea. I tried to get him to start off with the beauty he's already created but he said he's not ready to give her up."

Sarah raises her palms skyward. "He can't part with his truck but tosses me like yesterday's trash?"

"Sarah . . ."

"Sorry! I was just sayin' "—she wiggles her fingertips—"go 'head. Don't mind me."

"We have two trucks on the lot that he can start with but then we have to round up some inventory. I want to wait until he has several trucks done before we go public so we can have a grand opening of sorts." I give her a pointed look.

"I get it. You're tellin' me to keep my piehole shut."

"I wasn't going to say it like that, but yes. I especially don't want Carson to get wind of this. Next thing you know he'll carry a line of tricked out trucks and steal our thunder."

"I'm not stupid."

"I never said that you were."

Sarah looks ready to argue the point but then her expression softens. "I'm sorry, Candie. I don't mean to be so bitchy. This truck thing seems like an amazing idea. The town could use some excitement."

"And we could use the money."

"So now what do we do?"

"We need to start scouring the area for old trucks. Nick suggested some of the back roads. And of course we need to really push what we have here on the lot to stockpile some money. In the meantime I'm going to work on a business plan." I glance out the window and see a young couple pull onto the lot. "We've got a customer. Will you take them? They look like buyers."

Sarah puckers her lips. "My wrist is throbbin'."

I roll my eyes.

"Oh, *okay!*" she says with a chuckle. "You're a dog-gone slave driver."

"Get used to it."

"Get used to it," she mocks as she pushes up to her feet.

"Oh, Sarah?" I ask innocently, and she turns from pushing open the door to look at me. I stick out my tongue.

"Oh grow up," she says but then sticks her own tongue out at me and then we both burst into laughter. It hits me that even though she can be a drama-queen pain in the butt, I love her to death. I watch her head over to the young couple and strike up a lively conversation. She's much better at this than she gives herself credit for. Here all my life I thought Sarah oozed confidence and in reality she's much more insecure than I ever dreamed. I suddenly realize that Nick was right. Sarah is afraid to open up and give all she's got. I never imagined that my bigger than life daddy could ever become pale and physically weak. I guess that we make assumptions and take for granted things about those whom we love the most.

With a sigh I mutter a little prayer that this truck thing takes off like a rocket. Daddy needs a breather. Sarah needs her confidence boosted. And me?

I need . . . A vision of Tommy Tucker in red-hot chili pepper boxers skitters across my brain and I smile.

12

Here's Your Sign . . .

I'm in a darned good mood up until it's time for Tommy Tucker to pick me up for volleyball practice. Sarah ended up selling the young couple the Ford Taurus at a nice profit and I delivered two trucks for Nick to start working on, so it was a productive day. A sugar buzz from a Pepsi and a banana MoonPie has me sort of hyper but I thought I needed the energy for practice. Okay, it was a lame excuse to eat the treat but I know how to manipulate myself quite well. As I stand there in my Wrigley Field T-shirt and shorts I realize that I'm not so much hyper but nervous.

With a groan I plop down onto the lumpy sofa. "Well, hells bells." I grab a fringed pillow and hug it to my chest, thinking this is stupid to be nervous over a doggone date. The *bing-bong* ring of the doorbell startles me out of my musings and I peek around the ruffled curtain to find Tommy standing on my front stoop. Instead of a cowboy hat and Wranglers his shaggy blond hair is gleaming in the sunlight and blue board shorts are slung low on his hips. A white Nike logo T-shirt fits snugly enough to showcase defined pecs and biceps that look like they could crack walnuts. *Nice,* I think to myself and then swing the door open with a smile.

"Hey there," Tommy says as he comes inside. "You ready for a workout?" He might look like a surfer dude but his Southern drawl is slow and complemented by his good-ole-boy grin.

"It's been a while," I warn him. "I hope I don't disappoint you."

"That's not likely to happen," he says while sliding his Oakley's to the top of his head.

"We're talkin' about volleyball here, Tommy," I dryly remind him.

He widens his eyes and attempts an innocent expression. "Of course we were. What did you think I meant?"

I answer by giving him a playful shove and encounter rock-hard abs. "Are you always such a big player, Tommy Tucker?"

"The best."

"That's what I thought."

"Wait, we're still talkin' volleyball, right?" His Paul Walker blue eyes crinkle with teasing laughter.

"No, we most certainly are not."

"Well then," he says as he holds the creaky screen door open for me, "you know what they say?"

"I'm afraid to ask but I will."

"The bigger they are the harder they fall."

"So you're sayin' that a girl just hasn't swept you off your feet yet?" I brush past him and head toward his black Ford Ranger.

"Dudes don't get swept off their feet," he scoffs as he opens the truck door for me. The lift kit makes the step up difficult for a short person such as myself but as I start to grab the door handle for assistance Tommy puts his hands around my waist and hefts me onto the front seat as if I weigh nothing . . . making me feel all feminine and fluttery.

"What happens to dudes, then?" I'm trying to be flippant but he's leaning in close, looking all tanned, blond, and Paul Walker-ish, making my danged voice come out breathless as if I'm trying to flirt . . . but I'm not. I don't think. Okay, I am.

"I wouldn't know," he answers in a surprisingly serious tone, "since it's never happened to me."

"Then maybe you *will* get swept off your feet."

"Well, that would take quite a woman since I weigh just shy of two hundred pounds."

"You don't look it," I comment, and then feel a blush heat my cheeks. "Oh, I said that out loud, didn't I?"

Tommy's bad-boy grin returns. "Are you flirting with me?"

"I'm trying."

Tommy tosses back his shaggy head with a good-natured laugh. "Good, keep it up. I like it," he comments with a sideways glance in my direction after pulling out into the street. "So, you a Cubbies fan?"

"How'd you guess?"

"Your shirt," he answers with a grin.

"Oh . . . right. Yep, I could walk to Wrigley Field from where I lived in Chicago. I'm still a Cincinnati Reds fan at heart but I loved the atmosphere at Wrigley Field. You ever been there?"

"No, but I've always wanted to go. Maybe . . ."

"What?"

"Nothin'."

"No, what?" I reach over and shake his knee. "Tell me."

I'm surprised by his rather shy grin. "I almost said that maybe someday you might show me around Chicago and we could take in a game but I thought it might be too forward of me. But then you had to go and badger me into it."

"I didn't badger you."

"You touched my leg and that was all it took."

"Tommy Tucker, are you blushin'?"

"Hell no. I don't blush." He reaches over and cranks up the air-conditioning. "Is it getting hot in here or is it me?"

"Oh you're hot, all right, and you darned well know it."

Tommy laughs and I join him. After all that's happened today I'm surprised at how at ease I'm feeling. At a stoplight he turns and looks at me but doesn't say anything.

"What?"

"You're different than what I expected."

"Good different or bad different?"

"Fun different."

"So, then that's good, right?"

"Very good," he says as he shifts gears. "You seemed a bit uptight and serious before."

"Well, I have to admit that I'm having more fun than I've had in a while. I've been so worried about my daddy and the business. This distraction is just what I needed. Thanks, Tommy."

"Is that what I am? A distraction?" He asks as he pulls the truck into the sports center.

I'm not sure if he's kidding or offended. "Hey, that's a compliment. I'm not easily distracted."

"Well, you're welcome then. I think."

I chuckle as I open the door but before I can jump to the pavement Tommy is there to help me down. I put my hands on his shoulders and he takes his sweet time while we have one of those lingering moments that could lead to a kiss but instead is just a teasing promise of things to come. Then I remember that I shouldn't let things get that far since I won't be here for all that long.

"Okay, *what*?" Tommy asks with a shake of his head.

"What do you mean?"

"Candie, you're frowning at me."

"Oh." I paste a smile on my face.

"Now that was fake."

"Was not!"

He makes a funny face and I give him a genuine smile.

"Now that's more like it. There will be no faking anything when you're with Tommy Tucker."

"Really now." I cock an eyebrow at him. "What if I make a bad play? Can I fake an injury?"

"Well . . . okay, I guess," he says as he grabs the big mesh bag full of volleyballs. "But you can always use the sun in your eyes excuse."

I have to laugh. "Have you done that?"

Tommy looks at me in mock horror. "Of course not. The district baseball championship game senior year when I missed a routine fly ball happened because the sun *really* was in my eyes. That's my story and I'm stickin' to it."

"I had graduated by then so I don't remember."

"Good," he says as he hefts the bag over his shoulder. "Not one of my finer moments."

I confess some of my volleyball screwups as we walk over to the sand volleyball court.

"You're just tryin' to make me feel better," he says as he tosses me a volleyball.

"Oh, come on, Tommy. I'm sure you were a great baseball player."

He shrugs. "I was good at just about any sport I played and I tried all of them. I'm solid but I never got great, you know? I guess I should have stuck with one and really honed my skills but I love them all."

"Well then, you must really enjoy your job here at the park."

"Yes," he says with a wave of his hand in an arc, "that's why this job is like my dream come true. I'm surrounded by organized sports . . . baseball, softball, volleyball, and tennis. I'm proposing an expansion of our indoor facility so we can have indoor soccer and basketball leagues in the winter. Initially it will be costly but will pay for itself in just a few years."

"A good investment for the city, I'd say."

He grins. "Do me a favor and run for city council."

I smile back but it reminds me that I won't be here that long. With a mental shake I push that thought to the back of my mind. "Tommy, the improvements you've already made here are amazing. I've always loved this park and now it's even better. There's something for everyone here."

"Kids need to keep active so they'll stay out of trouble and be healthier. I also want to include an indoor walking track for runners and set up times for seniors who want to walk indoors so that . . . ," he trails off and shakes his head. "Mercy, Candie, you can tell me to shut my mouth any time now. Am I boring you to death?"

"Not at all," I answer truthfully. "I'd like to hear more of what you have planned and believe me I think that Pinewood needs this. I think your enthusiasm will be contagious."

"I won't make a million bucks but I love what I do. Okay, I *will* shut up now," he promises as he steps into the sand. "Let's warm up."

"Tommy, I'm interested. *Really.*"

"Then why are you frownin' at me again?"

"I am?"

"Yeah."

"I guess I was thinkin' that you're different than I expected too. And before you ask, yes in a good way. There's more to you than meets the eye."

"Don't give me too much credit," he warns as he bops a ball at me. "I still watch *South Park,* play video games, and eat cold pizza for breakfast."

"Yeah, well, sometimes I think that growin' up is overrated," I admit, thinking back to my conversation with Nick as we pepper the ball back and forth. "Hey, where's the rest of our team? Aren't we all going to practice?"

Tommy shrugs. "This practice was last minute, so I'm not sure who will show up."

"Who else is on our roster?"

"I've got the league set as four on four co-ed teams. You have to have at least one member of the opposite sex on your team and on the court at all times. So we have you, me, Bailey, and Nick. Bailey's sister and girlfriend signed up too but I'm hoping to get a few more players. If you can think of any of your high school teammates, then let me know."

"I've been away for so long that I'm out of touch but I'll see what I can do." I surprise him with a wicked spike but he dives in the sand and digs it out. His return goes a little cockeyed but I manage to get to it and hit it back.

"I'm impressed," he says and sends me a ball with more oomph to it.

I heroically make a running dive for the ball but come up with nothing but a mouth full of sand. To make matters worse I roll three times before coming to a stop faceup with my gritty mustache.

"You okay?" Tommy asks while kneeling over me. Of course I can't answer because of the sand. "Let's get you a drink of water.

I nod and allow him to assist me to my feet. Spitting and sputtering I follow him to the shelter house where he promises there's a water fountain. I really hope that this isn't a giant litter box for mangy stray cats.

"Here, let me," Tommy offers. As I bend over the fountain he politely turns the knob. Of course the water shoots up in a giant arc totally missing my sandy mouth and goes straight up my nose. "Sorry!" he says but I hear laughter in his voice.

I adjust the dip of my head to match the water but Tommy lowers the pressure so my poor mouth remains sandy. We do this little dance a few more times before I playfully slap at his hand and manage to squirt myself in the eyes. Finally, I'm able to rinse my mouth and get rid of the sand . . . well most of it anyway.

"Still impressed?" I ask with a shake of my head. When he looks at me as if he doesn't know what to say I help him. "There's no correct answer for that one but if you dare laugh I'll head-butt you into next week." My voice sounds nasal due to the water still up there, somewhere near my brain.

Tommy's look of concern changes to a grin at my comment. "You and what army?" he teases.

"Don't need one," I assure him in my nasal tone. "One of the few advantages to bein' short is that I can do a head-butt right to the stomach no pro-blem-o."

"You've never head-butted anyone," he scoffs.

"Wanna bet?" I challenge. He's right of course. I especially wouldn't want to ram my head into his rock-hard abs but I narrow my eyes and he takes a step back, looking kind of nervous. Just for fun I decide to take a couple of steps backward and then act as if I'm going to head-butt him as threatened. The operative word here is *act* but the toe of my shoe catches on a raised crack in the sidewalk (I swear there's one there) and I go airborne like a chicken trying to fly. Well, we all know that chickens can't fly, so I find myself flopping forward in an odd almost slow-motion tumble.

Tommy's eyes widen and he has the decency to catch me beneath my outstretched arms before I land on my face, this time without the cushion of the sand. "Wow, I thought you were just jokin' but you really were gonna head-butt me." He looks at me with a kind of wonder . . . as though he wonders if I'm crazy.

I'm not quite sure how to dispute his statement so I offer a lame, "Not really."

"No, I'm truly impressed. I don't usually get head-butted on the first date."

"I tripped."

"I know."

"I'm humiliated."

"Aw, come on, Candie, don't be." He eases me back up to a standing position. "You were just havin' fun." He tucks a springy curl behind my ear, reminding me that my hair gave up the fight against flatironing a while ago. "I think you're cute as a button."

Great . . . cute as a button. Sounds like something to say to a five-year-old or maybe a puppy. Suddenly I don't want to be best-friend girl or cute girl. I just want to be me.

"Hey, there's that frown again. Did I say somethin' wrong?"

"No," I assure him but when I try to take a step back he puts his hands on my waist.

"You're not really embarrassed, are you?"

"Only a little," I admit.

"Good, I didn't think you were like that."

I glance up at him in question. "Like what?"

"All prissy and worried about how you look."

"Oh." Suddenly I feel like the geeky jock I was back in high school. This time I make more of an effort to back away.

"Okay, now I *did* say something wrong. Tell me."

"Why don't you think I care about how I look? Because it's pointless?"

He gives me a confused look. "You lost me."

"Never mind," I tell him. "I don't know what's gotten into me. I'm not usually such a drama queen. Jocks aren't like that, right?" I start to pull away again but his blond eyebrows draw together and he stops me.

"Wait a doggone minute. So, you think of yourself as a jock?"

I shrug. "Yeah. Like in not prissy and not caring how I look . . . you know Sarah said somethin' similar to me the other day. Is my hygiene coming into question? Do Stacy and Clinton need to get hold of me?"

"Who?"

"Never mind. Look, I'm being an idiot and I'm not sure why. Can we drop this?"

"No," he surprises me by saying firmly. "I have two sisters so I think I'm catchin' on. I think you're gettin' the wrong impression and I want to clear things up."

I open my mouth but he silences me with a gentle finger to my lips.

"Yeah, you're not a high maintenance don't-mess-my-hair-up-or-smear-my-lip-gloss kinda chick. And *yeah*, you'll dive for a volleyball and eat sand in the process. But Candie, let me make myself perfectly clear. I think you're hot as hell." He rubs his fingertip over my bottom lip while looking intently at me with those blue eyes and then slowly lowers his head and kisses me. It's not an all-consuming, devouring me kiss but . . . warm, tender, oh so sweet. "Damn," he says, drawing out the word while shaking his head.

"What? Ohmigod. Did I have some sand left in my mouth?"

"Not that I noticed." Tommy chuckles, a low and throaty rumble that does funny things to my tummy.

"What then?"

"Kissing you was even more amazing than I imagined."

"Oh, so you've thought about it?" I ask in a surprisingly flirty tone.

"Since I saw you at the pub the other night."

I give him a shove. "You're so full of it," I joke, but he doesn't laugh.

"Yeah, I am, no doubt about it. But not this time," he adds softly.

I swallow hard when his blue eyes go all intense. For a minute I think he might kiss me again . . . and I think I might just let him.

"You wanna blow this place and go grab a beer?" he asks.

"Sure," I answer, but we both stand there looking at each other with that I-want-to-kiss-again hanging in the warm summer breeze. His head dips and my heart starts thudding.

"Damn," he growls and pulls back.

"What's wrong?"

"The rest of the team just showed up."

"Does that mean we're stayin'?"

"Hell no. I'll leave the balls for Nick. He'll get them back to me.

"You okay?" Tommy asks.

"Why, was I frownin' again?"

He grins. "No, you had this dreamy expression on your face.

"Maybe I was thinkin' about your kiss."

"Yeah, right," he scoffs. "Now whose full of it? Hey, you head over to the truck. I'm gonna tell Nick that we're headin' out."

I nod, but feel a bit guilty about not staying for practice. "Maybe we should stay," I offer when he meets me at the truck.

"Aw, quit feelin bad about skippin' out. It's gonna be dark soon anyway."

"Yeah, but still . . ."

Tommy opens the door for me and says, "Look, you played varsity ball like me and it's been pounded into our brains that you don't miss practice. But remember that this is a recreational league. Just for fun."

"Well, okay, we can play just for fun right after we kick Carson Campbell and Sarah's butt next week."

Tommy laughs. "Are you capable of playin' just for fun?"

I give him a level look. "What do you think?"

"Not on your life."

"You got that right. I fully admit that I like to win."

"Good, because I do too." He reaches over and gives me a knuckle bump. "You're a girl after my own heart."

I know he's just teasing but his comment makes me feel warm and fluttery.

"Damn, I want to kiss you again."

"You said that out loud."

"I do that sometimes."

"Me too! It's a curse."

"Sometimes a blessing. Puts it all out there, you know?"

I nod but I'm not really sure what he said because I'm looking at his mouth and thinking that kissing him might be nice. He leans a fraction closer and our lips brush, sending a warm tingle down my spine. My eyes flutter shut but then some guy honks his horn and we jump apart.

Tommy puts the truck in gear and then laughs. "I gotta admit it's been a while since that's happened."

"Since what's happened?"

"Since I've been so into a girl that I have a horn honked at me."

"Mercy, we're *so* high school."

He grins at me. "Yeah, we are but it's fun, isn't it? Hey, you wanna go someplace and park?"

"No, I want a cold beer and some hot wings."

"Okay," he says glumly. "But before the night is over I'm gonna kiss you again."

"You're pretty darned cocky."

"I'm not about to touch that line," he says as we pull into the parking lot.

I have to laugh as I watch him walk in front of the truck to come over and open the door for me. I'm not sure how serious he is or if he just has all the right moves, but he's cute and funny and I'm having a blast. For right now that's more than enough.

13

Just What the Doctor Ordered

Tommy Tucker has me in stitches. At one point I laugh so hard that I snort and almost aspirate a buffalo wing.

"Did you just snort?" he asks.

"Yes. Consider it a compliment. The snort happens only once in a blue moon. The last time I think was in a crowded movie theater."

"What was the movie?"

"*The Wedding Crashers.* So you're lucky I didn't embarrass you in a crowd of people."

"Do you think your snorting would embarrass me?"

"Uh . . . *yeah.* It sure embarrassed my date. He gave me a did-you-just-snort look and I sort of nodded in the direction of the lady sitting next to me but I think he was on to me. It was our first and only date."

"Because you snorted?"

"I guess he just wasn't that into me."

"His loss." Tommy crunches on a celery stick and then says, "For the record, it's pretty hard to embarrass me."

"Yeah right. Only because nobody heard."

He points his stubby celery stick at me and shakes

his head. "Not true. Go ahead. Snort when my sister walks by."

I lean forward and hiss, "No way!"

"Dare ya," he challenges with the arch of one blond eyebrow.

"How do you know I can't resist a dare?" I narrow my eyes at him.

"You're an athlete. You said you like to win. It goes hand in hand. I know because I'm the same way."

I groan. "Then don't dare me!"

He takes a slug from his beer mug and clunks it down onto the table. "Too late."

"Tommy . . . ," I plead.

"Here comes my sister. Get ready to snort."

I try to snort, I really do but all I can do is laugh.

"Chicken!" he says when his sister passes by our table.

"I tried! I can't snort on command. It just . . . happens unexpected-like. You know?"

"Yeah," he says with a more serious tone, "I'm finding that out."

Somehow I don't think he's talking about snorting. A quiet awareness passes between us, not an uncomfortable silence but more of a warm tingle as though we've connected on a level deeper than flirting . . . nothing mind-blowing exactly but a hint of something *more*. He seems to feel it too but then again it's been so long since I've been on a casual date that maybe I'm reading way too much into a few laughs, wings, and beer.

"Wonder what the score is?" Tommy asks as he glances up at the TV behind me.

"I don't know. I haven't really been following." The Cincinnati Reds are playing on several flat-screen televisions scattered around the rather spacious bar but I've been too entertained by Tommy to pay much attention.

"Me neither. I've had better things to look at," he says with a rather shy grin that keeps his statement from being a line. He's such a combination of bad-boy swagger and nice-guy sincerity that he keeps me a bit off balance.

"I hope Ken Griffey Jr. stays healthy this season," I comment.

"Won't matter much if they don't get any good pitching again this year."

"True. How long has it been since we've had an ace or a doggone amazing closer?"

Tommy makes a show of scratching his chin. "Let me think . . . oh yeah, *forever*." He bugs his blue eyes out and I laugh for the millionth time that evening.

"Ah, Tommy, my abs are gonna be sore tomorrow from so much laughing."

He reaches over and covers my hand with his. "Good . . . well not the abs hurting part but I'm glad I made you laugh. You said earlier that you needed it."

"Yeah, you're just what that doctor ordered."

He leans back in the booth and laces his hands behind his head. "Yeah, a big dose of Tommy Tucker is what all the ladies need," he teases.

Just then Tommy's sister walks over to our table. "In your dreams, baby brother," she says and rolls her eyes at me. "You're not buyin' what he's sellin' are ya?"

"I don't know. He's pretty hard to resist."

"See," Tommy says smugly.

"I think she was bein' sarcastic, Tommy."

"Were you?"

"Of *course* not," I say in a mock serious tone that makes his sister Connie chuckle.

"I like her," Connie says and gives me a wink. "Can I get y'all another beer? On the house for taking my brother down a notch or two."

"I'd better not. Two is my limit on a weeknight. But

thanks. Your place is really nice and the wings were amazing."

"You like 'em hot, huh?"

"Sure, she's with me," Tommy says and his sister teasingly smacks him upside the head.

"Ouch!"

"You deserved it," Connie says but then smiles at me. "Nice meeting you, Candie. Keep this guy in line okay?"

"No problem," I promise.

Tommy gets up and gives his sister a hug before turning to me. "You ready?"

"Yes, it's getting a little late. I can't believe it's almost ten o'clock."

He nods. "Me neither. Yeah, I have an early day tomorrow," he says as he tosses down some money even though Connie didn't leave a bill. "Silly girl always wants to give me food for free." He takes my hand as we walk out the door and I have to say that it feels really good.

When we arrive back at my house I'm suddenly sorry that the evening is over. After a moment's hesitation I take the plunge and say, "I know it's a bit late but it's such a nice night out. Would you like to sit on my front porch for a spell?" My heart pounds a little as I wait for his answer. I keep forgetting that he got into this as a favor to me.

"I was hoping you'd ask."

When I let out a breath of relief Tommy gives me a shake of his head. "You didn't think I'd turn you down, did you?"

I shrug. "This whole thing started out as a favor. I don't want to push you into something you don't want to do."

"You're kiddin', right?"

I give him a negative shake of my head.

"We need to clear some things up," he says, and then gets out of the truck.

I wait for him to help me down from the passenger side and this time instead of a lingering promise of things to come Tommy pulls me in for a long delicious kiss. "Clear now?" he asks gruffly.

"Um . . . no, maybe I need some more convincing," I tease back and it suddenly dawns on me that I have the bantering fun that Nick and I shared but with the spark we were missing. I suddenly understand what Nick means about wanting the whole package.

"I can definitely do that," Tommy says and tugs me toward the front porch.

"Can I get you something to drink?" I ask when we reach the steps.

"A bottle of water would be great."

"Comin' up." I head inside and grab a couple of bottles of water and then join Tommy on the top of the stoop. The moon is high and there's a gentle breeze bringing the scent of summer flowers our way. Maybe we can just enjoy the evening without any other worries.

I'm thinking about leaning my head on his shoulder when he says, "Okay, Candie, you have to be honest with me. Is there something between you and Nick? I didn't mention it before but he gave a strange vibe at the volleyball court. I know you said you were close friends but give it to me straight. I need to know."

"Oh, wow. Not what you might be thinkin'. Nick was engaged to my sister, Tommy."

"The whole town knows that and to be honest I'm not sure what I'm thinkin', only that I'm really startin' to like you. So tell me the score."

"Nick and I have been friends since we were little kids."

"I get that but you're dancing around somethin'. What is it?"

"It's complicated," I answer lamely, hating that I used that stupid phrase.

Tommy leans against the porch railing and stretches out his long legs. "Look, I'll be honest with you, Candie. Even though I sometimes come off as being a player, in truth I'm a pretty simple and down-to-earth kinda guy." He taps his chest and gives me a shadow of a Tommy grin. "Nothin' complicated here."

"Believe me, I like that about you," I assure him in a husky voice clogged with emotion, but then again, this has been one hell of a day.

Tommy shifts his weight so that he's facing me. "Hey," he says gently. "Like I said, I think you can already tell that I like you a lot."

"I can't remember when I've enjoyed myself so much."

"Same here," he says, and then pauses as if gathering his thoughts. "With my daddy on the road most of the time, my mama and my older sisters provided enough commotion to let me know that I want *simple.* Uncomplicated. Usually when I sense drama I run like the wind in the opposite direction . . . and I smell drama."

"So, are you gonna run?"

"No, but just be straight with me," he says, but then reaches over and runs a fingertip down my cheek. "Are you gonna fill me in? You can trust me to keep my mouth shut about anything you say even if it's not what I want to hear. You explained some things but I know there's more."

I hesitate, not because I don't trust him but because I'm not sure just what to tell him about the kiss or even if I should. I promised Nick that I'd keep my mouth shut.

"Look, maybe I'm oversteppin' my bounds. I should just go." He starts to push up to his feet but I stop him by putting a hand on his leg.

"No . . . don't go."

He hesitates but then sits back down on the step. "I feel like I'm putting pressure on you and that's not my way." He pinches his thumb and forefinger to the bridge of his nose. "Did I just sound like a girl? Please, tell me I did not just sound like Connie."

"Maybe a little bit?"

He groans. "Need any wood chopped or a tire changed . . . anything? Quick, I need to do something manly."

"You could kiss me," I suggest, but then clamp my hand over my mouth.

"You just had one of those I-can't-believe-I-said-that-out-loud moments again, didn't you?"

With my hand still clamped over my mouth I simply nod.

"I sure the hell don't know what kind of mess I'm getting myself into." He scoots closer and gently pries my hand from my mouth. "But damned if I'm not already knee-deep in it."

"Tommy, I—"

"You still want that kiss or not?" he asks very close to my ear.

"I—I don't mean to be a drama queen or to lead you on and I hate, *really hate*—"

"Do you realize that you talk too much?" he interrupts, and then nibbles on my earlobe.

I try to act all nonchalant as if it didn't just send me into orbit. "It's a Southern thing. I'm not as bad as Mama and Sarah. I talk too much only when I'm nervous."

"I don't want you to be nervous around me."

"I'm not in the way that you think. I just don't want to—" I lose my whole train of thought when he nips again and then moves his warm, moist mouth to my neck.

"To what?"

"You're distractin' me!" I protest, and then gasp when he sucks my earlobe into his hot mouth.

"I know."

"B-but I thought you wanted to know . . . things."

Tommy sits up straight and looks me in the eye. "I do. Sort of. Maybe not. Damn, I don't know." He runs his fingers through his hair, making the shaggy layers even messier. After a deep breath he says, "I can read between the lines, Candie. I think there's something more than friendship between you and Nick but you have your sister to consider. Am I right?"

"No," I protest softly. "I'll be honest—Nick thought that maybe there could be but believe me, I do care about him, but nothing would make me happier than to see him and Sarah get back together again. He was just hurt and confused and it's hard for me because I love him as a friend." I put my fingertips to my temples. "I'm just not cut out for this stuff. In truth, I'm a pretty simple girl too." I shake my head. "I feel like I'm caught up in a redneck soap opera."

Tommy tips his head back and laughs. "What am I gonna do with you?"

"I thought you were gonna kiss me."

"Yeah . . . I was. But before I do, I want you to make a decision."

"Okay."

"If you want this to go any further I want you to know that I just need to know the score, that's all. Honesty is all I'm asking for. I don't want to be a diversion or a substitute for Nick or anybody else for that matter. This might have started out as something fun, but Candie, it's already way beyond that."

"Nick and I truly are just friends. He and Sarah have issues but I have no doubt that he loves her." I'm about to tell him that one of the real issues at this point is that I'm planning on going back to my job in Chicago at the end of the summer. My throat closes up at the thought of telling him I'm leaving before we can take this to the next level. "Tommy . . . look—"

"No . . . *no*, stop. What in the hell am I doing? Here I give you a speech about me not being complicated and I'm way overthinking this thing between us."

"But—," I begin only to be silenced by a sweet kiss that has me wrapping my arms around his neck and threading my fingers in his hair. When the tender kiss ends he scoots back against the wooden railing and then pulls me into his arms. "Let's just chill for a while, okay? No worries."

"Now you're talkin'."

With a sigh I rest my cheek against his chest and he loops his arms lightly around my waist. We sit there for a few moments in thoughtful silence with the muted hum of insects punctuated intermittently by the ribbit-ribbit of bullfrogs singing in the background. When the cool night breeze carries the woodsy scent of pine and earth mixed with the sweeter hint of flowers I snuggle closer, enjoying the warmth of Tommy's skin through the soft cotton of his shirt.

"This is really nice," he murmurs close to my ear and I smile, wondering if he meant to say that out loud. "Hey, you fallin' asleep on me?"

"Mmmm, I'm so comfy that I could do just that but you'd be stiff as a board come mornin'."

He chuckles.

"Okay, that didn't come out right."

"Actually . . . ," he begins, and then his laughter rumbles against my cheek.

"Don't say it," I warn him. With a chuckle I place my palm on his chest and raise my head to look at him.

"Say what?"

"Whatever you were gonna say."

His attempt at an innocent expression has me giggling so much that I do the dreaded snort, which

makes Tommy laugh hard enough that I'm almost
bumped off his lap.

"Aw, Candie, what am I gonna do with you?"

"Lord, I don't know."

"Damn."

"What?"

"Well, the last time I said that you mentioned something about kissing you."

"Ah, so you were hoping I'd say it again?" I ask in
a lazy, teasing tone, trying to keep things light, but my
pulse kicks it up a notch.

Leaning in closer, Tommy focuses his light blue eyes
on my mouth. "Guilty," he whispers and then slowly
reaches up and traces his fingertip across my bottom
lip. I must have been born with extra nerve endings in
my lips or something because this simple gesture has
me feeling hot tingles that start in my lip and slowly
sink south. My throat goes dry and naturally I try to
swallow, which makes Tommy's finger get caught between my lips. His eyes widen and I try to say that I'm
sorry because I really didn't intend to suck his finger
into my mouth, but this just makes my tongue lick his
fingertip in a sexy way that takes us both by surprise.

He groans—wait, that might have been me groan-
ing; I'm not sure—but suddenly I'm back on his lap
and we're kissing like nobody's business . . . *not* as
though we have issues and complications or need to
get to know one another but rather a wild mating of
our mouths. Maybe it was all of the talk about why we
shouldn't be doing this—I don't know—but it's doggone exciting. I tug his Nike shirt from his shorts and
slide my hands up his warm, soft skin.

Tommy in turn reaches up and tugs my shirt over
my head and tosses it somewhere. I don't protest a
lick because his big calloused hands feel so good on
my bare skin. It should but doesn't even bother me
that I'm sitting on my front porch in my sports bra be-

cause all I'm thinking about is his hands caressing my back while my mouth is fused to his. I don't know where this wild behavior is coming from but I think it has something to do with pent-up frustration . . . I'm not sure but all I know is that I *really* want my hands on his bare chest. Our lips are still locked together, making the removal of his shirt difficult but I don't want to end the delicious kiss, making my frantic tugging pointless.

With a low rumble of laughter Tommy pulls back just long enough to tug the shirt over his head. "Is this what you want?"

"Yes," I whisper while reaching out to touch him. Oh . . . warm skin, the ripple of muscle, and the tickle of golden chest hair tease my fingers. "Lean back on your hands," I whisper in his ear.

"Hmmm?"

"I want to explore your amazing chest," I tell him, wondering where the hell this inner sexpot has been all my life. *I want to explore your amazing chest?* Did Sarah and I have a Freaky Friday thing happen, because this is *so* not like me? I'm about to tell him I'm just kidding even though really I wasn't until he leans back and I'm like a kid in a candy store wanting to touch and taste everything. His six-pack abs quiver when I trace the muscles with my fingers, making my way up to his nicely defined pecs. When I lean in and lick one flat nipple Tommy sucks in a breath.

"God . . . Candie." Inspired, I swirl my tongue and he laughs weakly. "You're driving me insane."

"I don't know what's gotten into me," I tell him as I nibble on his neck. "I've never been this brazen."

"I'm not sure what that means but I'm not complainin'."

"It means bold."

"Bold is good. I like bold."

"Good." I know that this is getting out of control but I keep right on kissing his neck.

"Candie," he says softly but firmly.

I stop kissing him and place my palms on his chest. "What?"

"You're driving me crazy."

"That's what I'm goin' for." I trace the shell of his ear with the tip of my tongue and he groans.

"But you know where this is leading . . . ahh." He sucks in a sharp breath when I nibble on his earlobe, "fast?"

"Oh . . ." I look down at his sincere eyes and slowly shake my head. "Too fast. You're right."

"Damn. I'm almost never right. Why now?"

I laugh and give him a peck on the cheek. "I like you enough to stop something that I'm not ready for . . . well, I was ready but you get what I'm sayin', right?"

"This ranks right up there as the worst good news/bad news scenario I've ever doggone heard. You like me enough not to have sex with me." He raises one hand in the air. "Great!" He lowers it and raises up his other hand. "No, not great."

Of course I laugh.

"It's not funny," he complains with a silly pout.

"You gotta admit that it's funny."

He points to his face. "Do you see me laughing?"

"Oh . . . Tommy."

"I'm just teasin'," he says but then gives me a tender smile. "But I like you too and when we do make love I don't want regrets."

"Me neither," I tell him as I slide off his lap. We laugh as we search for our clothes that ended up in the bushes. After we tug on our shirts Tommy kisses me on the cheek and heads for his truck. I wave from the porch, thinking that this had been a day for the Candie Montgomery record books.

14

Partners in Crime

Sarah practically pounces on me as soon as I enter the office. I'm a little late since I had a hard time getting to sleep last night after all that had happened throughout the course of my eventful day.

"Just who were you kissin' on your front porch last night?"

"You saw me?" I squeak.

"Well, *yeah*. You were on your doggone *front porch*. I was gonna drop in after volleyball practice but you didn't look as if you wanted to be disturbed. Is the man in question Tommy Tucker?"

I feel a blush creep up my neck.

"Spill, big sis."

"Yes, it was Tommy Tucker."

Sarah's eyes open wide and she gets so excited that she almost spills her coffee. "No way."

"Way."

"I'll admit, he's hot."

"I know."

Sarah blows on her coffee and then asks, "Is he a good kisser?"

"I don't kiss and tell."

"Then I won't either," she primly replies.

I gasp while pouring myself a mug of coffee. "You kissed Carson again?"

"You first."

After sitting down in the creaky swivel chair I take a sip of my coffee and then smile. "I really like him. He's cute and funny and yes, an amazing kisser."

"Are you going to see Tommy again?"

I nibble on my bottom lip and then shrug. "I guess."

Sarah frowns at me. "What do you mean, you guess? The women in Pinewood drool over Tommy. Why wouldn't you date him? He's a little young but who cares?"

"Well, I have a lot on my plate right now, Sarah. I don't know if I want to get something started if I'm going to end up leaving."

Sarah sits down on the edge of the desk and leans forward, making her long blond ponytail slip over her shoulder. "You don't have to look so serious. Have some fun for once, Candie. You're always so doggone straitlaced. Cut loose for heaven's sake. So what if it's just a summer fling?"

I think of my behavior last night and almost choke on my coffee.

"Well, shut my mouth. You slept with him."

"I most certainly did *not*! Why would you think such a thing?"

"Because you're blushing to the roots of your hair."

I reach up and tuck a curly lock behind my ear. There was no time to flatiron since I overslept once I finally fell asleep. I kept going over my incident with Nick and then my date with Tommy in my head and ended up having a weird dream that I was a mermaid.

"Okay, I admit that things got a bit . . . heated but I did not have sex with Tommy."

Sarah turns away and pours more coffee. "But you wanted to."

"The man is gorgeous, Sarah. But I have more self-control than to sleep with a virtual stranger!"

"I'm just teasin'. Geez, you're touchy. I do have to warn you though that Tommy has a reputation for bein' a bit of a player."

"There's more to him than that!"

Sarah puts her palms up in the air. "Whoa there. I was just sayin'."

"I'm sorry. I didn't sleep well last night so I'm a bit of a grump."

"I shouldn't go runnin' my mouth about Tommy. I don't know him all that well. The player rep is hearsay and you know that there's plenty of gossip in Pinewood. I just don't want to see you get hurt. Been there, done that."

Sarah rubs her bare ring finger with her thumb and I want to ask if she's considered talking to Nick, but she looks so sad that instead I change the subject. "What do you say we close early today so that we can start scouring the area for used trucks?"

"You think Daddy would be okay with us closing early?"

"Well, it's either that or we go separately and I don't relish driving the back roads by myself, do you? Besides, we'd still technically be working, not just goofing off."

"Okay, I guess. You think this truck thing is gonna fly?"

"Granted it's a bit of a risk but sometimes you have to just jump in and go for it, don't you think? You're in this with me right? If not tell me, Sarah. I don't want to railroad you into something you're not behind."

Sarah sighs. "I'm just such a big wimp. You like to venture out and I prefer to stay in my comfort zone."

I lean back in the squeaky chair. "Yeah, right. You love being the center of attention. Cheerleading in front of a crowded gym. Competing in the Miss Kentucky pageant?"

"Don't you see, Candie? That *was* my comfort zone."

"Was Nick your comfort zone too?" I ask before I can stop myself.

Sarah stares down at her coffee mug. "Maybe." She's quiet for a moment but then looks at me as though she wants to say something. She finally shrugs but gives me a look as though she wants to elaborate— but then clams up.

"We need to get to work but I want to ask you one thing—but you don't have to answer."

Sarah swallows but then nods her head. "Okay."

"How does it feel when you kiss Carson?"

"He's not as big a jerk as what people think."

"That's not what I asked."

She looks a bit uncomfortable but says, "It was real nice . . . pleasant, I guess. Hell, I don't know."

"Yes, you do."

"I know where you're goin' with this so just shut the hell up."

"Was it anything like kissing Nick?"

"Didn't I just tell you to shut up?" she says, but I can see the answer in her eyes. "Nothin' would come of me and Carson anyway."

"Why is that?"

"Oh come on, Candie. I amuse Carson in a Jessica Simpson playing Daisy Duke kind of way but I'm sure I'm not what he wants to take home to his mama."

"Candie, his daddy is Harley Campbell and he's as down-home as it gets."

"Yeah, but he was raised up east by his mama. Carson is Ivy League and I'm—"

"Stop," I tell her, and stand up so fast that the old chair rolls backward and hits the wall. "Don't you go sayin' that you're not good enough, Sarah Jane Montgomery!"

Sarah's eyes widen as she jumps up from the edge of the desk. "Lord, Candie, what's gotten into you?"

"I don't know but it feels good. Now, if you hook up with Carson, it's strictly your business. He's kind of a jackass but don't shy away from him because of who you are or where you came from. The way I see it a good old slice of humble pie might do high-and-mighty Carson Campbell some good."

"I don't know what that means . . . the humble pie thing."

I blink at her for a second. "Me neither, it just came into my head but just go with it, okay? I'm on some kind of roll here."

Sarah starts laughing. We high-five and knuckle bump even though we don't know what we're celebrating but it does feel good.

"Okay, ready to get to work?" I ask, still fired up.

"Yes!" Sarah shouts but then we look at each other. "What is there to do exactly?" she asks in a more low-key tone.

I shrug. "Do you want to help me work on the ideas for the truck promotions? I'm thinking a fun grand opening–style party. We can do a drawing of the lot and think up ways to display the trucks."

"Really? You want me to help?" She seems so pleased that I want her input that it makes me feel kind of rotten.

"Of course," I tell her even though I was planning on doing the work myself. It occurs to me that I've never really taken Sarah's opinion seriously. I was the smart twin and she was the pretty one and we are both so much more than that. Damn, it's so cliché.

"The wheels are turnin', Candie. Whatcha thinkin'?"

"I was thinkin' that we sometimes act like what

people expect of us, you know? Or even what we expect of each other. Let's break that mold, Sarah."

She looks at me for a long moment. "I'm not sure that I can."

"The hell you say!"

"Candie, just what *has* gotten into you?" she repeats with a chuckle.

"I'm not sure. I think with Daddy getting sick it made me think that life can be short and all of that hooha. I want to stop holdin' back. Am I making any sense?"

"You wanna kick a little . . ."

"Exactly! If this truck thing blows up in our face, then at least we tried."

"There's the attitude, um, I guess."

"You know what I mean."

Sarah nods. "Yes, I do. Now let's put our heads together and come up with some brilliant ideas." She rolls a chair over, pulls out a pen, and looks eager to begin.

"Eventually we'll have to run this by Daddy."

"He's not gonna say no to anything we decide to do. I think he really wants to turn this whole operation over to us and spend more time with Mama. He sure has earned it and so has Mama. She put up with his long hours and he worked his ever-lovin' tail off."

I nod while opening the folder with my notes. "I know but I want his approval, don't you?"

"You already have that."

"Sarah, Daddy approves of you too, for goodness sake."

She flips her ponytail over her shoulder. "Oh, I *know*. But he sure did miss you while you were in Chicago. I tried to fill your shoes but I could tell it wasn't the same for him.

"Sarah!"

"Oh hush, I'm just bein' whiney. I think I need some chocolate."

"PMS?"

"Big-time. I could eat an entire bag of M&M's."

"A whole bag? *Wow*," I tease, and wiggle my fingers over my head.

"I'm talkin' the one pounder."

"Oh that's serious stuff. There should be a Snickers bar in the top drawer." I start to look but she stops me.

"I ate it," she confesses with a sad shake of her head. "I can pass up a lot of things but chocolate is my downfall. Especially certain times of the month or when I'm stressed out, which seems to be a lot lately."

"Surely there are Reese's Cups in heaven."

"Oh, and Kit Kats? Have you tried one of those big ones?"

"The Big Kat?"

"Yeah," she says and groans. "We need a vending machine in here. No, that would be bad. Enough of the chocolate talk or I'll have to trot down to the store and get one."

"Two."

"Ten."

We laugh and then get down to business. We agree, disagree, argue and laugh, not realizing how much time has passed until it's well past lunchtime. The phones have been pretty much dead except for a call from Mama giving us an update on Daddy who is doing fine but being contrary. I had one lousy customer and Sarah waited on two without any luck.

"You need to work on a logo, Sarah," I tell her as we're wrapping things up.

"Me?"

"You always excelled at art. I have trouble drawing stick people. You're also good with color. Play around and see what you come up with. Once we have colors, a logo and some marketing strategies we'll have to consider a Web site."

"Really?"

I nod. "Yeah so we can reach people from all over. When they Google tricked out trucks I want our lot to pop up."

Sarah rubs her hands together. "This is exciting!"

I smile. "Yeah, it is. Let's hope that Nick and Bailey work fast so we can launch this thing soon. But we really should get on the road while we still have a few hours of light and try to locate more inventory for them to work on. I'm going to go home and throw on some shorts and a tank top. You want to meet me at my place? We can grab something and eat on the way if that's okay?"

"Sure. You go ahead and I'll lock up."

"Thanks. See you in a little while." I'm in a good mood and excited about our new venture but as I pull out of the car lot in the Jeep Wrangler I spot Nick across the street. He looks my way and I wave. Yesterday might have been awkward but I'm glad he's finally sorting out his feelings.

I don't realize that I'm lost in thought until my cell phone rings, making me jump about a foot off the seat. "Where is the doggone thing?" I dig frantically in my purse, telling myself that I need a designated spot rather than just tossing the phone in my unorganized mess. I answer while turning out into the street, drawing a horn blast from the car I turned in front of. Talking on my cell and driving does not mix well for me but I can never resist answering.

"Hello," I say while giving an apologetic wince to the horn blower. I glance over at Nick, who is looking at me as if I'm nuts.

"Connie just called me and wanted to know what a nice girl like you was doin' with a guy like me."

I chuckle. "Tommy, she did not."

"No," he admits, "but she did go on and on about how much she liked you. That's never happened before."

"I guess you date the wrong girls."

"Apparently. I've been given strict orders to ask you out again."

"You don't strike me as somebody who takes orders well."

"In this case it was easy."

"Ah, so are you asking me out again?"

"Yes and my orders included taking you someplace nice instead of a sports bar."

"I *like* sports bars. So I insist that we go back to Connie's place."

"I knew it. You're my kind of girl and you're defying my sister at the same time. Can I get any luckier?"

"Is that a loaded question?"

"Of course not. Connie made me promise that I'd be on my good behavior."

"But I like you just the way you are," I tease as I turn into my driveway.

"Are you real or did I just dream you up?"

"Well, if you dreamed me up will you make me ten pounds lighter and five inches taller?"

"No way. I like *you* just the way you are."

I'm laughing as I enter the house. "Oh good Lord are we laying it on thick or what?"

"I was only tellin' the truth," he says more seriously, making a warm rush of shy pleasure wash over me. If Tommy Tucker is playing me he's damned good. "So, can I see you tonight?"

"I have to work until dark," I answer as I toss my keys on the kitchen table and toe off my shoes.

"Meet me after dark, then? Wait, that didn't sound right."

I chuckle into the phone. "Tommy, I'm sure I'll be beat after such a long day."

"Oh," he says so glumly that I have to smile.

"If you don't mind chillin' on the sofa watching a movie or a ball game I think I can muster up the energy for that."

"How about if I bring over a pizza?"

"Perfect. I'll call you when I get home."

"See ya then," Tommy says and I click my phone shut. With a silly smile I head into my bedroom and slip into worn and comfy jeans shorts and a yellow tank top. "Lord Almighty." I moan as I check out my butt in the mirror and remind myself to start jogging. Maybe the sand volleyball league will help as well.

"Checkin' out your tushie?"

I yelp and spin around to face Sarah. "Must you always sneak up on a person?"

"I called out your name. You must have been daydreamin' about Tommy."

"I was probably in a zone," I admit while I search for my Nikes. "Is my butt as big as a barn?"

Sarah laughs. "No."

"All of that pizza and office work has landed right on my hips. Why not my boobs? And yet when I diet I lose it there first!" I yank my shoelaces harder than necessary and then have to loosen the bow. "And to think I told Tommy to bring a pizza over tonight."

"Oh, seeing Tommy-Boy again?"

"Casual. Just hangin' out," I explain to her as I straighten up. All the blood rushes to my head and I feel a little dizzy.

"You okay?"

"I think I need something to eat. All I had was a MoonPie this morning," I admit, sounding like a Southern diva. I barely refrain from putting the back of my hand to my forehead.

"We'll stop and get something first thing," Sarah says in a soothing tone much like Mama's.

"Yeah, like I couldn't live off the fat of my butt for a while," I say and smack my jean-clad cheek.

"Tommy sure must think you're bootylicious."

"Oh stop!" I plead as I follow her out to the Jeep. "You drive," I tell her and toss her the keys, "and I'll take notes of possible trucks we see and want to make offers on. Nick said that he'd have them towed if needed."

"Where do you want to eat?" Sarah asks as she backs out of the driveway.

"Are you okay with Wendy's?"

"Sure, I can find something on the menu."

"Then we should go the back roads into farm country and approach anyone who has an old truck sitting out in the side yard."

Sarah shakes her head. "That will be just about everybody."

"Yeah, but they can't be complete junk. Some rust is okay but Nick has to have a solid body to work with."

"He had one," Sarah says in a voice so deadpan that I have to chuckle.

"At least your sense of humor is coming back."

"Being angry all the time is tiring," she admits with a sigh. "Maybe I should just move on."

"Does Carson Campbell have anything to do with your decision?"

"In a roundabout way," Sarah says as she pulls into Wendy's parking lot and winds around to the drive-through. "It felt good to be kissed . . . to be desired again. I admit that my ego took a beating over this whole thing." She shoots me a grin. "Maybe I'm the one who needed a slice of humble pie." Sarah stops at the speaker and rolls down the window.

"May I take your order?" a high-pitched voice asks.

When Sarah looks at me in question I say loud enough for the high-pitched voice to hear, "A junior bacon cheeseburger, Biggie Fry, and Biggie Frosty."

"No way!" Sarah says in horror. "Biggie?"

"It's the *junior* burger," I protest. "Okay," I loudly proclaim again, "leave off the Frosty and make it a Diet Coke."

Sarah snickers.

"What?"

"Why bother with a Diet Coke?"

"Right." I narrow my eyes at her and shout to the speaker, "Change that back to a Frosty."

"You were the one complainin' about your butt. I was only trying to help."

"Well, you can kiss the butt in question!" I tell her, and then giggle when I wonder if they can hear us inside the restaurant.

Sarah sticks her tongue out at me and then turns to the speaker. "I'll have the mandarin salad."

"You can't get that. You're drivin'."

"Oh, right." She purses her lips as she reads the menu. A car behind us beeps the horn.

"Come on, Sarah."

"Hold your horses," she snaps and then says sweetly to the speaker, "Make that a grilled chicken sandwich and hold the mayo."

"Fries with that?"

"Lord no!"

"That will be seven sixty-three at the first window."

Sarah pays and pulls to the next window where she takes her small bag and hands me my biggie one. She eyes my Frosty with longing as she passes it to me.

"Don't even think about it," I warn her and take a big bite. "These are low fat you know," I tell her, trying to defend myself.

"Really?"

I nod and take another cold, delicious bite.

"One taste."

"No way."

"I need the chocolate," she whines.

"Oh . . . *okay.*" I relent and pass it to her. "We can share just like Mama used to make us."

After taking a big bite from the oversized spoon Sarah pulls out into traffic. "God, those fries smell so good," she says with a groan. "Eating with you is like being put into a torture chamber. You are such a bad influence!"

I have to laugh. "Me?" I ask drawing out the word into about five syllables. "You had me eggin' a dog-gone car, Sarah!"

Sarah laughs as she snatches a fry. She looks at it as if it's evil and then pops it into her mouth. "Salt . . . grease . . . *mercy,* that was good."

"Need a cigarette?"

"It wasn't *that* good."

I shove the fries her way. When she hesitates I say, "Come on, you know you want it."

"Of course I want one but are the consequences worth indulging?"

Her comment gives me pause but not of course about the fries. "That's the million dollar question, isn't it?"

She snatches another French fry. "We're quite a pair, aren't we?"

"Partners in crime." I lean over and give her a high five. "Now let's go find us some trucks."

15

Famous Last Words

"There! Stop!" I shout when I spot an old red Chevy truck half-hidden by tall weeds.

Sarah brings the Jeep to a screeching halt, making me dig my fingernails into the edge of my seat. "You've got to be kiddin' me," Sarah says. "That old piece of junk?"

"Wait here and I'll hop the fence to get a closer look."

"No way! The last time you did that an old mangy dog almost attacked you. Let's go up to the house and ask first."

"Yeah, right, and get stuck jawin' with some old farmer for almost an hour like the time before that?"

Sarah groans. "Can't we call it a night? I need a cold beer and a hot bath in that order."

"Sarah, we've only bought two trucks. Just one more try, okay? I'll take a closer look and if it's a bucket of rust we'll be on our way."

Sarah purses her lips but then nods. "Okay, but if you hear a dog barkin' hightail it back to the Jeep. I'll keep the engine runnin'."

"You are *so* overreacting. I'm not going to be in any danger checkin' out an abandoned truck."

"Famous last words. Whatever. Just hurry."

I narrow my eyes at her. "You got a hot date with Carson?"

"A late business dinner. I'm hopin' to get some decent used cars sent our way so we can afford something better than the junk we've been scouring the countryside for."

I point my finger at her. "Don't you dare tell Carson about our idea! He'll beat us to the punch and we'll be screwed."

She raises one eyebrow. "Something my life has been sorely lacking."

I chuckle. "Okay, poor choice of words."

"And by the way, don't you go pointin' that finger at me unless it's loaded."

Of course, I point it again and wiggle it for good measure. With a little squeal she makes a grab for me but I'm out the door before she can even blink. I'm laughing as I use flat rocks as stepping-stones over a narrow creek bed and then I climb a small incline leading to a split rail fence. Luckily there isn't any barbed wire to deal with like last time I attempted this feat. After scaling the weathered wood I turn and give Sarah a thumbs-up before pushing through the knee-high weeds while wishing I were wearing long pants.

At first glance the truck looks to be in pretty good shape so I venture closer to check for rust or body damage. There's a crack in the windshield that's totally fixable and some surface rust on the wheel wells but other than that the truck looks in surprisingly good condition, making me wonder why it's been put out to pasture. I'm thinking about raising the hood when I hear someone shout, "What the hell you think yer doin'?"

I shade my eyes against the setting sun and see a

gray-bearded guy in overalls and he has a—*holy crap, a shotgun*. After ducking for cover I wonder if I should keep quiet or explain my situation. I decide to go for quiet. Maybe he's been hitting the hooch and will think he's seeing things. With a pounding heart I scrunch behind the rear wheel and hold my breath. Why I think it's necessary to deprive my body of oxygen I don't know, but I do until my cell phone rings, blowing my cover all to hell; of course I yelp, bringing even more attention to myself. I wonder if I should just call out and state the nature of my business and offer him money? Yes, that makes more sense than cowering here in a ball of terror. I mean, I'm from around these parts. What's there to be afraid of?

"Come on outta there and show yerself. Come on now. I won't hurt ya."

I don't know who this guy thinks I am but in the movies when someone says to come out and they won't hurt you is the time to run like hell.

"You're not tryin' to steal from me, are ya?"

Steal a truck that won't run? And then it hits me that there must be something hidden in the truck worth stealing. I've heard rumors that some of the backwoods farmers grow marijuana. I text Sarah to keep the Jeep running and to be ready to roll. Then, after taking a deep breath I contemplate whether it would be better to stealthily crawl through the weeds or if I should get up and run.

I opt to get up and run.

"Hey!" the drug-dealing farmer yells. Of course the drug dealing is just speculation on my part but there must be something in the truck worth taking. I really don't care; I just want to get out of there in one piece. With that in mind I run faster than I thought I was capable of running but I guess adrenaline is powerful since I'm anticipating that buckshot might soon be pelting me in the ass! I fall once and do an impressive summersault to my feet. I scale the fence, flop over the top to the ground, but roll to standing as if I were a navy seal. After splashing through the creek I yank the door of the Jeep open, throw myself into the seat, and yell, "Hit the gas!"

"Okay!" Sarah says with wide eyes and presses her foot to the pedal so hard that we fishtail before shooting down the road. I smack against the headrest and tug on my seat belt. We fly over the county road as if we're Bo and Luke Duke except we're in an old Jeep instead the General Lee. A dip in the road has us airborne but then hitting the pavement so hard that we both come up out of our seats.

"Whoohoo!" Sarah yells and keeps the pedal to the metal until we're several miles down the road.

"Holy crap, Sarah, slow down! There's a tractor up ahead!" I grab the armrests, push back in the seat, and prepare to rear-end the John Deere. Sarah eases up on the gas but the tractor is coming up way too fast, so she veers into the left lane. I'm guessing that her plan is to pass the tractor but a pickup is coming straight at us. We both scream and she swings back into our lane in the nick of time. The truck driver blasts his horn but all I care about is the back end of the tractor that will soon be in my front seat.

We're both still screaming as Sarah stomps on the brakes and comes to a screeching halt inches from the clueless farmer who continues to chug along, not knowing that we almost crashed into him.

As the dust settles our screams become pathetic, hoarse squeaks until we fall silent. Sarah is clutching the steering wheel and I've got a death grip on the armrests and our chests are heaving. A leftover half scream bubbles up in my throat and comes out a gurgle.

"Holy shit," Sarah says in a husky voice strained from screaming. She looks my way but her hands are still gripping the steering wheel. "What the hell happened back there with that farmer?"

I blink over at Sarah. "He—he had a shotgun. He thought I was stealing something from the old truck. I was thinkin' maybe it was full of drugs!"

"Drugs?"

"Well, you know, *pot*," I whisper as if the drug-dealing farmer will hear me. "Do you think I overreacted?"

Sarah gives me a shaky grin. "Overreacting is in our nature."

"Okay, I think we're done for the day."

Sarah nods and starts down the road at a less hair-raising speed. "I'm still kinda shaky."

"Me too."

"It was sorta cool though. Exhilarating."

I gasp. "It certainly was not!"

"Makes me want to have sex."

"What?"

"Oh come on. Don't you feel all charged up?"

"Sarah, it's called an adrenaline rush. Get over it. Do *not* go having sex with Carson Campbell because of our near-death experience."

"Okay . . . ," she says glumly but not convincingly enough for me.

"Seriously."

Sarah glances over at me before putting her eyes back on the road where they belong. "It's your fault, you know."

"Okay, next time we'll go up to the house like you said."

"I didn't mean *that* but yeah, next time we will."

"What are you getting at then?" I ask while examining raw scrapes on my knees.

"It was the danged French fry."

"What?"

"A taste of the forbidden," she says dramatically.

"You're right, you know. Sometimes we act the way we're expected. I thought I had to be pissed and sad after Nick dumped me. But guess what? I don't."

"But are you?"

Sarah nods glumly. "But you know what? I don't have to always look like a damned beauty queen. So what if I pack on ten pounds? Huh? Maybe if I concentrate less on my appearance then I'll have to rely more on what comes from within."

"No!" I shout so firmly that Sarah's eyes widen. "You know what? You don't have to worry so much about your appearance if you don't want to, but if you like staying slim and fit and looking beautiful, then don't change that, Sarah. You don't have to pack on weight or change your appearance to get more respect. To hell with that. We shouldn't have to act dumb or hide our beauty or lose in a game or make less money. If a guy is intimidated, then he's not worth it." I look over at Sarah after my tirade and tears are streaming down her face. She steers the Jeep off to the side of the road and turns in the seat to face me. "Sarah, after working with you on the truck ideas I realized how very smart and talented you are. I'm sorry that I didn't recognize it sooner."

Sarah sighs. "I played the dumb blonde card because it was easy and safe and I didn't have to compete with you."

I shrug. "I played the geeky jock in much the same way. But we're not kids anymore. Let's make a pact to leave our old insecurities in the dust on this backcountry road. Visuals help," I explain. "I learned that in advertising."

"Gotcha," she says with a sniff.

"And let's find us some guys who want us and love us for who we *are* and not who they want us to be."

"To look beneath the surface," Sarah says and smacks the steering wheel.

"We're all different and yet all the same."

Sarah nods at my sage advice.

"It's getting deep in here isn't it?"

"Yeah. I still need that beer and a hot bath before my business dinner with Carson."

"We've solved enough of the world's problems for one day haven't we?"

Sarah leans her head against the headrest and laughs. "Yeah and it's damned tiring." She turns her head my way and looks at me with serious eyes. "But thanks, Candie. I really do feel better, don't you?"

"Yeah. I do."

"Do you think we'll stick with all of our grand proclamations?"

"I doubt it. But voicing them is a start."

Sarah nods. "Yeah." She turns on the radio and we sing along with our favorite country songs. We get lost only once before pulling into my driveway just before dark.

"Take the Jeep. I'm going to stop over at Nick's in the morning to see what he thinks of the trucks we bought before coming over to the lot, so I'll just walk."

"Okay. Have fun with Tommy," she says with a grin.

"It's just casual!"

"Yeah, right. Whatever you say," she says, and then starts backing out of the driveway.

"And your dinner is just business," I call after her. I'm only in the house a few minutes when Tommy calls my cell phone.

"Hey, I'm on my way if that's okay?"

"Tommy, I'm a mess. Can you give me time to shower first?"

"The pizza is hot and the beer is cold, but I'll wait if you want me to."

I groan. "You're killin' me."

"I'll take that as a 'come on over.'"

"Okay, yes, come on over," I answer with a laugh.

Of course then I run into the bathroom to get a good look at myself. "Mercy," I mutter when I see my reflection and almost call Tommy back but instead I drag a brush through my hair and quickly touch up my scarce makeup. I'm dabbing on a hint of perfume when the doorbell rings.

With one last glance in the mirror I wince and then head for the front door.

Tommy's got a pizza box in one hand and a six-pack in the other and such a cute grin on his face that I have to smile. "The pizza smells amazing," I tell him while holding the door open for him to enter.

"I forgot to ask what you like as toppings so it's just plain cheese."

"Works for me. Take it into the kitchen and let's dig in." My stomach embarrassingly rumbles with hunger and I glance at him to see if he hears but if he did he's gentleman enough not to say anything.

Tommy cracks open a couple of Bud Lights while I stretch up on tiptoe to get plates from my cabinet. Unfortunately at my height anything other than the first shelf is a challenge.

"Let me help," Tommy offers, and comes up behind me to easily reach the plates. The warmth of his body so close to mine sends a shiver of awareness through me and when I ease down from my toes I accidentally brush back against him. His quick intake of breath tells me he feels the rush too and he backs away so quickly that he bumps up against the edge of the table, nearly knocking over a beer.

"Impressive," I tease when he catches the bottle in midtip.

"Always save the beer," he jokes, but gives me a rather shy grin that I find way too cute. I'm feeling pretty good about how he's reacting to me when his eyes suddenly widen. "Oh my God, Candie."

"What?" My hand goes up to my hair and I'm thinking that he's finally noticing how bad I look. I knew I should have showered. Oh no, maybe it's not my appearance.

Maybe I smell.

Horrified, I barely resist the urge to take a whiff of my armpit. "I warned you I needed to shower," I remind him in a small voice.

"Do you know you're bleeding?"

"Um, no." My eyes widen and I immediately think he's referring to the monthly visit. God no! Please no!

"How did you manage to scrape your knees like that?" he asks gently.

"My knees?" I squeak and then look down and see that both knees are scraped raw and trickling blood. I had forgotten about my minor injury sustained in my race from the crazy farmer. "Oh. They don't really hurt," I bravely proclaim although now that I'm aware of the scrapes they do start to sting.

Shaking his head he presses a cold beer into my hand. "Do you have some first aid stuff?"

"In the bathroom."

"Let's get you patched up," he says firmly squelching my urge to ignore my stupid knees.

"Fine," I nonchalantly agree as I head to the small bathroom down the hallway.

"Have a seat," he says after he lowers the toilet lid. "Are your supplies in the medicine cabinet?"

"I suppose. My mama supplied me with most of my stuff."

"Do you mind if I rummage around?"

"No . . . ," I answer hesitantly while hoping that my tampons are beneath the sink. I realize he has sisters but still . . .

While sipping my beer I watch Tommy gather cotton balls, antiseptic, and bandages. His streaky blond hair is casually messy and he's hot surfer-boy sexy in white board shorts and a black Hurley T-shirt. Dark blond stubble shadows his jaw making me want to reach up and run my hand over his cheek. His male presence fills the small space and I'm able to take in minor details like a small scar on his chin that I didn't notice about him before.

"Okay, ready?" he asks as he turns to me.

Am I ever.

"This is gonna sting."

"Do you have a stick that I can bite down on?"

"Very funny. Seriously, this is gonna hurt a little."

"No biggie," I bravely proclaim but in truth both Sarah and I are wimps when it comes to physical pain. I would have been whining about my knees but I suppose the aftereffects of my near-death experience and the arrival of Tommy kept me from noticing the sting.

Tommy pours some of the antiseptic onto a cotton pad, kneels down in front of me, and gently dabs at my scrape. Fire. My knee is on fire! I bite my bottom lip to hold my moan at bay but when he dabs again I suck in my breath.

"Sorry," he says and his blue eyes really do look remorseful.

I swallow my pitiful moan and nod. "It's okay," I manage to assure him in a breathless my-knees-are-on-fire tone. When he tosses the cotton pad and soaks another one I close my eyes and flinch. "Ouch!" I squeak.

He chuckles. "I haven't touched you yet."

"Oh." With a sheepish look I open my eyes in time to see him cautiously dab at my knee. An embarrassing hissing noise comes out of my mouth and I squeeze the beer bottle.

"Damn, I'm so sorry, Candie. I know it smarts." He waves his hand over my knee and then blows to ease the sting. "You didn't want these scrapes to get infected, though." He raises his head to look at me. "I've got to do the other one."

"You'd think that bein' an athlete I'd be used to physical pain. During the heat of a game I could always tough it out but afterward I was always a big ole wimp."

Tommy leans in and gives me a light kiss. "You just need a little tender lovin' care. I just hate that I'm havin' to cause you any pain."

I smile at him and I have to admit that it's nice to have someone pamper me. Living on my own especially so far away from home could get rough sometimes. While I'm a pretty capable person, handling a bad cold or the flu without my mama there to bring me soup and sympathy was hard. "Havin' you fuss over me is kinda nice."

"I like fussing over you." He leans in and kisses me again. "Ready?"

I nod but decide to take a swig of liquid courage first. I neglect to tell Tommy this and just as I tip the bottle he dabs my knee. "Yeow!" I lean forward, showering his shirt with beer.

"Sorry!" we say together and then laugh.

"Let me put these bandages on and then you're finally finished."

"Okay."

"There," he says with a nod and then tosses the wrappers into the little trash can that matches my toothbrush holder and soap dish courtesy of my mother. "All done. Now, let's go eat the pizza." He stands up, offers his hand, and tugs me to my feet.

My stinging knees are stiff, causing me to stumble forward, but Tommy steadies me with both hands around my waist. Having my knees bandaged in my bathroom is about as unromantic as you can get and yet I don't think I've ever been as drawn to a man as I am right this minute. Apparently gentleness and caring are quite a turn-on.

"You okay?" His voice is gruff, sexy as hell.

"I think so. My knees sting a little and the bandages make it awkward to walk."

"I can fix that," he says and scoops me right up off my feet easy as pie.

"I can walk," I protest.

"Let me pamper you," he says softly. "I want to."

"Okay." I wrap my arms around his neck and hold back a sigh when something warm and wonderful blossoms inside me. I think I'm falling in love . . .

My heart beats wildly at the notion but I manage to say in a pretty steady voice, "Take me into my bedroom."

His eyes widen a fraction and he bumps his shoulder into the door frame.

"I've got some dry shirts in there." I'm quickly realizing that he was getting the wrong idea . . . or maybe the right idea? My heart thuds, wondering . . .

"Oh . . . good," he says and I swear he's blushing. "I hate smelling like beer."

I reach over and flick on the overhead light as he carries me into my bedroom. "Forgive the mess. I'm still in the unpacking stage."

"Just what could you have that would fit me?" he asks while gently lowering me to the floor.

"I've got some big T-shirts from the softball team I was on in Chicago." After locating the box full of shirts I squat down and rummage through them until I come up with a size large. "Here, this should fit," I tell him and toss the shirt in his direction. It lands on my bed, making my mind go in a direction that it shouldn't. But then again that seems to be happening every time I'm near Tommy Tucker.

"Thanks." Tommy tugs his wet shirt over his head and boy oh boy do I ever get an eyeful of man-candy. I got a glimpse of him in the moonlight last night but this is better. He's muscular without too much bulk and has just the right amount of golden chest hair that narrows to the happy line pointing south. When he glances my way I'm embarrassed that I'm ogling, so I quickly turn my head, making myself lose my balance. I tumble forward, landing on my tender knees.

"Fudge!" I shout, glad that I refrained from dropping the unlady-like F-bomb. I don't do it often but it always seems to happen in public when I've already done something stupid. I'm pretty talented at making a bad situation worse. Maybe it's about time I started making a good situation better . . .

16

Seriously . . .

"Candie!" Tommy rushes over and kneels down beside me. "You okay?"

"Well . . . no, not exactly."

"Here," Tommy says, offering his hands, "here, get up off your knees."

I grasp his warm hands and try not to think about the close proximity of his bare chest. He helps me up and then sits down on the bed next to me. "I don't know why I find it necessary to continually make a fool of myself in your presence."

"Now just how are you doing that?" he asks with a quizzical frown.

I put my index finger to my pinky and start ticking off my many blunders. "There was the eating sand incident, the snort in your sister's restaurant, the—"

"Candie," Tommy interrupts, "those weren't blunders. That was just you bein' *you*."

I raise my palms in the air. "Oh great, that's even worse!"

Tommy chuckles. "No. It's not. I want you to just be yourself around me. I find you endearingly cute but sexy as hell. Don't change a damned thing," he insists, but then shakes his head. "That wasn't very eloquent but you get my meaning, right?"

I think about the conversation I had earlier with Sarah. "No, I totally get it, Tommy. That was perfect. Just perfect."

"Really? Because I've always been good with a joke but when it comes to more serious stuff I pretty much suck."

"I take you seriously, Tommy."

He gives me a half smile. "Not many people do but I suppose it's mostly my own fault."

I put my hand over his. "It's funny, because Sarah and I were just talkin' about how we can get pigeon-holed into roles. We sure did it as sisters. It's easy to become what people expect and ignore who you really are."

"Like being the class clown. A screw off? A player?" Tommy looks down at the bedspread and then back up at me. "Yeah, I know."

"Look, I didn't know you in high school but sometimes those four years define who we think we are . . . or have to be. Tommy, I already know there's more depth to you than what meets the eye. Sorry, bad boy, but you've been outed as a nice guy. Funny? Yes, but smart as a whip as my daddy would say."

"Are you gonna tell and ruin my rep?"

"Oh, you're gonna do that all on your own. You're doin' some great things with the community center, Tommy. You should be proud of that." When he looks back down at the bedspread I give his shoulder a shove. "Don't go givin' me that aw-shucks attitude."

Tommy chuckles. "Do you know how great it is to be able to talk to a chick like this? I've felt that comfort with you from the get-go and I'm hopin' you feel the same way."

"I do."

"Excellent. But Candie, I have to warn you that

we'd better hightail it into the kitchen because sittin' here with you on this bed is givin' me all kinds of ideas," he admits with a slow, sexy grin that has me wanting to push him back on the bed and kiss him crazy.

"Me too."

Tommy flops back onto the mattress with a groan. "You're not making this any easier."

"I thought I could tell you *anything*." I lean closer and make the mistake of putting my hand on his chest. It was meant as a casual gesture but it sends a hot thrill right through me.

"Candie . . ." His eyelids droop as his gaze drops to my lips. "Damn, I want to kiss you. It seems like that's all I've been thinkin' about lately."

I *know* where this is leading since we're in my bed and it's inviting trouble but his warm, smooth skin sends my brain the command to lean in close. "Oh, Tommy," I whisper a hairbreadth away from his mouth. I warn myself to make the kiss brief . . . playful and then to sit right back up but the moment my lips graze his I'm a gonner. His mouth is hot, silky smooth and the friction of his tongue against mine is pure bliss. I open my mouth for more and he gives it to me with long delicious strokes.

In the back of my mind a frantic voice sounding suspiciously like my mother's is telling me that I've got to pull back or we're going to be having sex here shortly. My body, however, is responding like sex here shortly is a damned good idea, so I keep right on kissing him.

"Candie," Tommy says low and husky in my ear. "You know where this is headin', right?"

"Mmm, yeah," I respond in a dreamy, sex-induced voice.

"I want to do the right thing but in another few seconds it won't be my brain doin' the thinkin'."

"We should go eat the pizza, shouldn't we?"

"That's not a fair question, Candie," he complains with a weak chuckle. "But . . . *yeah.*"

I roll away from temptation and sit up. "It's all your fault bein' bare-chested and everything."

"You're the one who spilled the beer all over me."

"Because you were torturing me! Pouring that fire water on my poor raw knees." I look down at my bandages and try for a sexy pout that Sarah would be proud of, except I can't pull it off and end up laughing.

Tommy stands up and tugs me to my feet. "How'd you get those scrapes anyway?" he questions while putting on the shirt I had tossed to him. Darn, why'd I have to have a shirt that fit? I should have at least tossed him a snug medium.

"You'd never believe my tale so I'm not going to bother," I tell him as I walk out of the bedroom. My knees are even more tender so I'm walking sort of funny, but I figure that I've already done so many goofy things that marching like a penguin pales in comparison. "Let's just say that I'm clumsy and leave it at that."

"Oh, give me a break. You can't say something like that and not tell me the rest of the story."

I pause in the hallway to look at him. "It was business related and I have to keep it on the down low."

Tommy frowns. "You run a used car lot. How dangerous can that be?" His eyebrows shoot up and he puts a hand on my arm. "Were you collecting money from someone? If someone tried to hurt you, I'll—"

"No, nothing like that," I assure him but then think of the drug-running farmer and my flight of fear. "But it's nice that you want to kick some butt on my account."

"You're not gonna tell me, are you?"

When I reach the kitchen I open up the pizza box

and put a slice on a plate for him. "I know it sounds silly but I can't tell. Really."

Tommy arches one golden eyebrow and rubs his chin. "A woman of mystery. I like that."

"Yep, that's me," I reply with what I hope is a sly grin. "International woman of mystery. See, if I told you . . ."

"I know, you'd have to kill me."

"In truth I'd make a terrible spy."

I laugh as I reach in the fridge for a couple of beers and then join him at the table. I like that he didn't press me for the information and I guess I *could* tell him but after the speech I gave Sarah about secrecy I decide it's only fair to keep my mouth shut. She had better not say a doggone thing to Carson.

"Hey, what are you thinkin' about?" Tommy asks after swallowing a bit of pizza. "Looks like you're deep in thought."

"Oh, it's nothing," I assure him while I'm shaking off my worry. "Just business stuff. With my daddy sick our numbers have been down. Plus, that rat Carson Campbell doesn't trade with us like his daddy did, leaving us a little high and dry."

"I'm sorry 'bout that. So then why is Sarah playing for his volleyball team?"

"She's trying to stay on his good side. She claims he *has* a good side but I'm not so certain."

"Nick has befriended him a bit. Carson might end up being an okay guy after he learns the ins and outs of our small-town ways. After what went down between your sister and Nick the town folk have given Nick a bit of a rough way to go. He hasn't exactly been what you could call shunned but he definitely gets the cold shoulder," Tommy explains while watching me closely for my reaction.

I shrug as I come over to the table. "I don't think it's right for everyone to be all up in his business.

Nick is a good person. He's just confused and has managed to hurt people in the process."

"Including you," Tommy says. A muscle ticks in his jaw and I have to smile in spite of this rather uncomfortable conversation. "Now, just why are you smilin'?"

"You," I tell him with a shake of my head. "Gettin' protective of me again. It could go to a girl's head." I start to sit down but Tommy surprises me when he slips an arm around my waist and pulls me down onto his lap.

"Quit worryin' about everybody. People you love are gonna get hurt. That's just life. But you have to start thinkin' about what you need and what *you* want."

I look into those amazing eyes of his and swallow hard. Then, cupping both of his cheeks I lower my mouth to his and give him the kiss he so deserves.

"Hey, what was that for?" he asks in his husky voice that's so damned irresistible that I lean in and kiss him again.

"For being you," I tell him. "Plus I was taking your advice about taking what I want and what I need."

"So are you sayin' that you wanted and needed me?" he asks in a teasing tone but his eyes are serious. It hits me that I might not have known Tommy long but I think he's falling for me and I really do have the power to hurt him. I look away but he tilts my chin up. "Oh no you don't."

"What?" I try to smile but my lips do this wobbly thing that has Tommy shaking his head while gripping my chin more firmly.

"Don't go pulling back on me worrying that my heart will get trampled on. What I will regret is if you don't give me a chance. Now that would truly bite the big one."

I have to chuckle at his choice of words.

Tommy grins. "I told you that I wasn't very . . ."

"Eloquent?"

"Yeah, that."

"You get your point across just fine. How do you already know me so well anyway?"

"I don't know you nearly enough," he says, and then kisses me lightly.

"That's simple enough to remedy. Do you want to take the pizza into the living room so we can watch a movie?"

"Sounds like a plan," he tells me with a more relaxed smile but when I go to stand he tightens his hold around my waist. "We can take it slow. I do, however, have a tough time keepin' my hands off you. You might have to keep me in line."

"Now why would I want to do that?" I ask softly and then give in to the urge to kiss him before snagging the longnecks and heading into the living room. "You can put it on the coffee table. There are coasters there somewhere. Another gift from my mama."

Tommy holds up a cork disk with a butterfly embellished on it.

"The dollar store, I'm sure. I fully plan on givin' this place my personal touch in due time. In exchange for the rent I'm gonna do some painting and minor repairs."

"Say the word and I'll be glad to pitch in."

"Thank you, Tommy," I tell him as I dig around in the box holding my movie collection. "Okay, chick flicks, action, or comedy. I don't have any horror or scary stuff. In case you haven't noticed I'm pretty much a wimp."

"You choose," he offers.

"Hmmm . . . Sleepless in Seattle or The Wedding Crashers?"

"This is a trick question, isn't it?"

I laugh. "Have you ever seen Sleepless in Seattle?

"Between my mom and two sisters I've seen more than my share of chick flicks, believe me." He leans forward and says, "But I'll watch another one for you."

"Awwww. *The Wedding Crashers* it is," I announce and he looks so relieved that I chuckle.

"You were messin' with me, weren't you?"

"Yeah. I do love that movie but you don't want to see me cry. I'm not a silent weeper. I wail, kinda like Lucille Ball."

"No way."

"Way. It's worse than my snorting. Mama and Sarah are wailers too. We almost got ejected from a movie theater once, but come on, it was *The Notebook*," I explain and he looks at me closely to see if I'm teasing. "I kid you not."

Tommy takes a bite of pizza and chews it thoughtfully. I have to wonder if he's asking himself just what the heck he's getting himself into. After popping in the disk, I grab a slice of pizza and join him on the sofa carefully, wondering how close to sit. I can tell that he's wondering just how cuddly to get too and it makes me feel a little awkward. After the movie gets going though we're laughing at Vince Vaughn and Owen Wilson and the atmosphere gets more relaxed. The carbs and beer makes me mellow and without exactly planning it, my head is soon resting against Tommy's shoulder. He doesn't seem to mind so I tuck my feet up on the sofa and snuggle a little bit closer.

"This movie is hilarious no matter how many times I see it," he comments and like a true guy takes control of the remote. "Hey, you've yet to snort."

"I did once but you were laughing too hard to notice."

"I want to hear it."

"Fat chance. I can't do it on command and it's not exactly something I'm proud of."

"Fine," he says with a sigh but then starts rewinding the best parts in an effort to get me to do it and of course I finally do . . . a really big one that has me hiding my face in my hands.

"Happy now?"

"Yeah," he says, "I am."

Although there is still a lot of sexual tension crackling between us, I can't remember when I've been this relaxed and it feels good. I could definitely get used to this. All too soon, however, the movie credits are rolling and I'm holding back a yawn.

"I'd better get goin'," Tommy says and gives me a kiss on the top of my head.

After sitting up I stretch and yawn again. "This was real nice."

"Yeah, it was," Tommy says and leans in close as though he's going to kiss me but then straightens up. I have to say that I'm disappointed but then Tommy says, "Oh hellfire," before pulling me close and kissing me thoroughly. I'm blinking and a bit dazed when he stands up. "I can see myself out," he offers but I do the polite thing the way my mama taught me and follow him to the door.

"Listen, I'd like to see you tomorrow but I have to work at the softball fields overseeing the complex."

"Okay," I tell him, trying not to sound too disappointed.

He pauses but then says, "Look, I know this is lame and you don't have to do this but if you want to you can join me. All I really do is ride from field to field in a golf cart and keep an eye on things, check up on the concession stands and stuff like that. Not too exciting . . . aw, no, forget I asked. I'm sure you have something better to do with your time."

"Do I get to drive?"

"The golf cart?"

"Yeah."

"Maybe."

"Get free hot dogs and Laffy Taffy?"

Tommy grins and I swear he has the cutest dog-gone grin on the face of the earth. "One or two. If you get lucky I might even throw in nachos with those stale chips and fake orange cheese. I'm not sure if we have Laffy Taffy. Nerd Ropes are the 'in' candy."

"Okay, if you throw in a Nerd Rope I'm in. Just don't tell Sarah. She's all over me about my poor eating habits."

"My lips are sealed."

"Your lips are amazing," I tell him and then clamp a hand over my mouth.

"An out loud moment?"

I shake my head.

With his killer grin he leans over, gently pries my hand from my mouth, and then kisses me softly. "Your lips are amazing too."

"You are so full of it, Tommy Tucker," I tease, but my heart is beating like crazy.

"Normally I'd agree with you, Candie, but not this time." He looks at me as if he wants to kiss me again but takes a step back instead and shoves his hands in his pockets as if putting them there to keep from touching me. "I'll go by the ball fields and get things opened up and then swing by and pick you up around seven?"

"Sounds good." I watch him as he walks to his truck and I realize that I have a silly smile on my face. The smile remains while I get ready for bed and stays there when I put my head onto the pillow. It's been my habit lately to lie awake with worry as I watch the red digital numbers on my alarm clock but tonight I turn away from the nightstand and snuggle into the covers. I push away all of the uncertainties and complications that have been swirling around in my brain and let my body truly relax. For the first time in a long while I feel as if the future has something wonderful to offer and I'm damned well going to go after it with all I've got.

17

Love Hurts

The next morning I have a bit of a spring in my step in spite of my stiff knees. Nick had called to tell me that he's making quick progress on the trucks from our lot and the ones that we bought. Mama called right afterward to give me the good news that Daddy is feeling well enough to sit on the front porch swing. I'm in such a good mood that I don't mind when I burn my bagel or that I forgot to buy cream cheese.

"So my bagel is black and who needs cream cheese?" I proclaim, and then take a crunchy, brave bite. "Not so bad," I lie to myself but then toss it in the trash and search for a MoonPie. "Sarah will never know," I whisper as I tear open the wrapper and sink my teeth into the soft goodness that has yet to be copied. There is only one MoonPie . . . end of story. I'm polishing it off when Sarah calls me on my cell.

"Hey, want me to pick you up?"

"No, I'm gonna walk."

"Oh, ate a MoonPie, so you're gonna walk off the empty, nonnutritious, gonna-end-up-on-your-butt calories?"

"I burned my bagel so I had no choice, granola girl."

"Right . . ."

"Oh shut up."

Sarah laughs. "So are you stopping at Nick's to check out his progress?"

"I had planned on it. See you in a bit." I head into the bedroom and opt for a pleated skirt and floral blouse instead of my usual khakis due to my bandaged knees. The slight hint of rain in the air makes it useless to straighten my hair but I add a bit of styling gel to keep the frizz at bay.

"Hey," Nick says as he comes up behind me outside the shop.

"Mornin'."

"I'm getting a slow start since I stayed up way too late last night," he explains. "But I'm making lots of progress. I'm really gettin' pumped about the trucks."

"Good. I mean about the progress, not you stayin' up late," I explain with a smile.

Nick responds with a slight grin but there is an aura of sadness about him that makes me think of a basset hound puppy . . . not that he resembles one. A worn blue T-shirt tucked into low-rise, ripped and faded jeans coupled with his broody good looks has Nick looking like a Hollister model . . . except he's the real deal and not some manufactured imitation. As he bends over to pick up the newspaper, fingers of morning sunshine pick up highlights in his chestnut hair that were created from outdoor living instead of a bottle. His longish hair is from lack of time for a trim, not for a fashion statement. He and Sarah truly make a striking couple.

"I have a gut feelin' I'm gonna be burnin' the midnight oil quite a bit. I'm as eager as you are to get this goin'. Come on and see what I did with that Chevy S10," he says with a measure of pride.

With a nod I follow Nick inside. He pauses to flick on lights and check messages before opening the door to the shop. "Wow!" I put a hand to my chest. "Nick, it is so cool!"

"You think so?"

"Oh, *yeah*." When I nod he beams.

"I added a drop kit. It will handle better closer to the ground and gives the body a sporty appearance."

"It looks so sleek without the bulky bumpers. How did you do that?"

"The front bumper cover was easily installed over the factory one. The roll pan over the back bumper smooths out the rear." He walks to the back of the truck and squats down. "See, the gap between the tailgate and bumper is smaller, giving it a clean look. See here?" he asks while pointing. "The hitch is hidden behind the roll pan." He looks up at me and says, "I think it's turning out okay, don't ya think?"

"Oh, more than okay! I love the lime green and orange flames. Did you airbrush those?"

He nods.

"Nick you're really talented."

He shrugs off my compliment. "This is something I've always wanted to do but never had the reason to spend the money. If this takes off it will be a dream come true."

"Why did you keep it a secret?"

Nick stands up and says, "I had to concentrate on makin' a living. I never dreamed that this could be more than a hobby."

"Well, it should be," I tell him as I gaze admiringly at the truck.

"Bailey is gonna work on customizing the interior. That's more of his expertise. We're hopin' to use parts and accessories from the junkyard to cut down on costs but we do have to order some of this stuff. I'll keep track so we can figure out the profit margin. I figure with some of the trucks we can do some simple things like adding a custom hood and some accents to give a tricked out look without much time or money involved."

"I agree. Some customers will want something simple and sleek while others will want the full package."

"And hopefully as profits roll in we'll have more capital to work with. Bailey has a couple of buddies who are gonna help us out. I hope to have a front line for you within a few weeks."

"Wow, that soon?"

Nick's brows draw together. "I was under the impression that you wanted the trucks as fast as possible."

"I do."

"Then what's the . . . *oh no*, you haven't run this by your daddy yet, have you?"

"Well . . ."

"Why not?"

I nibble on the inside of my lip. "I didn't want to upset him. But Nick, I had to do something or we were gonna have to fold the business and sell. I know that the property is worth pretty much but I didn't want to have to go that route. I didn't realize how bad things had gotten and with Carson not sending us cars we were screwed."

"Do you think your daddy will have a problem with your idea?"

"No, and neither does Sarah but I wanted to see if it was even a feasible project before approaching him."

"But you're going to, aren't you?"

"Soon. Mama says he's up and about and in better spirits. I just didn't want to give him cause to worry."

Nick runs his boot across the concrete and looks

down at the ground. "How are your parents feelin'
about me these days?"

"We haven't spoken of it."

Nick nods while still gazing down. "And Sarah?
Still hatin' my guts?"

"She's been spendin' some time with Carson," I
comment casually.

His head snaps up and his green eyes widen a fraction before he shrugs. "Really?" he asks in a carefully
even tone. "Are they . . . dating?"

"I don't know if you would call it *that*. It's more
business-related. At least that's what she's sayin'." I
roll my eyes for good measure.

Nick swallows. "So . . . you think there's more to it
than business?" he asks but is unable to maintain the
even tone.

"Would it bother you if it were more?"

"No," he says with a quick wave of his hand.
"Sarah's free to date whomever she wants. Really. She
is." He takes a step closer to me. "It doesn't bother me
at all. In fact, I'm glad because then I can get on with
my life."

After inhaling a deep breath I blow it out and say,
"That's the biggest crock of bull I ever heard."

Nick's eyes widen. "What do you mean?"

"Get real." I decide that tough love is in order, here.
"You love Sarah and I damned well know she loves
you. Yeah, you might need more from her but did it
ever occur to you that you're gettin' what you ask
from her?"

He looks at me with troubled eyes. "Just what are
you gettin' at?"

"Did you ever try to reach Sarah on a deeper level?
Or did you always treat her like arm candy?"

Nick's green eyes flash at me in surprise. "I never
treated Sarah with disrespect. You know me better."

"Of course I do," I quietly assure him. "I didn't

mean it quite like that. But I'm comin' to learn that there's more to Sarah than she lets on. I can say this to you because I've done the same thing. Nick, she acts the way we expect her to." I put my palms up in the air. "She gets *surprised* when I ask for her opinion or input."

"Holy shit." He rakes his fingers through his hair. "Did I really do that?"

I take a deep breath of garage-scented air. "Don't feel so bad. We've been enablers but Sarah's to blame too. You're right that she had more to give but we have to expect it from her . . . treat her differently."

"So now what?"

I sigh. "That's up to you. But I suggest that you start with talkin' to her."

"I know. It's just that she's so pissed. I don't know if she'll ever want to be in the same room with me, much less have a conversation."

"Oh yeah? Well then, you'd better be okay with her hooking up with Carson." Of course I'm trying to get his reaction . . . oh I get it, big-time, when his eyes widen as big as silver dollars.

"Do you really think that could happen? He's not the guy for her, Candie."

"Really? Then who is?" I give him a pointed look.

Nick stares at me for a second. "I'm such a dumb-ass."

"If the shoe fits . . ."

"Gee, thanks, tell me how you really feel . . ." Nick shakes his head. "How am I gonna fix this mess?"

I come over and poke him in the chest. "That, my friend, is up to you." With that parting shot I leave the garage. Once out in the fresh air I drag in deep gulps to keep my emotions from spilling over. Now the question is: Do I meddle or stay out of it?

"Stay out of it," I whisper firmly but then shake my

curly head. Oh, come on, I'm a small-town Southern chick. Meddle is my middle name.

After crossing the street I wander around the car lot pretending to check out the inventory and pick up trash but what I'm really doing is getting my head together before facing Sarah. My own emotions are still a little strung out but it also feels as if a weight has been lifted off my shoulders.

"Hey," Sarah says when I finally enter the tiny showroom. "How'd it go with Nick?"

"The truck looks fabulous. He's making some quick progress. We'll have to tell Daddy soon."

"That's cool. I think Daddy will be excited, don't you? Mama said that they might winter in Florida this year, so I think he's more than ready to retire and turn the business over to us."

Us. Everyone just assumes that I'm here to stay. I drag in a big breath and manage a smile.

"Hey, what's the matter?"

"Nothin'."

"I'm your doggone twin. I can feel it right here when somethin's wrong." She taps her heart.

"You are so full of it."

"Well, sorta, but somethin' is botherin' you. Did Nick say anything to upset you?" She narrows her eyes as she gazes out the window at his shop. "That man needs his ass kicked."

"Go do it."

Sarah whips around from the window so fast that her ponytail comes around and hits her cheek. "What?"

"You heard me. Have you ever truly confronted him?"

"I fight like a girl, Candie." She makes slapping motions. "I can't really kick his ass."

"I mean figuratively. Have you ever truly confronted him about this whole thing? March right over there and give him a tongue-lashing."

Sarah's eyes widen and her cheeks turn pink.

"Not that kind of tongue-lashing."

"I wasn't thinking *that*."

"Were too.

"Sarah, it's obvious that you're still in love with him!"

"No! I *hate* the son of a bitch." She says it so vehemently that I shake my head.

"What?"

"I don't think so. Not that it's any of my business or anything."

"No. It's not," she says in a pouty tone that's so Sarah. She hesitates for a second and then says, "Tell me, just what did that jerk say to you?"

"No! You have to buck up and get your ass over there and talk to him yourself."

She sits down in her chair with a thump. "See, he'll talk to *you*. He'll confide in *you*. Damn him!" she hisses but then her anger dissolves and her eyes well up. "Why won't he talk to *me*?" She jabs her thumb into her chest and then yelps, "Ouch! Damn it all to hell and back!"

I sit on the edge of the desk and lean close to her. "Sarah, maybe Nick doesn't know that he *can* talk to you."

"Now just what the hell is that supposed to mean?" she asks while rocking back and forth in the squeaky chair. "Can't talk to me. Why that's a bunch of bull. We were engaged to be married for pity's sake. Candie, sometimes you come up with some crazy-ass stuff."

"I'm right and you know it."

"I know no such thing." She rocks even faster.

"Stop with the doggone rockin' and squeakin'," I demand so loudly that she actually stops and looks at me with wide eyes. "Sarah," I begin more calmly, "I've come to realize that there's a side to you that you've kept hidden. We sorta talked about it, remember? Open up with Nick and be yourself like we discussed. There's so much more of you to give than your pretty face and long legs. You said that you didn't think that you were enough for Nick but honey, you are. You just need to let him see it."

Sarah looks at me for a long silent moment and then a single tear slides down her cheek. "Candie, don't you see?" She swallows and then continues, "That's the scary part. What if I do open up . . . you know really put it all out there and then I'm still not enough? Huh? There were so many times when I wanted to talk about, you know, real stuff . . . and I was afraid."

"Sarah, afraid of what?"

"Sounding *stupid*. Nick's smart, Sarah. Graduated summa cum . . . whatever." She flips her hand in the air. "I guess I never felt like he would value or care about my opinion. All he ever cared about was how I looked."

"Because it was all you ever showed him. It might have been enough for a teenager but not a man. So it was safer to play dumb."

"It wasn't playin'."

"Oh bull!" I sputter.

"Hey, you just spit on me!"

"Sorry, but I'm a little upset here. It's hard to watch two people I love so much screw up their lives!"

"Why are you so pissed all of a sudden? This is my problem, not yours."

"No, Sarah, it's not."

18

One Way or Another . . .

I remain silent because I don't know what to say but I can see the wheels turning in Sarah's head and she's putting the whole, big-ole puzzle together.

"Are your forgettin' that Nick broke off our engagement," she says more to herself than to me, "because he—he realized that *you* were the twin that he wanted, not me."

"I'm not the damned twin he wants!" I assure her. "We're just friends! Am I gonna have to carry around a sign sayin' so? God, why won't anyone believe me?"

"Maybe because you two always had this . . . *thing*."

"Yeah, it's called friendship. He's always had eyes for you."

"Yeah . . . eyes! You said it yourself! Candie, I was enough as a teenager but seeing you at Christmas let him know how much he missed you. How much I was lacking."

"You're not lacking a damned thing except using the good sense that God gave you!"

"Oh, just shut up! I am! You were the golden child and I was merely pretty. When Nick came over to the house to hang out with you I would parade around in my bikini just to get his attention away from you and on me." She shakes her head. "I shouldn't have done it but I was a kid. Nick liked making out with me but he liked *being* with you. Still holds true today."

"But you love him, don't you?"

"Yes." She drags out the word as if it's coming from the bottom of her heart. "God help me, *yes*. He's everything a girl could want . . . bighearted, hardworkin' easygoin'. Not to mention drop-dead gorgeous." She sighs. "Too bad that he can't have your personality in my body and then he'd have it all. Two twins in one." She looks at me and says, "Not that there's anything wrong with your body."

"Or your personality, Sarah."

She looks at me as though she's not convinced and says, "So just what is goin' on here? This is just a fuckin' mess."

"Sarah!"

"Oh stop," she says and attempts a smile. "Still the golden child who won't say a bad word."

"I am not!"

"Say it then."

"No, that's stupid."

"I rest my case."

I stare at her for a long moment while she gives me a daring stare back. I open my mouth once, then clamp it shut, but then say loud and proudly . . . well maybe not proudly, *"Fuck."*

"There, that didn't hurt a bit did it?"

"Not so much but just what's your point?"

"You don't always have to do the right thing."

I roll my eyes even though she's hitting a bit too close to home. "Wait, let me write that down."

Sarah flops back down into the chair. "I mean it, Candie. When I came out in my bikini you should have pushed my ass into the pool."

I remember how often I wanted to do just that and

I grin in spite of this painful conversation. "Now you're talkin'." I come over and sit back down on the desk. "There's no pool to push you in but do this for me: March over there and tell Nick how you really feel."

"Oh, Candie, sometimes I feel like you're the twin he really loves. You're the main course and I'm just dessert."

I shake my head. "No, he doesn't! He values my friendship, but Sarah, Nick loves you. Sure, there's some repair work to be done on both of your sides but if you want to patch things up, now is the time before it's too late." I consider telling her about the kiss but I decide to leave that worm in the can. "Sarah, Nick is confused and hurting."

"Some of it he deserves," she says in a clipped tone.

"Agreed. But if you still love him, then you have to at least talk to him. I know that in some ways it's safer to cling to your anger than to face your feelings."

"God, why is life so hard?"

"Mainly because we make it that way," I tell her with a shake of my head. "I have to ask about Carson, though. Do you have any interest in him?"

"Dang, we're more complicated than *All My Children*. We should have our own reality show called *All My Rednecks*."

"You sidestepped the question."

"Oh, *okay* . . . I like Carson more than I thought I would. Beneath his uppity, jackass exterior, I think he's a decent guy. Although I don't know *why*—some sort of female radar I guess—but I get the impression that there might be a woman in his life that he's not tellin' me about. I think he came here to Pinewood for more than one reason." Sarah leans back in the chair. "To answer your question, I like him and he's sexy as hell but he's not Nick."

"So you've thought about all of this."

"Busted. Okay, sister, I'm tired of bein' in the hot seat. Now it's your turn. Fess up about Tommy-the-Hottie Tucker."

"I like him a lot," I confess. "He's funny and caring. I feel so relaxed with him. There's no baggage."

"No twin sister involved."

"Yeah, there's that." I give her a rather sad smile.

"Oh, don't go givin' me that woe-is-me look. We needed to have this conversation. I wish it had happened a long time ago instead of the little love triangle we've got going on here."

"It's not exactly a love triangle."

"Whatever. It's a mess."

"Okay, so now what? Are you going to talk to Nick?"

Sarah closes her eyes and lets out a long sigh. "Shouldn't he come to me?" Her voice is small yet hopeful.

"Yeah, probably. But what if he doesn't? Then what? Are you gonna let your pride get in the way of happiness?"

Sarah groans. "Candie, I still have all this anger and resentment built up inside of me. The man *dumped* me and the other woman I was so worried about was you. This is all a little too overwhelming if you ask me. I don't know if I could keep it together long enough to get my point across. Wait a minute. What is my point anyway?"

"That you love him. Simple enough?"

"If only!" She does her feisty head bop but then looks as if she might burst into tears.

"It really is that simple if you think about it."

"Do I get to give him a tongue-lashing first?"

"I'm stayin' outta that one."

Sarah laughs but then quickly sobers. "I don't know that I have the courage to approach him."

I put my hand over hers. "I understand how you feel. Maybe the opportunity will just arise."

"Are you fixin' to meddle?"

I widen my eyes and put a hand to my chest in mock horror. "Why of course not. How could you suggest such a thing?"

"Because our mother is Marilee Montgomery and she taught us well." Sarah suddenly points over my shoulder. "Well lookee there! We have a customer!"

I turn toward the window. "Hot damn, we do. You want them? I look kind of goofy in this skirt with these bandaged knees. I'll do paperwork."

"Sure." She scrambles up from the chair. "Wish me luck."

"Good luck!" I grin as she heads out the door and then I settle in at the desk with the truck file. A few minutes later Sarah comes rushing through the door.

"They're out on a demo ride in the Ford Escort that Nick polished up. It's a dad shopping for his daughter's first car. He's worried about safety and all she cares about is the color and the stereo system. They are too cute for words."

"Yeah, but are they serious buyers?"

"Seems like it. I'm going to try and close the deal when they get back. What's the bottom line on that one?"

I open the file and check the invoice. "You can come down a couple of hundred and we still have a decent profit margin. But don't let them walk. We don't want Carson to get them."

"Gotcha."

"Speaking of Carson, are you still having dinner with him?"

"It's business, Candie . . . okay, mostly business."

"Monkey business?"

Sarah rolls her eyes. "I'm still trying to convince him that sending us cars is in his best interest, so I'm not going to cancel. Plus, it would be rude." She stares out the showroom window for a second and then turns back to me. "You know I'm not blaming this entire mess on Nick, but Candie, intentional or not, he did jack us both around a bit."

"Granted, but I think you need to give him a chance. For your sake and for his too."

"You care about him, don't you?"

"Yeah," I admit but then point my finger at her. "But you're my sister. My *twin* sister. I've never lost sight of that and I never wanted a guy to come between us."

"Oh God," Sarah says, "I'm gonna start cryin'."

I swallow and then croak, "Me too and it's comin' on strong . . . bubbling up inside me." I press my lips together in an effort to keep the wailing at bay.

"I"—she sniffs and swallows—"*can't*! Mr. Mason and his"—sniff—"daughter . . . oh shit"—sniff—"are gonna be back in a minute . . ." Her chest begins to heave and she starts fanning her face. Her nose turns red and her lips start to tremble. It's like a volcano ready to erupt.

"Quick, think . . . mmmm"—I fan my face too—"mmmmm h-happy thoughts."

"Boo, our beagle," she says in desperation.

"No," I shake my hands in front of me, "Boo's *dead*," I wail and then inhale a deep breath. "Not good."

"Oh . . . oh . . . okay then, *French fries*."

"What?" I mutter brokenly as I'm swiping at a tear.

"Good thoughts . . . greasy ole French fries."

"MoonPies!"

"Pepsi!"

"Keith Urban."

"What?"

"What the hell! I don't know. I'm thinkin' good thoughts doggone it!"

"Crisis over?" I breathlessly ask.

"Yeah, I think so," Sarah answers in a voice full of unshed tears. "Thank the Lord. Our caterwauling would have scared Mr. Mason and his daughter right off the lot."

"Hey look. Here they come." I point out the window.

Sarah takes a deep breath. "Okay, here goes," she says and pushes the door open.

I watch through the window as Sarah approaches the father and daughter with a big warm smile. I get a good feeling she's going to sell the car and as it turns out I'm right. Sometimes attitude is just everything.

The rest of the day slips by in a flash since it's fairly busy. I end up selling the old Jeep we've been driving around in and Sarah has a be-back with an older couple looking for a car for their soldier grandson who's coming home from Iraq.

"Ready to call it a day?" I ask as I stand up from the desk and stretch.

Sarah looks over from where she's rearranging the grid of keys hanging on the far wall. "Yeah," she says with a glance at the clock. "I'm going to stop out to see Mama and Daddy before my dinner with Carson. This Sunday after Mama's chicken dinner we need to tell Daddy our business plans with the trucks. You agree?"

"I do. I'm guessin' the chicken will be baked and not her famous fried, for Daddy's sake."

"I'm sure of it. Fried food is bad for you, Candie."

"Oh hush," I tell her as we head for our cars.

"Have fun with Tommy," she says in a singsong voice while wagging her eyebrows.

"I plan on it," I tell her.

"I want details."

"I'm not givin' you details."

"I'll get it out of you. One way or another."

"Will not!" I shout as she gets inside of an old Chevy Beretta, but she probably will. I head over to

the 1998 Toyota Camry that I've chosen mostly because it has half a tank of gas. I slip inside and crank
up the radio even though I have only about a two-
minute drive to my house. Tim McGraw's "Live Like
You Are Dying" comes on and I belt it out along with
him. My voice cracks as I try to hold on to that impos-
sibly long note at the end of the song, mostly because
I'm thinking of how we almost lost Daddy. Robust and
full of energy, it never even occurred to me that any
kind of disease could have taken him down.

But it almost did. I exhale a shuddering breath
thinking that my long-overdue crying jag is bubbling
up and about to burst forth. I might not be quite the
drama queen that Sarah is but *dang* this has been an
emotional day. "Happy thoughts," I whisper as I sit in
my driveway, gripping the steering wheel.

My cell phone rings breaking into my concentration
and making me jump so high that the seat belt grips
my chest. "Holy crap!" I mutter and search in the deep
dark recesses of my purse for the ringing phone. I finally spot the blue blinking light and grab it.

"Hello!" I answer in a husky yet agitated tone.

"Hey," Tommy says in his lazy, Southern twang,
"you okay?"

"I'm fine," I assure him as I turn off the car. "It's just
been a long day."

"Listen, if you don't want to come tonight I understand," he offers but sounds so disappointed that I
have to smile.

"I'll be right as rain after a hot bath and a cold beer."

"Aw, Candie, *damn.*"

"What?"

"Nothin'."

"No, come on . . . *what*?" I ask as I toss my keys onto
the kitchen table and toe off my shoes. The cool floor
feels good beneath my feet as I pad over to the refrig-
erator and grab a bottle of water.

"I was just picturin' you in a bubble bath with your hair all damp and curly while you're sippin' on a longneck. Girl, I just broke out into a cold sweat."

I chuckle into the phone. "I'm sorry, Tommy. I wasn't tryin' to get you all fired up."

"It comes natural. All you gotta do is breathe and I'm there. Heaven help me if you try to get me goin'."

I laugh harder.

"You think I'm kiddin', don't you?"

"Yeah."

"I'm blottin' my forehead as we speak."

"You're full of hot air."

"No, I'm a ball of sweat."

"Well, be sure to shower before you come over . . . oh man. Same thing just happened to me . . . you all naked in the shower . . ."

"Now who's full of hot air?"

I laugh again as I head to the bathroom. "You still plan on getting here around seven?"

"Yeah, if that's okay?"

"Sure. I'm looking forward to it." After flipping the phone shut I turn on the faucet and gather up my toiletries. As I'm dumping some bath salts into the steaming water I catch a glimpse of myself in the mirror. I'm grinning . . . and humming. When was the last time a guy had that effect on me?

Hmmm . . . I'm going with never.

I'm smart enough to know that Tommy might be what I need right now . . . funny, kind, and uncomplicated—oh yeah, and hot as all get-out, but a part of me is thinking that he has the potential to be *the one.*

After shedding my clothes and peeling off the bandages on my knees, with a long sigh I sink into the fragrant hot water. The silky heat is soothing and sensual, relaxing both my mind and my body. For a long while I soak while allowing my thoughts to drift here and there. I worry about Daddy, the car lot, the trucks, but then just as I'm almost asleep, Tommy's face floats across my brain, bringing with it some seriously sexy thoughts. A slow smile spreads across my face when I think that I just might have to see what happens when I really do try to get Tommy going . . .

19

All the Right Moves

"You look nice," Tommy comments right after I open the front door. Now that's the way to greet a girl.

"Thanks, I changed my outfit only about a dozen times," I admit with a grin.

"What?" He gives me a perplexed frown. "But why?"

"Nothin' was right. I looked too dorky, too dressy, too sleazy, until I finally settled on these old khaki shorts and this plain old blue T-shirt. I even called Sarah for assistance but of course I didn't take her advice. Tommy, you're turning me into a girlie girl," I complain with a shake of my head.

"Candie, you could wear a paper bag and you'd look good to me," he says taking my hand. When I open my mouth to protest he says, "Don't you go tellin' me I'm full of hot air. It's true."

"That's not what I was about to say."

"What then?"

"I was gonna go change into a paper bag," I tease.

"I wouldn't do that."

"Just why not? Would I embarrass you?"

"Hell no." He gives me a Tommy grin. "But it'd be danged easy to rip right off."

"Maybe that's what I was goin' for," I toss right back, but when his jaw drops open and his eyebrows shoot up I have to laugh. "My, my, did I just render you speechless?"

"Yeah, that may be a first," he admits but then pulls me closer. "You're forever surprising me, Candie Montgomery." He gazes at me with those intense blue eyes and my heart beats faster with the anticipation that he's going to kiss me. He dips his head but then seems to catch himself and pulls back. "We've got to get to the complex."

"Why?" I ask a little dazed and disappointed.

"Because if I kiss you I don't think I'll be able to stop and I really need to get back to the ball fields." With a regretful smile he gives me a gentle tug, leading me out the door and down the driveway to his truck. He doesn't let go of my hand and I think to myself that it's such a simple gesture but somehow makes me feel special. After opening the door he spans my waist and helps me up.

"What?" I ask when he hesitates before closing the door.

Tommy shakes his head. "I'm still picturin' you in a paper bag. You know I'm gonna be thinkin' about that all night long. Candie, *Candie*, the things you do to me."

Oh, the things I *want* you to do, pops into my head but I don't say it. "Only a guy would think a paper bag is sexy," I tell him with a laugh.

"It's not the bag but the rippin' it off part," he explains and leaves me with that image as he walks to the driver's side of the truck.

"Sorry," he says as he hops with ease into the truck.

I turn and give him a frown. "For what?"

"I should keep my thoughts to myself."

"I egged you on."

"Still . . . ," he says as he fires up the engine.

"Hey," I say so softly that he turns to look at me before backing up. "One of the things I like best about our relationship is that I feel so comfortable around you. I want you to feel the same level of comfort with me."

"Are you tellin' me I'm tryin' too hard?"

"No! I'm just tellin' you that you don't have to worry about sayin' somethin' wrong."

"Fine, no worries." He points his fist my way for a knuckle bump and then puts both hands back on the wheel as he backs into the street. "I guess I shouldn't tell you that I'm sorry that this is such a lame date."

"No, that violates the no worry rule. Listen, I know that this job entails some nights and weekends. But if you want to know the truth I think this will be fun. This is my kind of atmosphere, I'll have you know, so this is actually a darned good way to entertain me."

"Good . . . not that I'm worrying or anything," he says with a grin.

I angle my head at him. "Tommy don't *worry* about not bein' *worried.*"

He shakes his head. "You've got me pegged."

"Yep, bad-boy, devil-may-care Tommy Tucker is really a nice guy who worries too much about pleasing others and making them laugh. How right am I?"

After stopping for a red light he turns toward me. "You're giving me too much credit. I'm not as selfless as you're making me out to be but you hit pretty close to home." He shrugs. "Like I said, my image is mostly my own fault. If I want to be taken seriously I've got to work a little harder at it than most people. But I'm willing."

"Just be yourself around me. Because I like you."

Tommy gives me a shy smile that tugs at my heartstrings. "I thought that after working at that big ad

agency in Chicago and mingling with executives in designer suits that I might not measure up." He points to
his navy blue golf shirt with the Pinewood city logo
stitched on the front. "This is about as dressed up as I
get," he says as the light changes to green. "So many of
my friends said that they couldn't wait to get out of
this small town but not me. I couldn't wait to graduate
from college and make my way back here. I was so
glad when the recreation manager position opened
up."

"You're lucky. Some people never learn to appreciate what they have because they're too busy looking
for more."

"I bet you're glad to be back home."

"I am." This is where I should tell him that I'm still
planning on leaving at the end of the summer but I
don't want to ruin the evening, so I file it away to discuss with him later. Our relationship is moving at a
fast pace and it's only fair that I'm upfront with
him . . . and I will be, just not this minute. "I didn't realize all of the little things that I had been missing."

Tommy nods in agreement as he pulls into the parking lot. "I think part of the reason is that my dad had
to be on the road so much that he really loved his time
at home. He had to eat and shower in so many truck
stops that he never took my mother and us for
granted. He used to say that sleepin' in his own bed
and eatin' my mother's cookin' was like heaven on
earth."

"I'm sure he hated missin' you play ball."

"He did but he called me after every game. If I can
be half the man that he is I'll be doin' well."

An out of the blue thought hits me that Tommy will
make a good father but I decide that it might sound
too much like I want to have his baby, so I keep my
thought to myself. I seem to remember from a *Cosmo*
article that mentioning babies or marriage is one of the

ten best ways lose a guy this early in the dating process. I smile though, thinking I'm right. My mama's tire swing pops into my head and I can picture a miniature version of Tommy pumping his little legs . . .

"What are you smilin' about?" Tommy asks when he opens the door and sees me grinning like a fool.

"Oh . . . nothin'." I don't dare tell him! "I tend to daydream. Bad habit of mine."

"I can think of much worse habits than that," he comments as he helps me down from the truck. Instead of releasing his hands from my waist he pulls me against him and gives me an unexpected kiss. "Sorry, I just couldn't wait any longer," he offers with a boyish grin that is so doggone irresistible that when he starts to take a step back I pull him for another kiss.

"Me neither."

Tommy leans his forehead against mine. "This is gonna be a long night. I can't wait to get you all to myself. I'd call in sick but I'm the boss."

"Then you'd have to fire yourself."

"Yeah, that would suck," he says, and then laughs with me.

"Oh come on," I tell him, and tug on his hand. "This will be fun and the night will pass quickly. Just feed me junk food and I'll be happy."

"You got it," he says as he leads me to the golf cart and tosses me the keys.

"I get to drive?"

"As long as you don't get too reckless."

I give him a solemn nod. "Daddy used to let me drive as a kid. This brings back fond memories."

"You don't golf?"

"Never took it up."

"Well, I'll have to teach you."

I nod, liking the notion that he sees us doing couple-type things together.

"I'll bet you're a natural. Southpaws usually are."

We chat about the advantages and disadvantages of being left-handed as we head over to the concession stand for a big soft pretzel that we share. Although he had played down his job he's actually in charge of everything from going on an emergency hot dog run to breaking up a fistfight over a close call at the plate.

"Is it always like this?" I ask after he umps the first inning of a game when the umpire shows up late.

"Pretty much."

"You handle yourself well," I tell him.

"Thanks," he says with an appreciative smile and then pauses to answer yet another call on his walkie-talkie. "Head on over to the playground. A little girl is lost."

"Oh! Okay!" I put the pedal to the metal, which translates to slightly faster than walking. When we arrive over by the swing sets, Tommy hops from the golf cart and heads over to his teenage employee who looks totally frazzled. He's holding the hand of a tearful little girl in pigtails who looks to be around five years old.

"Hey Ben, who do we have here?" Tommy asks as he kneels down next to the sniffling little girl.

"Chloe," Ben answers. "She got separated from her mother."

"I want my *mommy*," she says and her big blue eyes fill with tears. "Will you find my mommy?" Her bottom lip trembles but Tommy keeps his cool.

"I wanted to take her over to the announcers stand so that we could call her mother but she wouldn't go with me," Ben complains.

"I'm not 'posed to go with strangers," Chloe explains to Tommy in a trembling voice. "I want my *mommy*." Her eyes open even wider and she inhales a shuddering breath. I know that look. Chloe is about to wail.

Tommy takes both of her small hands in his. "What's your mommy's name?" he asks gently.

"Lindsay."

"Is your daddy playing softball?"

She nods.

Tommy looks up at Ben.

"I'm on it," he says, and hurries off.

"Your mommy will be here is just a few minutes. I promise. And I have to tell you that you are one brave little girl. You were right not to go with a stranger. Give me a high five on that one!"

Chloe smiles and smacks him a good one.

"You know what else?"

"What?" she asks softly but without the tremble.

"Brave little girls like you need a reward. When your mommy comes to get you, tell her to take you over to the concession stand and you may have an ice cream from Tommy."

"Are you Tommy?" She points her chubby index finger to his chest.

"Yep, I am. What flavor is your favorite?" Tommy asks, and I know it's to keep her mind off the fact that her mother hasn't arrived yet.

"Chocolate chip!" she chirps.

"Mine too! Another high five!"

"Chloe!"

"Mommy!" Chloe shrieks and starts clapping her hands. "Mommy, Mommy!"

A pretty young woman rushes over. "I was looking all over for you!" she says and lifts her daughter up into her arms. "I told you we could swing after Daddy's game was over. Baby, why did you run off like that?"

"I went with Cooper," she says, "but he left with his big sister and I was afraid all by myself."

"Chloe, you shouldn't have left like that."

"Sorry." Chloe sticks out her bottom lip and I think

of Sarah. She points to Tommy. "He said that I can have an ice cream at the concession stand."

Lindsay looks at Tommy. "Thanks, but I'm not sure that Chloe should be rewarded for running off."

Chloe is smart enough to look to Tommy for help. Oh, this little girl is good.

Tommy pushes up to his feet. "I'm inclined to agree but even though Chloe was wrong for wandering off, she did the right thing by not going with Ben. She told him that she didn't go with strangers and I have to say that she was a very brave little girl and kept her head on her shoulders."

"Well, okay," her mother reluctantly agrees. "But no more running off like that!"

Chloe nods. "Sorry," she says gravely but then turns to Tommy with a smile. "Thank you, Mr. Tommy." Then without warning she leaves her mother's side and rushes over to give Tommy a fierce hug just above his knees. "You are very, *very* nice."

Chloe's mother smiles and says, "Thank you."

"No problem," he answers, but then shakes his head. "You're gonna have your hands full with that one."

"Tell me about it. So she gets an ice cream, huh?"

"Yes, just tell them that Tommy said to give her a big dip of chocolate chip."

"It's Mr. Tommy's favorite too," Chloe tells her mother as they walk away.

"You handled that well, Mr. Tommy," I tell him as we head over to the golf cart.

He flops down onto the seat with a weak chuckle. "You know I kept thinkin' on how you said that you wail when you cry and I just knew that little Chloe was gonna do that in about a minute."

"Yes, the signs were there. I felt for her."

"I don't do well with crying females. My sisters would always take advantage of that."

"The ice cream was genius."

"Her mother didn't think so. Dang, this has been one hellava night. I could use a cold beer."

"I've got some chillin' in the fridge."

Tommy glances at his watch. "Not long now. Couple of hours and I'm all yours," he says.

"You got that right," I say so low that he almost doesn't hear me.

"What'd you say?"

I shrug. "You'll find out soon enough I guess."

He gives me a sideways glance. "Now just what does that mean?"

"I don't really know," I tell him with a laugh.

"Candie Montgomery, you're not like any other girl I've ever known."

"Judging from the glares I've been gettin' all night long that's been pretty many. You even had little Chloe eatin' outta your hand."

"Candie, I know you're thinkin' that I've got all the right moves and I guess I've got a few . . ."

"Ya think?" I joke, but Tommy looks at me with serious eyes.

"I probably shouldn't be sayin' this but this feels different."

"Different . . . good?" I try to tease, but my voice is soft and breathless.

Tommy reaches over and cups my chin in his big hand. "Different . . . *right*." He tells me but then leans back in his seat. "I'm comin' on too strong. You've got a lot on your mind and I don't mean to complicate things even more. I'm not usually so intense. You can tell me to back off and I will."

I lean over and give him a quick kiss. "Let's just take things as they come, okay?"

"I'm worrying aren't I?"

I nod. "Yeah. Don't," I tell him but I find this unsure, vulnerable side of him endearing and so appealing that I want to haul him over and kiss him crazy. He's right. My life is complicated right now and the very last thing I want to do is hurt him.

"Oh no you don't," he says with a shake of his shaggy head.

"Caught me worrying," I admit with a small smile. "We need to quit and just enjoy each other."

"Sounds like a plan. Now if this shift would ever end we can do just that."

20

Don't Worry . . . Be Happy

After flopping down on the sofa with a sack of leftover hot dogs and a couple of longnecks, Tommy lets out a long sigh. "Man, this beer tastes good." He clicks his bottle to mine.

"You got that right." I nod in complete agreement. "There's a whole lot more to your job than I ever imagined and you handled it well. I'm impressed."

Tommy gives me one of his *aw shucks* looks. "Thanks," he says quietly, making me think that he doesn't get complimented nearly enough, so I make a mental note to do it more often. Perhaps he was overshadowed in that house full of women. "But it isn't exactly rocket science."

"Tommy, the park was full of people young and old. The Pinewood Sports Complex means quite a lot to this town. Don't sell yourself short." I give his shoulder a shove. "You've got a lot on the *ball*."

Tommy groans.

"Sorry, couldn't resist the pun. They don't come to me often. I guess your jokin' around is rubbin' off. Let's see if the Reds are still playing," I suggest and point the remote at the television. "Wow, look, it's into extra innings. Bottom of the eleventh."

"Sweet." He settles against the cushions, clearly pleased at my choice of entertainment. When they break for a commercial he reaches in the paper sack. "Hot dog?"

"I shouldn't, but after a soft pretzel, nachos, and an ice cream why worry?"

"That's our new motto."

"Why worry?" I ask with a grin.

"Yep." Tommy nods as he takes a big bite of his hot dog. "I'm coming to find that worry doesn't do a damned bit of good, so . . ."

"Why bother?"

"Exactly." He chews up another bite but then elaborates, "Don't get me wrong. I still believe in gettin' the job done right but without the extra hassle of frettin' about everything."

"Sounds good to me." I take the hot dog from the bun figuring that at least I'll forgo the carbs.

"You're gonna eat the wiener without the bun?"

I put my head back against the cushion and giggle. "What?"

"Hearing you say the word wiener struck me as funny. I know. I should be more mature than that."

Tommy is in the middle of a swallow of beer and almost spews it out. Half laughing, half coughing, he looks at me and shakes his head. "Weiner," he says, his voice deadpan, and then we both crack up.

"We're a couple of dorks, aren't we?"

"Hey, I resent that," he jokes but gives me a smile as though he's really enjoying my dorky company. "But bein' mature is overrated."

I think of my egg-throwing incident and laugh. "Between you and Sarah I'm finding that out."

"Yep, bein' a bad influence is a tough job but I take it seriously. Oh look, the game's back on."

While sipping on our beer we focus on the television screen. It's the bottom of the eleventh with the home team, the Colorado Rockies, up to bat. The first batter walks.

Tommy slaps his knee. "Will we ever get any decent relief pitching?"

"Yeah, but he's the cleanup batter, Tommy. Maybe Harang is playin' it safe. A walk-off home run would suck."

Tommy turns to me. "A walk *means* a run in my way of thinkin'—oh, *crap!*"

We both turn back to the television just as centerfielder Ryan Freel makes a running dive for the fly ball and misses. The ball gets behind him and rolls to the warning track.

"There's gonna be a play at the plate," Tommy says and scoots to the edge of the sofa in anticipation.

"Come on and throw the ball!" I yell as Freel bobbles the ball, comes up with it, and wings so hard that he falls to the grass with the effort, but the run scores and the Rockies win the game.

"That was a stupid mistake," Tommy complains. "Freel should have kept the ball in front of him instead of going for the catch."

"Oh, you gotta admire his hustle though, Tommy. Freel gives it all he's got."

Tommy's beer is halfway to his mouth but he sits the bottle down on the coffee table and clicks off the television. "So are you sayin' that playin' it safe is overrated too?"

Since I know that he's not really referring to the game, my heart hammers harder but I nod. "Way overrated. Of course he missed the ball and the Reds lost the game," I add, pointing my half of a hot dog at him.

"So, Candie, what would you have done?"

"I would've let the ball bounce and fielded it cleanly."

"Me too," he admits as he reaches for my hot dog and puts it on the coffee table next to his beer. "But then later, replaying it in my head, I would have wished that I had dived for the ball."

I swallow and whisper, "Yeah . . ."

He reaches over and tucks a lock of hair behind my ear. "Even if it meant losing in the end, at least I would've given it my all without regrets."

My heart pounds even harder when Tommy scoots closer to me on the sofa.

"I don't want to be lying in my bed later tonight wishin' I had . . ."

"Made a play for me?"

Tommy grins, "Yeah. Think I can make it past second base?"

I chuckle. "Depends upon how big your bat is."

"We could go on and on with the baseball analogies," he says in my ear.

"We . . . mmmm"—I shiver and then melt when he takes my earlobe between his teeth—"could."

"Or we could find something better to do . . . ," he murmurs hot and sexy in my ear.

"I . . . vote for that one."

"We think alike," Tommy whispers, and eases me back against the plump cushions.

After one last sensual tug on my earlobe that has me arching my back, he begins a warm, moist trail of kisses along my neck and then down my jawline to my chin. I dip my head, hoping to give him the message that my lips are being sorely neglected but he bypasses my mouth, making me crazy for a doggone kiss. Finally, he trails the very tip of his tongue over my bottom lip, back and forth as if savoring . . . teasing with a little nip and another lick until he covers my mouth with his.

The kiss is soft, subtle, making me crave more but

he holds back, easing into the kiss like a butterfly landing on a rose.

Leaning his weight to the back of the sofa Tommy
slides one hand beneath my shirt, exploring with fingers that are warm and with calluses that tickle my
bare skin. His touch is lightly caressing in contrast to
his kiss that becomes deeper, *hotter,* making me wish I
were wearing the doggone paper bag so he could rip it
right off. Needing to feel his skin, I slip my hands beneath his shirt and slide my palms up his smooth back.

As if reading my mind he eases up and tugs his
shirt over his head in a mouthwatering display of rip-
pling muscle and golden skin. I slide my hands up and
down his back lightly raking my fingernails until I'm
rewarded with a low moan deep in his throat. Unable
to resist, I cup my hands over his butt, dearly wishing
it was bare too. Just when I'm gathering up the nerve
to slide my hands beneath the waistband of his shorts,
he rolls off me and stands up.

I blink up at him in confusion but before I can make
my sex-drugged brain form a word of protest, he slips
his arms beneath me and scoops me up against his
chest. "W-what are you doin'?"

"I want you in bed where I can do this right."

"Oh." My sigh of relief makes him smile. "I thought
you were gonna run out the door or somethin'."

"Not on your life. Which way?"

"Way?"

"To your bedroom."

"Oh, down the hallway on your left."

Tommy heads that way with long-legged strides.

"Oh no!"

"Somethin' wrong?' He looks down at me with concern.

"It's a mess."

"What is?"

"My bedroom. My entire closet is unloaded onto my bed."

"Candie, that will take one sweep of my arm."

I arch one eyebrow. "Cool."

He kisses me on the nose and starts walking again. "Oh no!"

He stops again. "What?"

I feel my cheeks grow warm. "I don't have any . . ."

"Any what?"

"Condoms," I whisper like someone might hear.

"Got that covered. Or I will in a minute," he adds with a grin and starts walking again. As promised as soon as we're in the room he sets me down and then turns on the small bedside lamp that casts a soft glow. "You mind?" he asks eyeing the cluttered quilt.

"Go for it."

With a grin he sweeps one long arm across the mattress, sending my clothes scattering to the floor. Then, he turns down the covers . . . yes, my bed was made beneath the mess.

With trembling fingers I start taking off my clothes but he stops me.

"I want to do that."

My fingers stop and I look up at him. He's so big and tall and although I'm not a girlie girl, he makes me feel small and feminine. His long fingers could make quick work of the buttons on my blouse but he takes his sweet time, revealing my bare skin little by little, making me think that this is truly special for him and not just a roll in the hay. After easing my blouse over my shoulders he pauses to look at my black lace bra before tugging the sleeves all the way off. He cups my breasts and, even though there's not much of me, he doesn't seem to mind; he lets his thumbs rub over the lace until my nipples harden and pucker.

Just when I think he's going to unhook the front clasp, he unbuttons my shorts and slowly tugs the zipper down. With a quick intake of breath he then slides the waistband over my hips, revealing my matching black panties. After taking a step back he slides his gaze over me and says, "You're beautiful."

The quiet admiration in his gaze makes me feel as if I'm gorgeous. "Thank you." I look down at the floor but he tilts my chin back up. "I've never thought of myself as beautiful." Until now.

"And you're sexy as hell," he adds with a slow smile and then my heart just about stops when he kisses my neck, the curve of my breasts, and then kneels down to start a hot trail of kisses down my torso. My head lolls to the side when his tongue swirls over my navel and then *mercy*, he cups my ass and kisses me *there*, making the black silk hot and wet.

My knees give way and I flop back onto the bed . . . not exactly a sexy move. "I meant to do that," I tell him.

Tommy gazes down at me and shakes his head. "Ah, Candie, I would say 'What am I gonna do with you?' but at this point I already know."

I would laugh at his comment but he shucks his shorts and then *holy cow* he's standing there in very revealing white boxer briefs molded to muscular thighs and well . . . *other things* and my mouth goes dry. When I realize where I'm staring, I make a point of gazing back up at his face.

"You do it," he says and comes to the edge of the bed.

Do what? I'm not really very practiced at this sort of thing so I'm not sure what he means. I'm wondering if I should ask but then that would let him know how inept I am, so I say in what I hope is a sultry voice, "My pleasure," but it comes out more like a croak than a sexy suggestion and I still don't know what he wants me to do. Finally in exasperation I ask, "Just what am I supposed to be doin'?"

"I was hopin' you'd remove my underwear," he replies with a slow smile.

"Oh, well why didn't you just say so?"

"Point taken," he says but then laughs. "Candie, take off my underwear," he says but then shakes his head. "It sounded better in my head."

"Am I killin' the mood?" I ask in a small voice.

"Candie, there's no way in hell that you could possibly kill the mood."

"That's a relief," I say with such actual relief that he laughs harder. "Oh, I *am* killin' the mood!" I hit the mattress with my fist. "I just want to be sexy. Is that askin' too much? But nooo, I can't purr or pout or—" The rest of my tirade is smothered when Tommy covers my body with his and kisses me crazy. I wrap my arms around his neck and my legs around his waist and suddenly whatever I don't know how to do fails to matter. Apparently Tommy doesn't need a sex kitten, just plain ole me.

His hand slides up my thigh and grazes my belly, making my muscles quiver and my skin tingle. With one quick flick of his deft fingers my bra opens and my breasts spill forth with happy freedom. Tommy licks and teases one nipple and then the other until I'm arching my back while holding on to his head. Maybe smaller breasts are more sensitive . . . you know all the nerve endings compacted or whatever because he is driving me *crazy*! But then I suddenly realize that his hands have replaced his mouth on my breasts and his head is dipping south . . . licking and kissing until his head is between my thighs.

With a gasp I decide that I have to sit up and make him quit because no one has done this before and I'm not certain that I'm ready for such an intimate act, but my body feels so heavy and warm that I can't quite manage to move. I decide to just tell him to stop but his finger slips beneath my panties and although I mean to say *stop*, it comes out, "God . . ."

"Candie, arch your hips."

I swear I mean to say *no* but again I say, "God . . . ," and arch my hips; my panties come off in one easy tug to my feet, making me shiver when the cool air hits my hot body. He flings the panties somewhere and before I can protest, his mouth returns and I forget all about saying no or being shy. My fingers thread through his hair and my heart pounds hard while Tommy turns my body into liquid heat. I'm hot on the outside and getting all melty on the inside like a toasted marshmallow. Somehow I have the sense to untangle my fingers from his hair and fist my hands into the sheet instead. Two big bald spots on Tommy would be difficult to explain.

Throbbing pleasure starts to build and tighten until I'm saying random words because even in the throes of passion I can't keep my mouth shut. With tender intensity Tommy sends me higher and higher until I'm reaching for blessed release. Finally, with an embarrassingly loud cry I explode with joy and then melt into the mattress like hot fudge sliding down a scoop of vanilla ice cream.

I'm having little aftershocks of shivering bliss so, until I miss the heat of his mouth, at first I don't realize that Tommy is sitting up in bed. For a horrible moment I wonder if I've done something wrong but then I realize that he's putting on protection. I hate to tell him but I want a short nap to regroup and recharge because I'm certain that I've blown all of my sexual circuits. I know that this was all about me but my body feels heavy and sated and . . . I'm suddenly so tired. *Maybe in the morning . . .* , I think with a yawn and a stretch, and close my eyes.

"Oh no you don't. " Tommy's low, sexy voice rumbles in my ear. "We're not nearly finished, Candie girl."

"Mmmmm," is my answer. But then he kisses me, caresses me with his silky mouth and slow hands. Desire comes flooding back, hot and potent. When I wrap my arms and legs around him he thrusts inside of me with one delicious stroke. I gasp, loving the feeling of him buried deep. Tommy, ever the gentleman even now, stops, allowing my body to accept the sheer size of him.

"Candie . . . ," he says husky and ragged in my ear while starting a slow and easy rhythm. I hug him tighter, arching up, encouraging him to go deeper and harder while pleasure intensifies and builds. When he takes me over the edge right along with him he kisses me . . . on and on until his arms tremble and he rolls to the side but keeps me wrapped in his embrace.

With my head on his chest I listen to his rapid heartbeat and draw little circles on his damp skin. He tips my face up and kisses me with such tenderness that if my body could move I would make sweet love to him all over again. "Stay with me tonight."

"Wild horses couldn't drag me away," he says, but then groans. "That was really corny, wasn't it?" he asks while staring up at the ceiling.

With effort I come up on one elbow and put a hand on his chest. "If you feel as depleted as I do, wild horses would have to drag you away. Tommy, I can barely move. You are one thorough lover. I am spent."

Tommy reaches up and tangles his fingers in my damp, curly hair, pulling my head down for a long, luscious kiss.

"Okay . . . well maybe not totally spent. Give me a minute," I tell him with a smile and lay my head back down on his chest. His arms come around me and I snuggle close. With a contented sigh I'm thinking that the sex was amazing but just being in his arms is the best feeling of all.

21

Wake-up Call

I'm humming as I pour a cup of coffee for Tommy, adding cream and a hint of sugar, and thinking that if he doesn't like it that way I'll drink it and pour him a new cup. I cinch the belt on my short terry cloth robe tighter and even though I'm thinking that a trip to Victoria's Secret might be in order, I'm feeling a little naughty since I'm naked underneath. I've showered, shaved my legs, and brushed my teeth just in case he wants a little wake-up call before I have to head to the car lot. Working on Saturday has always been a big drawback in the automobile business but we don't open until ten so there's still plenty of time . . .

I pad on my bare feet to my bedroom but when I reach the doorway I stop in my tracks. Tommy is on his back sprawled across the bed in golden tanned splendor. The white sheet is pushed past his navel and one foot is peeking out at the end of the bed. When he shifts, the sheet slides lower, making me hotter than the steaming mug of coffee.

It's his face, though, that makes me smile. Although dark blond stubble shades his strong jaw making him seem like a tough guy and his shaggy hair is bed-head sexy . . . his mouth is what draws my attention. Soft, full lips that drove me wild last night are slightly parted as he breathes, making him appear somewhat vulnerable. Tommy is strong and virile but what I find most appealing is his boyish charm; now that I'm getting to know him I know that his devil-may-care attitude masks a bit of insecurity and a really big heart . . .

A heart that I could break if I'm not careful.

Sure, we talked about taking the risk with no regrets but all of that is a bunch of bull once the hurting begins. My heart starts pounding and I'm thinking that I should be honest with him that my plans are to leave at the end of the summer. What began as a silly plan to thwart gossip has quickly turned into something deeper but I'm afraid that telling him means losing him. While I'm standing there getting scared, Tommy opens his eyes, but instead of the smile I was expecting, I get a sleepy frown. "Hey, does my hair look that bad?"

"Say what?"

He scoots up to a sitting position. "You're looking at me like you're scared to death. Do I look that bad in the mornin'?"

"You look sleep rumpled but sexy as hell."

"Then why are you starin' at me like you're fixin to . . . ," he begins but then hesitates and narrows his eyes. "Oh no you don't, Candie."

"Don't . . . what?" I ask nervously. How does he already know me so well?

"I'm not even going to say it but the word begins with a *w*. Just get your cute butt over here with that coffee."

I walk over to the bed and hand him the mug. "Cream and a bit of sugar."

"Perfect. Now sit down here by me." He pats the mattress before taking a sip of coffee. "So, when do you have to be at work?"

"Not until ten," I answer, grateful that he refrains from addressing our relationship and seems willing to live in the moment. Tommy seems to know just how to put me at ease and I can't help but smile. After sitting down on the edge of the bed I lean in and give him a coffee-flavored kiss. "I've got cinnamon buns in the oven. They won't be ready for another fifteen minutes if you want a quick shower."

"Ah, so that's what I smell. Cinnamon rolls. I haven't had those since I was a kid. I used to beg my mom to let me pop open the can with the edge of the spoon. Then I'd use up the icing before my sisters would wake up."

"I always make extra icing. That's why I'll never be skinny."

"Skinny is another overrated notion you can put to rest."

"Easy for you to say, Mr. Hard Body."

"Candie, there isn't one inch of your luscious body that I'd want to give up," he says but then grins. "Mr. Hard Body, huh? I do believe that I earned that name last night." He slides his fingertip down my cheek that's warm from blushing. "Damn girl, just when I thought I was worn out you'd get me going all over again."

"Yeah right," I try to tease but my doggone voice is breathless.

"Well, now, those buns might just have to burn."

"Are you talkin' about my buns?"

Tommy laughs. "You're getting good at comin' right back at me."

"I'm learnin' from the master. But the *cinnamon* buns are going to be done in about five minutes, now."

"Mmm, you're bringin' me breakfast in bed, right?"

I trail a finger down his chest. "Do you want me to?"

"Naw, I was just teasin'. You don't have to pamper me."

"Oh, but I want to!" I give him a quick kiss. "Now, hop in the shower and when you come out you'll have hot cinnamon buns with extra, *extra* icing."

"I can't argue with that," he says and my eyes about pop out when he slides from the bed and I get quite a nice view of buns that are even more enticing than the ones baking in my oven.

I hurry into the kitchen and whip some buttercream icing to supplement the tiny little bag. The timer buzzes just as I'm finishing up. It's been so long since I've cooked for anyone and it feels nice. I start humming again as I take the golden brown buns from the oven but just about jump out of my skin when Tommy comes up behind me and wraps his arms around my waist.

"Somethin' smells good," he says in my ear.

"Oh I know. I love the scent of cinnamon. I'll have to get me a Yankee Candle."

"I was talkin' 'bout *you* and I'll only settle for the real thing, not a candle." He nibbles on my neck. "Taste good too."

A hot tingle goes all the way to my toes and I lean back against him. "You smell good too."

"Yeah, like a danged coconut. Your shampoo smelled like a piña colada." He steps away to pour himself a cup of coffee. "Need some?" he asks holding up the carafe.

"Please." I turn to him with my cup and just about swallow my tongue. His hair is still wet and slicked back from his face, making the planes and angles more pronounced. The dark blond stubble on his cheeks is thicker, causing his eyes to appear even bluer. And *mercy*, he's wearing nothing but a short white towel loosely knotted at the hip and a killer smile that says that he knows just what he's doing to me . . . but two can play that game. Barely swallowing my urge to give the towel a swift yank I slather icing on the warm roll and hand him the plate. While he takes a big bite I dip my finger in the excess icing and slowly lick the creamy white goo off with the tip of my tongue. "Do you want it in here or in bed like I promised you?" I ask with wide eyes but then giggle. "I'm not good at this whole seduction thing." I tug his hand to my mouth and take a bite of his bun. "And you," I tell him after swallowing, "with that tiny towel leaving very little to my imagination . . . could you be any more obvious?"

"I was goin' for obvious but I couldn't bring myself to walk in naked."

"You don't beat around the bush, do ya?" I ask but then realize the double entendre and clap a hand over my mouth. "I am such a dork."

He feeds me another bite of cinnamon bun. "Yeah, but a very sexy dork."

"Thank you . . . I think." I pick up another bun and feed him this time. I giggle when a glob of icing drips to his chest but when I reach for a napkin he shakes his head.

"No way. Lick it off."

I look at the icing and then raise my gaze to his face. He has just a hint of a smile but his eyes are intense. My heart hammers in my chest because I know where this is leading. After last night you'd think I couldn't possibly have a shy bone left but this is in the light of the day standing right here in my kitchen. When I hesitate he doesn't say anything else, but simply watches me as I lean in and oh so slowly lick the vanilla sweetness from the center of his chest. "Clean as a whistle," I tell him with pride but he reaches into the small bowl and swipes another bit of icing near his navel. This time I don't hesitate and I lick with a swirling motion that has him sucking in a surprised breath. My heart hammers harder but when he reaches for the bowl I move it out of his reach.

"Hey," Tommy protests but I give him a sultry smile, only this time I don't giggle. While watching his face I dip my own finger in the icing and swipe a dab over his nipple and then slowly flick my tongue back and forth until he's leaning back and gripping the countertop. "Candie," he says low and sort of pleading but I ignore him and give his other nipple the same treatment. Then, with a swift tug I toss the towel to the kitchen floor.

I've never done anything even close to this bold, but with a shaking hand I dip my finger into the sticky icing, swirl it over the head of his penis . . . and then lick it off. When I look up at him his eyes are closed and his chest is rapidly rising and falling as if he's having a hard time catching his breath. While lightly caressing him I gaze at his face. Sunshine is streaming in through the kitchen window, bathing him in soft-morning light and I think to myself that I've never seen such a golden, gorgeous sight. In that moment all I want to do is please him.

And so I do . . . until his hands are tangled in my hair and he's calling out my name.

"God, Candie," he says and gathers me into his arms. After kissing me so long that my head is spinning, he lifts me up and carries me back to the bedroom. After slipping on protection he lifts me up to straddle his lap and I'm amazed that he's already recovered and ready to go. "I want to watch your face," he explains and then kisses me as I sink down on top of him. With his hands around my waist he guides me, helping when my legs tremble.

All the while he gazes at me as I grip his shoulders. It's so intensely erotic this way . . . as he watches while filling me fully . . . deeply. The rest of the world fades until there is only Tommy and me.

With a hoarse cry I grip his shoulders and arch my back. He thrusts his hips upward and pushes against the headboard, and I come with such pleasure and emotion that I lean in and kiss him over and over until finally I fall against him with a weak but so pleased sigh.

"Did I mention that you are amazing?" Tommy asks.

"I think so."

"Okay, it's worth repeating. You're amazing. I'd come up with something better than that overused word but my brain is officially mush right now."

I lean in and lay my head on his chest. "Oh, how I wish I could stay right here all day long," I tell him with a sad moan. "But I have to muster up the energy to go to work."

He wraps his arms around me. "I wish you could stay too. I have to work tonight and I don't have the nerve to ask you again to ride around in the golf cart with me all night," he says but there's a hint of hope in his voice.

"I would do just that but I promised Sarah that we'd go grab a bite to eat and talk over business. We're going to stop over at the pub later on if you want to meet me there."

"I'll try to get out of the park early," Tommy promises. He kisses my shoulder. "Will you hang out there until I arrive?"

"You bet," I promise with a smile but I suddenly feel sort of shy after my wild behavior.

"Hey," he says softly, "don't go looking like that."

I shake my head. "I don't know what's gotten into me."

"Well whatever it is I hope it stays. You're beautiful and your spontaneity is refreshing . . . unpracticed and without motive."

I raise my eyebrows.

He shrugs. "I know that was pretty deep for me but I have my moments. It's true so don't laugh."

"I wasn't thinking that was deep for you, Tommy. I was thinking that you bring out this side of me that I never knew existed." I lean in and kiss him. "And I like it. But unfortunately I do have to get dressed for work."

He nods. "I'll let myself out so you can get ready."

"Okay." Unable to resist I give him one last kiss before heading for the bathroom. When I look at my reflection in the mirror I have to smile. My eyes are wide, my cheeks are rosy, and my lips are swollen from Tommy's kisses. I have the look of a woman well loved and I decide that it agrees with me. Even after putting on makeup and taming my curls I'm still glowing and I wonder if Sarah will notice anything different about me.

After putting on a white polo and khakis I step it up when I notice the time. I'm late! But instead of being frazzled like I normally would be, I laugh. As I head out the kitchen door I notice the mess on the counter that would usually bother me and I shrug. So I'm a few minutes late? So the countertop is a sticky mess? Who cares?

Not me! I'm still walking on sunshine or air or whatever . . . I'm happy, so engrossed in my bliss that I don't notice the loud voices . . . well, make that Sarah's loud voice coming from the office until I'm about to open the front door.

22

Loud and Clear

"Candie's not here, Nick, so you'll just havta deal with me," I hear Sarah say in a biting tone.

"Did I say that I wouldn't?" Nick replies in that steady voice of his that rarely gets rattled.

"Weren't you looking for her?" she asks, but in typical Sarah fashion doesn't wait for an answer. "Well too bad. It might come as a surprise to you but I'm a partner in this truck project. I have opinions and ideas that are pretty damned good if I say so myself. So whatever you need you can go through *me*," Sarah says in a progressively louder tone. I peek in the window to see her jabbing herself in the chest. *Wow* that's going to leave a mark. Color is high in her cheeks and she's rapidly blinking as if she might start crying.

"It's fine, really," Nick says a little less calmly. "I just need to know if it's okay to order the lift kit for the Chevy Silverado? I want to get started."

With a frown I peek in the window. A lift kit for the Silverado? Nick already ordered it. A *something's up* feeling tingles along my spine.

"Of course," Sarah answers in a clipped tone.

"Candie and I were just going over the budget yesterday. I recall seeing a lift kit on the list."

"Good," Nick answers, and then there's a long moment of silence.

"Anything else?" Sarah asks tightly but with a slight
quiver in her voice.

"Sarah . . . ," Nick says, but then falters.

"Look, I'm busy," Sarah says even though there's no
one on the lot. "Unless you have business to discuss I
suggest that you leave." In case Nick didn't quite get
her meaning she points to the door.

Nick clears his throat. "Actually, there is."

Oh my . . . I peek in the window and see Nick jam
his hands in his weathered jeans pockets. Sarah's
pointing finger drops to her side and then she leans
against the edge of the desk as if her legs are giving
out. She tries to keep her face impassive but her eyes
are wide and her mouth trembles at the corners. "You
know on second thought you should just deal with
Candie. She should be here soon."

"Probably not. When I passed her house Tommy
Tucker's truck was still in the driveway," he says and
I put my hand over my mouth. Who else might have
seen Tommy's truck there this morning? I push that
thought to the back of my mind and continue to eaves-
drop.

"I'm surprised that you didn't stop to kick his ass."

Barely refraining from stomping my foot I put my
hand over my mouth harder to keep a huge squeal at
bay. Sarah was supposed to talk to Nick and she's
making the whole mess worse by letting pride win out
over her true feelings.

"What's that supposed to mean?" Nick asks.

"Aren't you jealous?"

"Sarah, where are you goin' with this?"

"Oh come on, Nick. I was arm candy. Good enough

to sleep with but I just wasn't smart enough or clever enough, was I?"

"No, you *weren't*," Nick tosses back and I want to scream! What are they doing?

"Well, at least you're finally man enough to admit it. I deserve that much," she tells him, but I notice that her fist is clenched as if she wants to whack him a good one.

"Bullshit!" Nick shouts and this time a little squeal escapes me. I've rarely seen Nick lose it and I have the gut feeling that this is about to get crazy. "Every time I tried to talk to you—ask you something worthwhile— you'd show me your new shoes or manicure! What I wanted . . . needed from you, Sarah, you simply wouldn't give to me. Yeah, I admit that you're beautiful. But the sad part is that I would see glimpses of your intelligence before you'd catch yourself and morph into the dumb blonde routine. You know what? You're right. It just wasn't enough. But the thing that hurt is that you could have been so much more. *We* could have been so much more than just a damned cute couple. Yes, I wanted to have with you the closeness I had . . . still have with Candie."

"Then maybe she's the one for you."

"Sarah, damnit, stop! Candie will always be special to me like a—a *sister*—a friend." He takes a step closer. "Sarah, only you can make me weak at the knees."

"But I want to be more that that!" she says in a broken tone that makes me want to cry. I sigh and lean against the building. But thank the Lord she finally admits it!

"Then do it!" he demands more softly this time and I risk peeking in the window once more. Nick is standing in front of Sarah so I can't see her but I just bet her doggone head is hanging. "Look, I should have asked for more from you." He runs his fingers through his hair again. "It was just too easy, too uncomplicated being us, you know? I want it all from you, Sarah. Are you willing to give it to me?"

Say yes! I suppress another squeal and if ever there was a twin connection I wish it were now. Closing my eyes I put my fingers to my temples as if that would help make it work and I send Sarah a silent message: *Fight for Nick. Tell him your feelings.* And then I add *you big dummy* for good measure.

"I'm afraid," she finally answers.

"Sarah, afraid of *what*?"

"Sounding stupid, okay? I know it's lame but the truth. If nothing is expected then you can't disappoint. Mama was always happy with the whole beauty queen thing so I just ran with that. You have to admit that it worked with you for a while too."

"No, it didn't . . . well maybe at sixteen it did. But Sarah, there were lots of pretty girls out there, especially at the University of Kentucky."

"Are you sayin' I was a dime a dozen?" she says so incredulously that I almost burst out laughing.

Nick chuckles and for the first time I think that there is hope for this conversation. "No. I'm sayin' that I always knew that there was more to you than a pretty face. Ah, Sarah, I miss your laughter and holding you in my arms."

"Are you forgetting that *you* are the jerk . . . excuse me, the *one* who broke off our engagement because I wasn't enough?"

"Don't you get it? In the past few minutes you just gave me everything: honesty, humor, insight, and intelligence. Don't ever hold back on me again, do you hear me?"

"Loud and clear," she answers, and then I suspect they're kissing but I decide not to look. Hey, I do have my standards.

"What did you do with the ring?" Nick asks hesitantly.

Sarah's silent for a moment.

"You didn't flush it down the toilet or toss it off the bridge did you?"

"Oh course not. I'm not that crazy."

I roll my eyes and I imagine that Nick is barely refraining from doing the same thing.

"Okay, I thought about it . . . the toilet part but only after too much wine and I was hugging the commode anyway."

"Where is it then?" Nick persists.

Sarah sighs. "In the bottom of my purse where it's been since you broke it off over Mexican food, which I have not been able to eat since, I'll have you know. Just the smell of refried beans makes my stomach do flip-flops. Just another thing I've been holding against you." She sighs again. "I had this whole scene planned out in my head where I'd march over to your shop and I'd throw the damned ring at you. And then trash your place or something equally satisfying."

"Why didn't you?"

"Because I knew I'd end up throwing myself at you instead and I didn't want to suffer the humiliation."

"Oh, Sarah, I'm so damned sorry. When I told Candie that I was a jackass she said that I was just confused."

"Yeah, a confused jackass."

"Guilty. But I want you to know that I never wanted to hurt you or Candie either and I managed to do both."

"I keep telling you that we're not a package deal."

Nick is quiet for a moment and I wonder if they're kissing but then he says, "If I dig that ring out of the bottom of your purse, will you put it back on?"

"Hell no," Sarah says and I barely keep from bursting in the office and shaking some sense into her.

"I guess I deserve that," Nick quietly responds and

even though I have my own issues with how he handled the whole thing, my heart breaks for him.

"Yeah, well, I contemplated all sorts of things that you deserved along with throwing the ring at you, including a punch in the nose or maybe a drink tossed in your face or my favorite, which was keying your truck. You caused my eyes to get puffy and my face to break out and I gained five pounds! But you know what? I'm gonna give you what you really deserve."

"And what would that be?"

"A second chance. I want a second chance too. I'm giving you the ring back and *if and when* the time is right I want you to ask me again on bended knee and all that. Fair enough?"

"How will I know when the time is right?"

"I'll tell you," she says, trying for a snippy tone but her voice cracks. "Oh Nick . . ."

When I peek in the window Nick and Sarah are hugging and then kissing. I put a hand to my heart and sigh. Sometimes life works out no matter how hard you try to mess things up. While smiling I wonder if it's okay to enter the office when Sarah says, "Speaking of the time being right, Candie, you can come in, now."

What? She knew I was here? After taking a deep breath I enter the office with a whatever-do-you-mean look plastered on my face.

"Don't even try it," Sarah warns with a grin. "I spotted your big eyes and curly hair a while ago. And then you made some weird squeaky noise."

"Busted," I admit with a wince. "Sorry, this was none of my business."

"Actually it was," Nick says.

"Yeah, you were a part of this love triangle," Sarah agrees with a shake of her head. "Oh, wow, that sounded *way* sexy."

Nick and I both shoot her a look.

"Hey, I'm just sayin'," she answers a bit defensively. "I wasn't suggestin'—"

"Stop!" Nick and I say in unison and then we all three laugh.

"So sorry if I have sex on the brain. It's been a dry spell," Sarah complains and gives Nick a pointed look.

"Um, I can handle things if you want to take this *conversation* elsewhere."

"Okay." She licks her lips and then says to Nick, "We have so much to talk about."

He nods and tries to frown but looks positively giddy. "And I would like for you to see the trucks."

"Oh puh-lease," I tell them and roll my eyes. "I wasn't born yesterday." I make shooing motions with my hands but Sarah comes over and hugs me.

"I'm well aware of when you were born. You pushed me out of the way, remember?" she says with a laugh.

"I'm tellin' ya, I paved the way," I insist. "Hey," I tell Sarah as they head out the door, "you two make plans for tonight. We don't have to go to the pub."

Sarah gives Nick a questioning look but he shakes his head. "Bailey's comin' over to work on the trucks. I could meet you over there but it would have to be late."

"That's okay," I tell him with a shrug. "I was just putting it out there. Tommy's meeting me after he's done at the park so that will work out fine," I tell them but they barely pay any attention to me since they're so wrapped up in each other as they head out the door. I watch through the window and they don't even make it across the parking lot without pausing to kiss.

"Thank goodness," I say, and breathe a huge sigh of relief but then I realize that Nick was right. I'll always love him and it would have worked between us but it *would* have been like friends with benefits and I want it all too . . . friendship and passion and I think I might have found it with Tommy.

I start humming again as I do paperwork while keeping an eye on the lot. Although I don't expect to see Sarah again for the rest of the day she comes back in a little over an hour and she's smiling.

"So did you two do much talking?" I ask in a tone suggesting otherwise.

Sarah sits down on the edge of the desk. "Actually we did. Really talked. You know, it's scary how easy it is to screw things up. Pride, anger . . . jealousy." She shakes her head. "Fear."

"Don't beat yourself up. We're all just human beings. Prone to mistakes and ruled by emotion."

"I'm still afraid. How can I ever shake that?"

I put my hand over hers. "Love. I believe it's the strongest emotion of all. Just love him with all you've got."

Sarah smiles. "We still have some making up to do but I'll remember that."

"So, what did you think of the trucks?"

"Oh, they were amazing. We're going to make a killing! And Nick is so excited. This is like a dream come true for him. Isn't it weird how you came up with this idea sort of out of the blue?" Her eyes dance and she says, "Oh, and I want to show you my logo. Now if you don't like it you just say so okay? I promise I won't be offended."

"Yes, you will."

"Okay, I will, but be honest anyway."

"Lay it on me."

Catching her bottom lip between her teeth Sarah pulls out some sketches from a leather case. "What do you think?"

"Oh my goodness!" I look down at the little cartoon magician pulling a truck out of a top hat.

"You know . . . *trick my truck*?"

"Sarah, I totally get it. It's cute and clever . . . and memorable. I love it!"

"You do? Really?" She gives me an anxious look.

"Positively! I saw a lot of this kind of thing at the ad agency and believe me, this is excellent! High five!" I slap her palm. "The little guy rocks. I can see him on a sign and business cards and of course a Web site."

"Okay, we have to think of colors," Sarah says and we start to brainstorm. She brings around a chair and we put our heads together, eat candy bars for lunch, and don't look up until a customer walks on the lot. I end up selling the Ford Taurus and Sarah moves the Chevy Cavalier.

"Whew, this has been one productive day," Sarah comments as we're locking things up.

"Yeah, we're running out of cars to drive home," I tell her as I toss her keys to an old Camry. "You didn't by chance have any luck convincing Carson to send us some inventory, did you? We never really talked about your dinner with him in all of the other excitement."

"He didn't budge much. But he did say that he might consider sending us cars that he can't move on his lot."

"Oh so generous of him." I wrinkle my nose.

"He's not such a bad guy, Candie."

"Coulda fooled me." I arch one eyebrow.

"Oh, stop. I was all Business Barbie with him. I acted pleased and everything with his lame offer, figuring it was a start. Once we get the truck thing goin' it won't matter, will it?"

"We can ask Daddy's opinion tomorrow but I was thinking that perhaps we should keep some cars here along with the trucks. Maybe over on the far side of the lot?"

"I was thinking the same thing," Sarah agrees with a nod.

"Don't be hesitant to voice your opinion, okay?"

Sarah arches one eyebrow. "Oh, don't worry. In fact you're going to be wishin' I'd keep my mouth shut," she warns me as we head out the door. "Hey, I'll pick you up around eight so we both don't have cars in town."

"Did you want to grab a bite to eat first?"

"No, first I'm going to head over to Gayle's Glamorous Nails to repair my manicure. I seriously need to quit pokin' myself in the chest. Then I want to indulge in a long, hot shower and take a nap if it's all the same to you. Besides, when I dine with you I eat all the wrong stuff. Pretty soon my butt will look like yours."

"Hey, guys like a little junk in the trunk," I tell her, defending my rear.

"Tommy-the-Hottie sure must," she says while wiggling her eyebrows. "You've got to tell me all about last night."

"I will not."

"Will too! You listened to my private conversation. You owe me."

"You knew I was listening the whole danged time!"

"But you didn't know that I knew."

We argue all the way to our cars and then she calls me on my cell, begging for details, which I don't give to her. Eventually she'll get some information out of me, especially after a couple of beers, but for now I want to keep the memories of last night all to myself.

23

Hell Yeah!

When Sarah opens the kitchen door a little after eight I hurry to toss the Biscuits and Burgers takeout remains in the trash. I truly meant to order a grilled chicken sandwich with light mayo and baked apples as a side but seriously, who can resist the smell of French fries?

"Hey," Sarah says as she enters the kitchen. Her hair is big on top but otherwise sleek and shiny. "You like my new do? I only meant to get my nails done but I saw this style on Lindsay Lohan in *Glamour* and asked Gayle to copy it.

"Modern redneck. I like it. You look great."

"Well, these doggone jeans are tight thanks to my recent indulgences," she complains and then sniffs the air. "I smell fries! Got any left? No . . . *no!*" She puts her hands in the air. "Forget I said that."

"Sorry. I gobbled them up anyway. Listen, you have to start ordering your own fattening food. I'm tired of being the fall guy."

"Yeah, but every fry of yours I consume is one less that you do."

"True. You're gonna gain weight and I'll lose it.

Works for me. Okay then, how do I look?" I ask and turn in a circle. My jeans are low rise and my blue tank has scalloped edges of lace while showing just a hint of my torso. "It's a little sexier than I'm used to but I want Tommy to take notice."

Sarah narrows her eyes. "Wait a minute. Where'd you get those boobies?"

"It's a push up bra," I whisper. "After work I did a little shopping at Victoria's Secret."

"Why the hell are you whisperin'?"

I shrug. "I feel . . . a little naughty. Guess what?" I wait for her to say *what* and then whisper, "I'm wearin' a . . . *thong*."

"You're kiddin'."

"No!" I tell her in an excited squeaky voice.

"I mean you're kiddin' as in you've never worn one?"

"Never!" I squeak again.

"So what have you been wearin'? Granny panties?"

"Nooo!" I defend myself as I grab my purse and we head out the door. "Not granny panties!"

"Oh, let me guess," Sarah says over the hood of the Camry. "You wear high-cut briefs . . . *cotton*. Oh, but sometimes you shake it up a little with colors."

"Oh, thanks for tellin' the entire neighborhood what kind of panties I wear," I grumble as she backs out of the driveway. "I have other silky things. Just not thongs."

"No one cares about your underwear," Sarah assures me but then grins, "except for maybe Tommy-the-Hottie."

"Stop callin' him that!"

"My, *my*, you're touchy," she teases, but then stops at the end of the driveway and turns to me. "You really like him, don't you?"

"Yeah, I think it could lead to somethin' special."

"Whoohoo, things are finally lookin' up for the

Montgomery twins," Sarah says. "Come on, Candie, give me a *whoohoo*."

"You know I don't *whoohoo*."

"How 'bout a *yeehaw*?" she says and then demonstrates so loudly that my neighbor Mrs. Cartwright who happens to be hard of hearing looks up from her front porch swing.

"Um . . . no."

"Well then, march right back in there and put your granny pants back on, you big fuddy dud."

I narrow my eyes at her. "I am not a fuddy dud. Need I remind you of my egg throwin' prowess?"

After pulling out into the street she says, "One little egg throwin' incident does not exempt you from your fuddy-dud status. Okay then, how 'bout just a little bitty *hell yeah*."

"Gawd." I take a deep breath and say, "Hell yeah. There." At least she didn't ask me to drop the f-bomb.

"Weak, Candie. So weak. Come on now. A little louder like this, HELL YEAH!" She feels the need to speed up as she yells.

"You're gonna get us a ticket."

"Oh loosen up, Granny Pants!"

"I'm wearin' a doggone thong!"

"I know, so give me a *hell yeah* to celebrate!"

"No!

"Chicken."

"Okay . . . ," I tell her before taking a deep breath. "HELL YEAH!" I shout out the open window right as we hit Main Street and of course draw attention to our crazy selves. A couple of teenagers walking down the sidewalk laugh and then yell back, "Hell yeah!"

"Felt good didn't it?"

"A little," I admit.

"Okay now shout, 'Hell yeah I'm wearin' a thong.'"

"You're pushin' your luck, Sarah. And by the way if you go and tell anyone of my thong wearin' status I will kick your butt all the way into next week, you hear me?"

"Okay," she readily agrees but I don't like the mischief in her eyes as she parks the car.

"I'm warnin' you," I tell her as we walk across the parking lot.

"You can trust me with your naughty little secret."

"Oh like you're not wearin' one."

"Of course I am. It's just not a secret. In fact I think I'll just have to announce it in Pete's Pub."

"No you won't!"

"Just messin' with ya. Although that hard up and horny comment landed you Tommy-Boy."

"Oh don't take the credit for that! I already knew him. He offered to play my boyfriend when the whole doggone town was shunning me!"

"So I did bring you two together. You can thank me now."

I roll my eyes, "Okay, thank you for turning the town against me and branding me a fiancé-stealing hussy."

"You're welcome," she teases.

I have to laugh but then say, "Isn't it weird how life works sometimes? How one thing leads to another?"

"It was meant to be." Sarah puts her hand over her heart and flutters her eyelashes.

"Oh stop."

Sarah pulls me close for a hug. "I'm happy for you, Candie. I'm happy for me too."

I laugh as I hug her back. "Me too."

Sarah pulls back but then frowns. "The thing about bein' this happy is that I have this fear that somethin's gonna come along and ruin it. It kinda puts pressure on a person not to mess up."

"Sarah, that's called being a pessimist." I take her by the shoulders and give her a gentle shake. "Let's be optimists."

"Yeah, keep lookin' for the good in everything."

"Hell yeah!" I shout just as the door to the pub opens and of course everyone turns our way but you know what? I don't give a damn. "Hell yeah!" I shout again while raising my fist for good measure and a few people in the bar toss a *hell yeah* right back at me. A moment later Sarah and I are handed a cold beer.

"Watch this," Sarah says in my ear. She raises her beer bottle in the air and this time we get the entire bar to yell and I have to laugh. Sarah will forever love being the center of attention.

"A *swaller* and a *holler*," someone shouts. Sarah and I join in by taking a swallow of beer and then we holler with the rest of the bar. This goes on a couple more times before interest is lost.

"Hey, y'all put on some David Allen Coe!" A big burly dude shouts from his perch at a tall table and a moment later his request is honored at the jukebox. Soon half the patrons in the pub are singing along. I have to smile when I think of myself sitting in a martini bar with a glass of white wine while politely listening to classical music.

"Whatcha grinnin' about?" Sarah asks over the music.

"Nothin'. It's just good to be back in Pinewood. Let's snag those stools," I suggest and we hurry over to the long bar that runs the length of the room. Bar stools in Pete's Pub on a Saturday night are hard to come by.

"You girl's sure livened things up in here," Pete, the owner says from behind the bar. He's about Daddy's age, a big bear of a man with a warm smile and a tender heart but will toss you out on your ear if you cause a ruckus. "The next one's on the house."

"Thank you, Pete," I tell him and Sarah joins in.

"How's Dan doin'?"

"Drivin' Mama crazy," Sarah answers.

"Must be getting better then if he's back to his ornery self."

"He is," I answer this time. "Mama's makin' him toe the line. She can handle him."

Pete fills a mason jar with draft beer and hands it to a customer. "Dan's lucky to have you girls watch over the family business. And Candie, it sure is nice to have you back in Pinewood. You plannin' on stayin'?"

"I . . . um . . . ," I stutter, not wanting to answer.

"Sure she is," Sarah says.

After putting a bowl of pretzels in front of us Pete says, "I'm glad to hear it. Pinewood needs the young folk to stay here and keep this town thrivin'."

"Bloom where you are planted, Mama used to say," Sarah continues. "Chicago was a learning experience but you're a small-town girl at heart, right, Candie?"

"Um . . ."

"Here's to big timin' in a small town," Sarah says, and clicks her bottle to mine.

I click her bottle and take a long pull on my beer, wondering how I'm going to leave but I push the thought away to ponder later. We laugh and chat with friends while keeping an eye out for Nick and Tommy. Around ten o'clock a band starts setting up in the far corner and Pete clears away some of the tall round tables to make way for dancing.

"Hey," Sarah says, and puts a hand on my arm. "I just spotted Carson playing pool in the back room."

"You wanna go say hi?"

She shakes her head. "No, I don't want Nick to get the wrong idea."

"Hey, speak of the devil, he just walked in and Tommy's not far behind him."

Nick is looking all tall, dark, and broody and Tommy has his usual smile on his face, but both guys are turning female heads. When we wave, both of them make their way over to our stools at the bar. I

tares at a tall brunette goddess who walks in the
place.

Or should I say *sashays* in?

Yes, I should. Looking a lot like Cindy Crawford
minus the mole, she sashays over to the bar and I
swear it seems like she's in slow motion. With Toby
Keith's "I Love This Bar" playing in the background it
feels as though I'm watching a music video. She's definitely sophisticated but she sure isn't a redneck . . .
and this bar is *not* her kind of place.

Both Tommy and Nick are watching sort of slack-
jawed and as if on cue Sarah and I give both besotted
boyfriends a quick elbow to the gut. They grunt and
dutifully look away from the brunette and try to focus
back where their attention belongs. On us!

"Now where were we?" I ask rather tightly but I
have to admit that I'm watching the Cindy Crawford
look-alike over Tommy's shoulder.

"I'd like a dirty martini," she tells Pete in a rather
haughty tone. Pete, though, doesn't bat an eye or look
as besotted as the men seated at the bar, bless his heart.
I guess at this point he's just about seen it all.

"No problem," Pete says, "but give me a minute to
round up one of those fancy glasses."

The goddess doesn't audibly answer but gives Pete
a little flick of her fingers before turning around and
casing out the room as if searching for someone. I'm
thinking that whomever she's looking for isn't likely
to be in this pub or even in Pinewood for that matter
when her eyes suddenly narrow and her shiny pink
lips thin over her very white teeth. I look in the direction of her gaze . . .

Carson Campbell. Sarah turns to me with raised eyebrows and I shrug but then like me Sarah turns around
to watch the unfolding drama.

"I smell trouble," Tommy says in my ear.

"Me too," I whisper back.

was wondering how I would feel seeing Nick
Tommy at the same time and although I will al
have a soft spot for Nick, it's Tommy who capture
attention. He appears freshly showered and
cowboy than surfer dude tonight in his Wran
boots, and plain white T-shirt that shows off his l
shoulders and golden tan. My heart kicks it up a
when he reaches my side.

"Hey there, Sarah." Tommy gives her a peck d
cheek before turning the warmth of his smile o
"Candie . . . ," he says low and sexy in my ear, m
me feel all warm and tingly. Man oh man does h
smell good. "Sorry I'm late gettin' here. I h
shower the ball field dust off me," he says and s
Pete for a beer. "You ladies need anything?"

"We're fine," Sarah answers. "Pete gave us d
the house since we got this place rockin'."

Nick shakes his head. "I won't even ask," h
but slips his arm around Sarah's waist and give
kiss on top of her head. "Hey, I like your hair,
comments.

Sarah smiles as she flips her sleek locks ov
shoulder. "I call it sophisticated redneck."

Nick laughs. "And you wear it well." He l
her with amusement but there's a softness in h
that tells me that he's missed her so much.

"Sophisticated redneck sounds like it should
name of a magazine," Tommy says as he lea
elbow on the bar.

"It does," Nick agrees. "I think Candie and
should be on the cover.

"That would be an honor . . . I guess," I com
I reach for a pretzel.

"Of course it would," Tommy says as he han
a beer. We chat about Nick's trucks and Tommy
at the park until the front door of the pub o
hush falls over the crowd when everybody st

Pete hands the goddess her drink but before she can even think of paying, about ten guys reach into their wallets. Expecting her to take a polite sip of her martini I'm pretty danged impressed when she tosses back half of the drink without even blinking or coughing as I would be doing. I learned the hard way in Chicago that even the candy-flavored martinis pack quite a wallop. One night after consuming three appletinis that deceptively tasted like green apple Jolly Ranchers I was suddenly belting out "The Way We Were" with the lounge piano player. Barbra Streisand I'm not.

The goddess tips her glass up to her lips but then decides to think better of it. At first I'm thinking she might have had a similar experience after chugging martinis and is using better judgment but her eyes take on a predatory gleam as she heads for the billiard room. The crowd parts the way for her purposeful strides that are accentuated by the sway of her hips in very tight, white designer jeans. Either by chance or more likely on purpose the next song playing is Trace Adkins' "Honky Tonk Badonkadonk." Whatever. She appears to be a woman on a mission with Carson as her main target.

Sarah briefly turns to me and mouths, "Ohmigod," and I nod my agreement. Everyone in the place is watching her except for Carson who is innocently bending over to take his shot at the pool table. He straightens up, smiling, clearly pleased after sinking the shot but then turns when the goddess taps him on the shoulder. The crowd inhales a collective intake of breath . . .

Carson's smile fades and his eyes widen just before the goddess tosses the remainder of her martini in his face. The liquid splashes his shocked features while the olive bounces off the tip of his nose. A murmur ripples through the crowd but no one moves as if we're all in a freeze-frame.

Carson finally blinks and then lifts the tails of his untucked shirt to blot the gin from his face, giving the women in the pub a nice peek at his abs. The goddess seems unimpressed with his six-pack and after handing her empty glass to the closest person to her she pivots on her spiked heel, I'm guessing with the intention of leaving. I have to wonder how far she traveled in order to toss a drink in his face and just what Carson did to deserve it.

Carson's arm shoots out as if to grab her and I feel the testosterone level in the bar immediately rise as if every man in the joint is ready to come to her rescue. Carson's aim misses but instead of following her he simply watches her exit with a scowl on his face and a muscle ticking in his jaw. Everyone else follows her progress to the door but with her chin tilted upward and her head held high she seems not to notice or even care that she's the center of attention.

A moment goes by where we all stare at the door as it swishes shut but then the band starts warming up and soon Saturday night at Pete's Pub in Pinewood goes back to the usual barroom activities.

Sarah leans over closer to me. "I wonder what that was all about?"

I shrug. "I dunno."

Sarah purses her lips. "Hmmm, well somehow we're gonna find out."

"Sarah . . . you need to keep your nose out of it," Nick warns with a shake of his head.

After opening her mouth as if to protest Sarah gives him a wide-eyed smile. "You're right, Nick. I should."

With a sigh of relief Nick smiles back but as soon as he turns his head Sarah mouths to me, "I'm gonna find out."

I smother a laugh behind a swig of beer but Tommy says in my ear, "You two are quite a handful."

I jab my thumb at my chest. "Me?"

"Yeah, you."

"Maybe you should run like the wind . . ."

"Not on your life," he says, and while slipping his arms around me from behind he plants a warm kiss on my neck, making a hot shiver sizzle down my spine. "God, I want to get you alone. Can we leave yet?"

After swiveling on my stool to face him I say, "Not just yet. I promised Sarah I'd stay a while."

Tommy sighs. "Okay. But no longer than an hour."

"I promise," I tell him even though I'd be fine with leaving too. But there's still some underlying tension between Sarah and Nick and I did promise that I'd stay until she gives me the okay to leave without her. While she seems happy I can tell that her guard is still up.

"I'm guessing that they're back together?" Tommy asks low enough so as not to be overheard.

"Workin' on it," I answer.

"I suppose this means you're back in the good graces of Pinewood."

"Yes, I'm no longer being shunned, so you're off the hook," I tease but then anxiously wait for his reply.

"Good," Tommy says making my heart skitter like a flat rock across a pond.

"Good?" I echo.

"Yeah, this makes us official. No more pretense," he says in a light tone, but his eyes are serious. My heart skips another beat when I realize that he's falling for me. I must have a talk with him about the possibility of my leaving although I am beginning to wonder if I even want to. Still, he needs to know the truth.

"Tommy . . . we need to—," I begin but the band starts playing "Redneck Girl" and Sarah grabs my hand. She tugs me to my feet and we join just about every other chick in the place, dancing with our hands above our heads and singing along at the top of our lungs. When it's over we double high-five but then stay on the dance floor to sing along to "Friends in Low Places" before heading back to Nick and Tommy to finish our beers. By this time the older crowd is thinning out as younger people flood into the bar. Pete props the door open to let in the cool evening breeze but it's getting hot and smoky so I'm about ready to leave when the band starts playing a slow song.

"Wanna dance?" Tommy asks and of course I do. At first, I simply have my hand tucked in his and we sway together but halfway through the song he pulls me closer. With a sigh I slide my arms around his neck and rest my head on his shoulder, wishing that I were tall enough to press my cheek to his. I can feel the warmth of his skin through the T-shirt and the solid wall of his chest feels wonderfully masculine against my breasts. When I slide my fingers into his hair he pulls me even closer. My heart thuds and desire pools in the pit of my stomach and sinks lower, and by the end of the song I'm breathless with wanting him. "The hour isn't officially up but, Candie, do you mind if we leave now?"

"You were readin' my mind," I tell him with a smile. "Let's say good-bye to Nick and Sarah, okay?"

"Sure," he says, and tucks my hand in his warm grasp.

I lead him back over to the bar where Nick and Sarah are talking quietly. "Do you mind if we take off?" I ask, but give Sarah a look that tells her that I will stay if she wants me to.

"No." She waves us off. "Go ahead. It's getting too crowded in here."

I give Sarah a pointed look that's asking if she's going to sleep with Nick and she gives me a very discreet shrug of her shoulders. I give her a slight nod back and she knows I'm telling her that if it seems right she should go for it.

"You ready?" Tommy asks with such hope that I have to smile.

"Yes. See you around, Nick. And Sarah, I'll see you at Mama and Daddy's tomorrow. If you want to ride together just give me a call, but not early, okay?" I give Tommy's hand a squeeze so he catches my meaning.

"Okay." She leans over and gives me a hug. "I'm such a nervous wreck," she whispers and my heart goes out to her.

"Go with your gut and don't overthink it," I whisper back and give her one final, fierce hug. I don't really know who I think I am to give advice and I should probably just keep my mouth shut but at this point I think that Sarah needs some reassurance.

As soon as Tommy has me outside I take a deep breath of fresh night air that holds the promise of rain. Then out of nowhere Tommy puts his hands around my waist, hefts me up in the air, and twirls me around. A little squeal escapes me as I hug his neck. "What are you doin'?"

"I don't know. I just felt like spinning you around," he says with a grin that makes a beeline for my heart.

"You are a crazy person, Tommy."

"I know," he says, and twirls me around again, "but you bring it out in me."

When he sets me down I'm still clinging to his neck so I take advantage of the situation and give him a slow, sweet kiss until someone yells, "Get a room!"

Tommy laughs and then kneels down.

"Just what are you doin' now?"

"Hop up on my back and I'll piggyback you to my truck."

I think about refusing but then with a giggle I wrap my arms around his neck and my legs around his waist and hold on tight while he sprints to his truck. I'm laughing so hard as I bounce from his long-legged strides that when he stops at his truck I slide to the ground but my legs give out and I land in a giggling heap at his feet.

"Whoa there." Reaching down Tommy helps me to my feet but instead of opening the door to his truck he presses me against the door and kisses me senseless as though we're a couple of teenagers. "My God, Candie, you've got me all fired up like I'm about sixteen years old," he comments, echoing my thoughts.

"You wanna make out in your truck?"

"What if someone sees us?"

"The chance of gettin' caught would be part of the fun," I bravely tell him, but my heart is pounding hard.

"Okay," Tommy agrees with some uncertainty as he opens the truck door. "You sure you want to do this now, right?"

"Hell yeah!" I tell him but then lean my head against the headrest and laugh.

"You are such a liar," he accuses me with a grin.

"No I *want* to . . ."

"But you don't want to get caught."

"My luck runs that way."

Tommy nods. "Mine too."

"Then I guess we shouldn't risk it," I tell him, but he looks so good sitting there in the moonlight that I'm having second thoughts. "Should we?"

"No, but fasten your seat belt," he warns with a gleam in his eye that has my heart pounding. "Because you're about to be in for a wild ride."

"Tom-meeeee!" I yell when he takes the truck off the road through the park. "You're gonna get us in big trouble drivin' through here."

"It's a short cut," he explains. "I'm a little anxious to get back to your place."

"I get that," I tell him but yelp when he takes us through a ditch, up a hill, and through a narrow path that's just barely wide enough for the truck to fit through. Tree branches are whacking against the roof of the truck. I'm bracing myself with one hand on the armrest and one on the ceiling while my foot is pressed against the dash. "Holy crap!" I squeak when we go airborne.

"Oh come on, Candie. You're a country girl. Surely you've gone muddin' and four-wheelin' before."

"Yeah, on my daddy's farm; not in the city park!"

"I'm only on the edge of the park."

"Yeah, but T-Tommy, there's a creek up ahead."

"Hold on tight," he warns me.

"I am!" I assure him and grit my teeth as we splash through the creek and then somehow end up on my street. When he turns the truck off I sit there for a long moment breathing hard and wondering how he got us here in one piece. "I thought I knew this town inside out but I have no idea how you got me here in five minutes flat."

"That might be because you had your eyes shut half the time," he says with a grin. "Did ya have fun?"

"No! You scared the daylights right outta me!" I put a hand to my chest and try to glare at him but fear is turning into something altogether different. "My heart is beatin' like a jackhammer." I'm trying to sound angry but my voice is breathless.

"Mine too," Tommy says with a smile that tells me that there was a method to this madness. In a flash he's out the door and over to my side. He pulls me from the truck and into his arms, lifting me up and kissing me all the way to the front door. "Where's your key?"

"It's open."

"I know this is Pinewood but you shouldn't do that."

"I know. I was more careful when I first got back," I tell him as he quickly carries me to the bedroom. I'm pleased that he's worried about my safety and I pull his head down for a kiss as we fall to the bed in a tangle of arms and legs and passion.

This time instead of slow and easy we're tearing off our clothes, naked and making crazy love in nothing flat. His kisses are deep and demanding as he takes control, making love to me with bold, hard strokes that quickly take me over the edge with such sharp intensity that I arch my back and cling to him while tumbling back down to earth. "I guess that was the wild ride you were referrin' to, huh?"

Tommy's laughter rumbles beneath my cheek. While I know that I don't have much to compare it to, I can't imagine anything better than this . . .

22

Kickin' It into High Gear

With getting the car lot ready for our grand opening, playing in the sand volleyball league twice a week, and dating Nick and Tommy, Sarah and I have kicked our lives into high gear. The past month has passed in a blur of activity. Although I haven't officially quit my job in Chicago, at this point I can't see myself leaving Pinewood.

"I don't believe I've ever been this tired," I comment while swaying on Mamma and Daddy's front porch swing.

Sarah looks up at me from her perch on the steps. "Tell me about it," she agrees with a big yawn.

"You girls should run along and get yourselves a good night's sleep," Mama suggests as she glances up from her big wicker rocker where she's working on her needlepoint. "Tomorrow's a big day."

"Is Daddy already asleep?" I ask before taking a sip of freshly squeezed lemonade.

Mama nods. "He was out before his head hit the pillow.

"We haven't worn him out have we?" Sarah looks at Mama with concern.

"A little," Mama concedes, "but he's lovin' it."

"Mama, be honest," Sarah pleads. "Is Daddy okay with our new business? I mean we could have called it *Dapper Dan's Tricked Out Trucks* instead of leavin' his name off," she says and gives me a disgruntled look since keeping Daddy's name on the sign was her choice.

Mama puts her needlepoint down and shakes her head. "Your daddy is more than happy to turn the reins over to you girls. He's worked so long and so hard over the years that he's looking forward to travel, a little bit of fishing, and a lot of golf."

"I hear there's talk of a second honeymoon," Sarah says in a singsong voice and wiggles her eyebrows.

Mama blushes a deep rose color that's visible even in the waning sunlight. "We've always wanted to go to Maui," she tells us and then puts her hand over her mouth before saying, "I've booked it! But don't tell your daddy. I want it to be a surprise for our wedding anniversary."

"Oh Mama!" Sarah and I say in unison . . . something we've been doing a lot lately. I do believe that the twin connection thing has finally happened.

"There's somethin' else," Mama says, and does the hand over her mouth thing again. I wonder for a moment if she's going to confess to buying a thong, and then I have to erase that picture from my brain. "I've been takin' golf lessons so I can play with him."

"No *way*," we say in unison once more.

Mama laughs, a beautiful tinkling sound that's finally back after her scare with Daddy. "You girls are doin' it again."

"What?" we ask together.

"That. Sayin' the same thing at the same time like when you were little girls." Her voice breaks and she says, "It does my heart good to see you two so close. It just goes to show that if you try hard enough things have a way of workin' out." She sighs. "There's only one thing left to make my life complete." She looks out over the lawn at the tire swing that's swaying in the summer breeze. "Grandbabies."

"Mama, we have to get married first," Sarah reminds her before taking a sip of her lemonade.

"Oh, I *know*. But I do believe that wedding bells are right around the corner. Both of you girls are head over heels in la-ove. Don't even try to deny it." She clasps her hands. "Wouldn't a double wedding be *won*-der-ful?"

"Mama!" we say.

"*What?* It would save on expenses."

"Neither of us is engaged," I remind her.

"Well hells bells, kick it into high gear, girls!" she cries and then her eyes well up. "One thing I've learned from your daddy's heart troubles is not to waste one doggone day because you never know what tomorrow will bring. Not that I'm bein' pushy or anything."

"You pushy, Mama?" Sarah says with a laugh.

"Heaven's no," I add with wide eyes.

"Oh, you two just hush!" she says with an elegant wave of her hand. "Well, I think I'm going to retire early. You know beauty rest is not an old wives tale," she comments with a pointed look at us both.

"We'll be on our way as soon as we finish your tasty lemonade," I promise her. "See you and Daddy tomorrow."

Mama nods as she gathers up her needlepoint. I notice that she moves a little more slowly than I remember and it makes my chest feel tight. "Bright and early."

After Mama goes inside Sarah says, "Should we go over the list of things one more time?"

"Okay," I agree, knowing that telling her no would be pointless.

"Oh don't give me that look," Sarah protests.

"What look?"

"The rollin' your eyes without even rollin' them look. I just don't want to forget any important details," she insists as she starts ticking off the long list of things to do, starting with the caterer, the tent in case of, heaven forbid, *rain*, the photographer even though we will have lots of media coverage. When Sarah drones on my mind sort of wanders since I know the list by heart.

"And we'll unveil the sign right before we open," Sarah continues. After several heated arguments Sarah and I finally decided on *Tricked Out Trucks* as the name of our new business. Even though I didn't want to hurt Daddy's feelings I knew that we needed to leave off the Dapper Dan part to keep the cool factor. We'll still have used cars, but a limited supply and perhaps give them up all together if we can keep the lot stocked with the custom trucks. The sign has been erected but covered up, much to the sorrow of the town. In fact, Pinewood has been all abuzz about the secret that Sarah and I will be revealing *tomorrow*. It's an absolute miracle that word didn't slip out but Nick is trustworthy and he threatened Bailey with all sorts of blackmail since Bailey had a steady girlfriend but has a wandering eye.

Then there are the trucks that have been carefully hidden in a storage garage at the back of Nick's property. He has eight amazing works of art ranging from mild to wild and is going to have his own masterpiece displayed on our tiny showroom floor even though he made it quite clear that it's not for sale at any price.

Because Sarah's so excited I'm trying to keep a low-key attitude even though I'm going crazy with excitement and worry. Tommy has been my rock over the past month, giving advice and sharing his opinion when asked but mostly just being there for me when I felt as if I were coming apart at the seams. "Okay, Sarah, are you ready to call it a night?" I ask with a yawn as I stand up.

"I guess," she replies absently while peering down at her list. After nibbling on her bottom lip and making a few more notes she looks up and nods. "Okay, I'm ready."

After taking our empty glasses inside we head to the old Camry I'm still driving and set out for home. "When this business takes off we're gonna have to get us a couple of cool trucks to drive."

"Yeah, with our logo on the hood!" Sarah suggests with a smile. I've already been talking to Nick about an idea to have more chick-style trucks to bring in the female demographic. I'm havin' a hard time though convincing him that a hot pink pickup would be really tight."

I stop at a red light and look at her. "I think that idea rocks! We can try it out with demos for us to drive and go from there. You need to do some sketches. You and Nick make a great design team."

Sarah beams at the well-deserved praise. "I've been trying to sketch after work but I'm just too danged tired."

"You'll have time after we get this off the ground."

"Lordy, I'm more keyed up than the night before the Miss Kentucky pageant. I don't think I'll sleep a wink."

"I know! I'm hoping that a bit of bourbon on the rocks will do the trick."

"Or maybe a little bit of Tommy Tucker," she suggests with the arch of one eyebrow.

"There's nothin' little about Tommy," I tell her as I pull into my driveway.

"Candie!"

"I'm just sayin'."

Sarah grins. "Wait a minute. Did we just have a role reversal?"

"You're rubbin' off on me."

"Good," she says, and I'm glad to see the lines of worry fade into a smile. "You're rubbin' off on me too. Makin' me a responsible adult and all that nonsense."

I laugh as I hand her the car keys. "I'll walk in the morning. Tommy isn't comin' over. He has a huge softball tournament that he's settin' up for but he promised to drop by when he gets a break. He feels terrible that he's so busy but I told him not to worry," I tell her, and then get out of the car.

"Just why do you have that grin on your face?"

"I'm thinkin' of Tommy. We're both worryaholics."

"Wait, is that a word?"

I shake my head. "No, but it should be. We try to keep each other from freakin' out too much."

Sarah frowns. "Tommy seems like a happy-go-lucky kind of guy. I would never have guessed."

I lean against the hood of the car and say, "There's so much more to him than that. He really is a good guy."

"Do you love him?"

My heart hammers at the question. "Yes," I admit softly as I drag the toe of my shoe across the concrete.

"Have you told him?"

"I've come close, but no."

"Let me guess, you're waiting for him to say it first." When I remain quiet Sarah folds her arms across her chest and gives me a you-gotta-be-kiddin' look.

"Isn't that the way it's supposed to work?"

"Oh, come *on*, Candie. We might be small-town girls but you're not that old-fashioned."

I shrug. "I guess I'm afraid."

Sarah pushes away from the car and puts her hands up in the air. "Of what? Commitment?"

"No!"

"Happiness?" She raises her hands higher.

"What if he doesn't say it back?"

Sarah's hands fall to her sides. "Aw, Candie . . . this falls into the excessive worry category. You know what?" she asks but, on a Sarah roll, doesn't bother to even take a breath. "If Tommy is a worrier like you he might be thinking the same thing. Tell him how you feel."

"Dive for the ball," I tell her with a slow smile.

"What?"

"You're telling me to dive for the ball instead of playing it safe."

Sarah rolls her eyes. "Athletes. Always have to use sports lingo that I don't really get. If you're asking me if you should take the risk, then yeah. Catch the ball."

"Dive."

"Whatever."

"I might not catch it but I won't wake up in the middle of the night with regret."

Sarah blinks at me.

"Thank you baby sister!" I tell her with a hug. "You're brilliant."

"Tell me somethin' I don't know."

"Now as Mama said, we need our beauty sleep."

"Speak for yourself," Sarah says, but then laughs. "I can't wait for tomorrow!"

"Me neither." We hug again while jumping in a small circle as if we're ten instead of grown women who are about to launch a new business. "Now go get some rest. It's gonna be a big day."

After getting ready for bed I pour myself a generous splash of Maker's Mark knowing that it's going to be difficult to fall asleep. I turn the covers down, settle in against the fluffed up pillows, and then take a sip of my drink. The smooth bourbon sends a trail of warmth all the way to my tummy and I already feel my eyes growing heavy. I toss back the rest, hoping to fall asleep before Sarah's list starts playing in my head. Telling myself that we have everything under control, I place my empty glass on the nightstand and slip beneath the covers.

With a bourbon-scented sigh I tuck my hands beneath my pillow while letting exhaustion and the whiskey lull me into la-la land. The last thought I have before drifting off to sleep, however, isn't of Tricked Out Trucks but of Tommy Tucker. With a sleepy smile I imagine the look on his handsome face when I finally tell him that I love him.

23

Why Waste Another Day?

When my alarm goes off I groan and slap at the snooze button but a second later I sit up straight in bed and blink into the semidarkness. "Today is the day!" I whisper in high-pitched excitement. My heart starts bumping against my rib cage as I hurry into the kitchen to start some coffee brewing. I pad over to the back door and pull back the frilly curtains, nervously peering upward in search of rain clouds; I'm relieved to see nothing but blue sky and fluffy white cotton ball clouds. There was only a slight chance of showers but any chance was enough to have Sarah and me on edge.

I pour a cup of coffee before the pot is even finished brewing and add a generous amount of fat-free flavored creamer that Mama turned me on to. Since Daddy's heart attack she's been all about fat free and all things healthy. I do believe that between my busy schedule, sand volleyball (that Sarah says I take way more seriously than I should, but I do believe that's because we whipped her team twice), and Sarah mooching my fast food, that I've lost about ten pounds and a dress size. Since Tommy is Mr. Buffness it's nice to have a little bit more confidence. Not that I needed any reassurance since Tommy makes me feel as if I'm the most beautiful girl in Pinewood with or without the extra ten Chicago pizza pounds.

At the thought of Tommy I smile. I really do love him and it's about time I told him so. Sarah was right. Why waste another day?

After topping off my cup of coffee I hurry to the bathroom to shower and get ready. I decide to flatiron my hair in the interest of looking businesslike. The midnight blue golf shirt with Sarah's little magician logo stitched in gold looks so cute that I grin at my reflection. We ordered several and in time we hope to sell the shirts and other cool stuff on our soon to be launched Web site. The sky is blue and I slept like a rock, I think with a contented sigh. "Everything is comin' up roses," I say out loud as I try to squelch any bit of nervousness threatening to bubble up in my throat. After spraying on some floral perfume and fluffing my hair I give myself a thumbs-up and head out the door.

Since I'm a good thirty minutes early I decide to stop at Nick's to check and see if all is well in truck land. I find him in the huge storage shed taking the tarps off the tricked out beauties. "Oh my God." I put my hand to my chest and give Nick a smile. "You finished the SUV! Nick, it's gorgeous!" The pearl white ghost flames over storm gray are stunning. "You outdid yourself on this one." I trail my fingers over the glossy paint.

"You like it?"

"Are you kiddin'? I love it! If I could afford it, I'd buy it right now."

Nick grins. "You mean you don't want hot pink like your sister?"

I have to laugh but I point my finger at him. "You know she's onto somethin' with trucks geared toward women."

"Uh yeah, pink would be a chick thing." Nick winces. "You're not seriously gonna make me do that are you?"

"We'll see what kind of sketches she comes up with," I answer with a shrug.

"Sarah sure hid her talent from us all, didn't she?" Nick says with a long sigh. "I don't know what the hell she was afraid of."

"Rejection, ridicule . . . laughter. Probably the same reason you didn't approach your father about customizing trucks."

"It's hard to rock the boat," he admits. "Especially when there's a family to feed."

"I know. But I wonder how many people out there never pursue their dreams because of fear of failure?"

"Countless I imagine." He comes closer and takes both my hands in his. "Candie, I'm so grateful for this opportunity. I can't remember when I've been this happy."

"Hmmm, love will do that to ya," I tease and I swear he's blushing. "So is marriage is the near future? Mama told me yesterday that she's waiting for grandbabies."

"A baby?" His eyes go wide and I think that he must be imagining a little version of Sarah to contend with.

"Oh you'd make a wonderful daddy. So are you gonna pop the question?"

"I messed up so bad the first time that I don't know if I have the nerve. But I think tonight might be the night. Don't you dare tell, though. I wanted to wait until after the hoopla of the grand opening."

I squeeze his big hands. "This makes me so happy."

Nick hugs me hard. "I'm glad, Candie, because I never wanted to lose you. You've always meant so much to me." He pulls back and looks down at me.

"For a while there I was confused and I'm sorry for that."

"That's over. But now we're all right as . . ." I stop and put a hand over my mouth.

"Rain?"

"Shhh! Don't utter that four letter *word*!"

Nick laughs. "It's not supposed to . . . *do that* today. Besides, Sarah had it on her list of things taken care of."

"You've seen the list?"

"I can recite it for you. So then, what about Chicago?"

"What about it?"

"Do you have things squared away with your job and everything?"

I nod. "Pretty much."

"And you don't regret your decision?"

"Not at all."

"Good for you." Nick arches a dark eyebrow at me. "Sarah says you're going to have a heart-to-heart with Tommy."

I gasp. "She told you!"

"We talk about all sorts of stuff now."

"So it's one of those be-careful-what-you-wish-for kind of things?"

Nick smiles slowly. "Not at all. I wouldn't have it any other way."

I laugh but turn around when I hear a door slam. "Who was that?"

Nick shrugs. "Must be Bailey. We're gonna start movin' the trucks over to the lot as soon as he gets here. I told him he'd better not hit the snooze button and fall back asleep like he always does."

I glance down at my watch. "I'd better get over there and try to keep Sarah under control. Not that I'm not a nervous wreck myself."

"You just don't let it show."

I sigh. "Yeah, I'm a master at hiding my feelings but it's about time that I put myself out there."

"Are you referring to Tommy?"

I nod.

"He's a good guy. It's none of my business but if you love the guy let him know."

"I think I just might do that."

Nick takes a big breath and blows it out. "This is gonna be a big day, isn't it?"

I give him a high five. "The best! See ya in a bit." With a smile on my face and a nervous tingle in my tummy I head out the door. I'm surprised when I see Bailey pulling onto the lot since I thought he was already there but I give him a wave before crossing the street.

"Where have you been?" Sarah all but shouts as I enter the showroom.

"I'm a few minutes early, Sarah," I remind her as I head over and pour a cup of coffee. "But I stopped over at Nick's to make sure everything was all right."

Her blue eyes widen. "It is, isn't it?"

"Yes," I tell her calmly. "And he has the SUV finished. It's gorgeous. I want it for myself."

"Oh Candie, what if nobody shows up? Maybe this whole mystery thing wasn't a good idea?"

I set my coffee cup down on the desk. "Sarah, you said yourself that even the women were buzzing about it at Gayle's Glamorous Nails. Tommy says it's been the talk of the town at the park and we've heard people speculate over it at Pete's Pub. Daddy even said the nurses were chatting about it when he went for his checkup. Just when was the last time there was any kind of mystery in Pinewood?"

"Ummm . . . I guess never," she admits, and actually grins. "So you think people will show up?"

"In droves."

"Do you think we'll sell some trucks?"

"I hope! Okay, enough of the worry. Let's get down to business."

"Gotcha," Sarah says, and whips out her list. "Don't look at me like that. I've added a few things."

I put my hands in the air. "I wasn't gonna say a thing."

"But you were thinkin' it," she says but then points out the window. "Oh, here come the trucks. And the tent."

"And the caterer."

"Lordy, Candie, and a news crew." She turns to me. "How do I look?"

"Perfect as always. Me?"

Of course she just can't say fine. Instead Sarah reaches over and tucks a lock of my straightened hair behind my ear. "Put on some lipstick," she says, and reaches in her pocket for her own tube.

After we gloss our lips we stand at the window and watch the commotion for a minute. "Wow, this is really happening, isn't it?" I say to Sarah, who nods at me with big eyes. "You ready?"

She smiles and we do our usual knuckle bump. "Let's get this show on the road."

Once we step outside the rest of the morning flies by in an absolute blur of crazy activity. I'm finally glad that Sarah's list is imprinted on my brain or I would have forgotten something. In spite of the constant commotion I keep hoping to see Tommy arrive but so far he hasn't shown up and my messages have gone unanswered. I chalk it up to his being busy with the softball tournament but I'm a little disappointed that he hasn't at least called.

We've covered the trucks with tarps and the new sign at the end of the lot is draped as well but at ten o'clock sharp we are set to unveil TRICKED OUT TRUCKS. Sarah and I take our places at the sign with Daddy whose booming voice will do the announcing. Nick and Bailey are going to take the tarps off the trucks one at a time while Daddy reads the make, model, and description.

"Oh my goodness, here comes the local news," Sarah squeaks to me and then points at a van with a satellite dish perched on top. Following closely behind is a white van with a radio station logo painted on the side. Sarah and I stare wide-eyed. Then just as we're ready to pull the tarp off the new sign sporting our little magician, I hear the boom-boom of a base drum. Sarah and I turn toward the sound and see the Pinewood High Marching Band heading down the street that has been blocked off by Sheriff Combs.

"I pulled some strings," Daddy proudly proclaims from behind the microphone.

"He's been at it all week," Mama, leaning over, says before turning to snap a picture of the band.

"You got any other surprises up your sleeve?" I ask Daddy with a shake of my head.

"I arranged for a shuttle to bring folks from Pinewood High School over to the lot," he admits. "Good thing I know the superintendent and the mayor of Pinewood," he boasts looking like Boss Hog in his white suit but without the big belly that he used to have before the heart attack.

"Do you really think that will be necessary?" Sarah asks just before the band strikes up a tune. Daddy doesn't need to answer because we can see that people are flooding onto the lot.

"Mercy," I say, but my voice is drowned out by the music and the buzz of the growing crowd. It looks as though the entire population of Pinewood has turned out and then some. When the band stops playing there's silence except for a ripple of excitement that buzzes through the crowd. Daddy turns on the microphone and says in his booming voice, "Ladies and gentlemen . . . boys and girls. May I present," he

pauses for a drum roll and then shouts, "Tricked
Out . . . *Trucks!*"

Sarah and I yank the cover from the sign and Nick
and Bailey take the tarp off the first truck, a souped-up
Ford Ranger lowrider in shiny deep purple with gold
flames licking down the front panels. Daddy proceeds
to describe the truck in detail while the crowd cheers!
Yes . . . *cheers!* Daddy does this scenario one by one
with the onlookers applauding harder for each subse-
quent truck. I notice two other sheriff's cruisers arrive
and I'm thinking, *holy cow*, we need crowd control!

When the very last truck is announced, a 1999
Chevy Silverado, the crowd roars. "The flaming paint
job has hidden graphics and a very cool sci-fi interior,"
Daddy booms, and the crowd collectively sighs.
"There is an '01 Tahoe front bumper and notice the
Street Scene side view mirrors. The stock air dam was
smoothed and painted with billet accents. A set of
super hi-tech solid LED lights was added behind the
tailgate and Sir Michaels roll pan. A Gaylord's X2000
Tonneau cover keeps the rear end looking hot while a
set of Pontiac Grand Am door handles finishes it all
off." Daddy has to pause until the crowd calms down
and then continues, "Try to control your excitement
when you check out the fabulous twenty-inch
Colorado custom slotted Slater rims up front and dan-
gerously sexy twenty-two-inch Slaters in the rear. The
V-8 was juiced up thanks to an ATI Procharger and
Nick added a PowerAid throttle spacer and K&N air
cleaner. If that isn't *enough,* the three-inch custom bent
exhaust flows through an aluminized Flowmaster
muffler, giving this beauty just the right *rumble . . .*"

Daddy goes on to describe the interior while the
crowd seems to be chomping at the bit to check the
trucks out. Although it wasn't on Sarah's list, Nick
must have anticipated the eager crowd and had Sheriff
Combs rope off the trucks with police crime scene

tape. Seeing this Daddy says, "We will begin the up close and personal viewing of the tricked out trucks but a line must form to ensure safety. Then we will begin bidding starting with the price listed on the window."

I look over at Sarah. Bidding? And then I get it. Daddy knows that these trucks are going to sell for way over the asking price.

Holy cow.

"For those of you who aren't interested in viewing or bidding we have refreshments provided under the tent," Daddy says and then steps down from the podium.

"Girls, I think you have a winner," he states in a calm voice but Mama lets out a little squeal and suddenly we're all hugging. "Okay," Daddy says after the hugging is over, "You two need to go up to the office and wait for the bids to come in. Obviously the highest wins but we have to wait to give everyone who is interested a chance."

"Daddy, do you really think that there is gonna be a bidding war?"

"I don't think. I *know.* I'll have Sheriff Combs keep things under control and the bidders in single file."

"Okay." I nod my head vigorously. "Sarah, let's go get set up."

"I'll watch over the hospitality tent," Mama offers.

"Thank you, Mama," Sarah and I say in unison and then we hightail it up to the office.

The rest of the afternoon is nonstop activity and by the end of the day Sarah and I are running on caffeine and adrenaline. All of the trucks sell for way over the asking price that already had a nice profit margin built in. This is wonderful of course except that now we are once again without inventory. We negotiated in the contracts that the trucks would be delivered in two weeks, giving us the opportunity to showcase them while Nick has the chance to trick more trucks.

"At least we have some profit to work with," Sarah points out with a smile that turns to a huge yawn. "But Nick is gonna have to hire some help. He and Bailey can't keep up with this kind of demand. Any Mountain Dews left?"

"I think we're out." With a moan I ease my neck from side to side. "Look," I tell her and point out the window, "Mama and Daddy are still chatting it up with people. It's great to see him up and about, isn't it?"

"Sure is." Sarah gives me a warm smile. "We did it, didn't we?"

I feel myself getting all choked up. "Yeah, we did."

"God, it feels *so* good!" Sarah closes her eyes. I know she's fighting it but a lone tear slides down her cheek.

"Sarah . . . ," I warn. *"Don't."*

"I'm tryin', doggone it," she says, and swipes at the tear. "This was a good day, wasn't it?"

With a smile I nod in agreement but other than a brief text message from Tommy telling me that he stopped over once but I was busy, I haven't heard from him. My something-is-wrong radar is standing at attention.

"I'm starving! Nick's interviewing with a reporter but then we're going to get a bite to eat. Want to come? Or do you have plans with Tommy?"

"He's got that tournament goin' on so I think I'll head over there." I keep telling myself that he must be terribly busy not to return my messages. I wonder if Nick will repop the question tonight and I try to keep a straight face.

"What?" Sarah asks. "You have a somethin's-up look on your face."

"Do not."

She gasps. "Are you gonna tell Tommy that you love him?"

I look at her for a moment and then proclaim, "Yes. Yes I am!"

With a squeal Sarah jumps up. "Come here!"

I meet her in front of the desk, preparing myself for a huge hug. We jump in a circle like little kids until we've used up the very last of our caffeine and then lean against the edge of the desk.

"I'm plum tuckered out," Sarah moans.

"Me too."

"I hope to get my second wind after a nice dinner."

I pat her on the hand and say, "I'll lock up but call me later, okay?"

"Sure thing."

With a big smile I wave to Mama and Daddy through the window and then watch them leave. This has truly been a wonderful day ... one for the record books. The only thing left to make it complete is to have Tommy in my arms. Pushing the weird feeling of unease away, I hop in the old Camry and head over to the ballpark.

When I pull into the Pinewood Sports Complex, the first thing I notice is that the parking lot is empty. I'm about to call him when I see him sitting on the back of a tractor, guzzling a bottle of water.

"Hey," I call out, and I'm expecting a smile but my heart plummets when he frowns at me. "You about finished?" I ask with a nervous edge to my voice. Apparently my something-is-wrong radar was right.

"Yeah," he says, and tosses his empty bottle in the trash with more force than needed. "Just about." He jumps down from the tractor, looking tired and dusty but I still want to hug him. When I take a step closer I'm taken aback by the wary look on his face.

"Tommy, what's wrong?" My stomach starts doing weird things but it has nothing to do with hunger.

He takes a deep breath and blows it out. "Is there something you've been neglecting to tell me?"

"As a matter of fact . . . yes."

"Candie, why are you even here?" He looks at me with such sadness in his eyes that the urge to hug him gets stronger even though I'm really confused.

"I'm here because we—we closed up for the day. It was a huge success, by the way."

"I'm glad," he says, and at least sounds sincere. "I did come by once when I caught a break but you were knee-deep in customers."

Even though he's acting strange I decide to just go ahead and tell him that I love him. Surely that will ease whatever is bothering him. "Tommy," I begin but emotion has me clearing my throat. "There *is* something that I've been meaning to tell you."

"You don't have to tell me. I already know." He adjusts the bill on his dusty cap and avoids looking at me.

"You do?" I ask brightly. "Well yeah, I guess my feelings are obvious, which is why I should have already told you. Tommy, I—"

"No, don't." A muscle ticks in his jaw. "I can't take it. I believed in our future but I was wrong." He shakes his head. "I can't believe what a dumb-ass I was."

24

All Jacked Up

Tommy's eyes widen and he opens his mouth but I turn on my heel and take off like a bat outta hell. I'm all turned around and suddenly find myself in the middle of a ball field, but I hear Tommy in swift pursuit so I zigzag, figuring I can throw him off . . . stupid, I know, since his stride is twice that of my short legs.

"Candie!" he shouts. "Get off the field!"

Oh, he's broken my heart and he's worried that I might mess up his precious ball field? I'm thinking that I might just flip him off when the sprinkler system suddenly kicks on, sending water spraying everywhere. "Eeeeek!" I run in circles instead of my former zigzag. To make matters worse I trip and fall right on top of a sprinkler head. Wow, that's going to leave a bruise. I stumble to my feet while rubbing my left butt cheek and slip on the wet grass, almost going down again. By now Tommy is upon me.

"Candie," he says, breathing hard and having the nerve to look good even when he's dripping wet but I'm so pissed off that I push him away. He backpedals from the force of my shove and actually falls down, giving me the chance to run again.

I make the mistake of looking back and get a pang of guilty concern when he doesn't get up right away. Is he hurt? Does he have a sprinkler head shoved up where it shouldn't be? Should I care?

Of course I care. I still love him even if he doesn't love me back. How's that for a big kick in the teeth? With a squeal of pure frustration I head back into the spray, muttering under my breath the whole way back to him.

"Tommy, what are you doin'?" I suppose it's a pretty dumb question but he's lying on the ground directly beneath a continual shower of water. "Can't you get up? Ohmigod is something broken?" Besides my heart? I leave that last part out even though I want to scream it at him.

"I'm havin' a back spasm," he gasps, and the sprinklers take pity on him and abruptly cease. "Old football injury . . . damned special teams." His face contorts in pain.

"Is there anything I can do?"

"No. It runs its course and then stops."

"Should I call for help?"

"No. It'll be . . . ahh—over in a few minutes."

"Okay," I say while dripping down on him. "If there's nothin' I can do then I'm leavin'."

"No! Candie! Wait!"

I ignore his plea even though it's difficult to leave him in pain.

"Candie! I . . . overheard you and Nick this morning."

I stop in the wet grass and slowly turn around. He tries to sit up but can't, but I inch a little closer so I can see his face.

"I—I wanted to see you before I came to work. I even brought you cheese Danish," he says hopefully, but all I give him is a scowl. "When you weren't at the dealership I figured you were at Nick's so I headed over there."

"Okay . . ." I'm still not getting it but then I raise my eyebrows. "You were upset that I hugged Nick? Damn it all to hell and back! We are just friends!"

"No"—he pauses to grimace in pain—"but you've been lying to me the whole summer—"

"About *what*?"

"Leaving! This whole damned time you were planning to go back to Chicago. Don't you think I deserved to know?"

I shake my head so hard that water droplets fly. "How could you think that of me?"

"I heard you say so! I feel like I've been played for a fool."

"Well, here's a news flash for you. You were wrong. You completely misunderstood."

"So you're not leaving?" He tries to sit up again but fails.

"No! I was on a leave of absence but I gave my official resignation." I shake my head sadly. "I didn't think there was any reason to go back to Chicago but now I'm not so sure."

"Candie, you have to put yourself in my shoes. It sure *sounded* like you were leaving. I'm sorry! I was so upset that I ran off half-cocked."

"I thought you knew me better." I take a step backward. "You know how important this day was to me and you *missed* it."

"Candie . . . ," he pleads and makes a valiant effort to sit up but hisses and his head drops back to the wet ground. "I was a mess. I did stop over . . ."

"I'll call Bailey to come and look after you," I tell him and then walk away. I hear him shout my name again but this time I don't look back.

It's a miracle that I make it home in one piece since I'm crying so hard. It's like driving without wind-

shield wipers in the pouring rain. "Damn him for ru-
ining my perfect day!" I shout as I get out of the car.

"Good day to you, honey," Mrs. Cartwright shouts
from her rocking chair.

I turn and give her a feeble wave. She puts her hand
over her mouth and I do believe she's stifling a scream.
I wonder what that was all about until I slosh into the
bathroom and get a load of myself in the mirror. I almost scream too until I realize that I'm looking at my
own reflection. Mascara is running down my face like
Alice Cooper. There's a clump of grass in my hair and
mud on my chin. I blink at my sorry self and promptly
burst into noisy tears.

"I look like a drowned cat . . . ," I wail. I have a habit
of saying random oddball things when I cry. "I scared
old Mrs. Cartwright . . . ," I continue to wail as I strip
off the wet clothing and drop it to the floor with a
splat. With a loud sniff I reach to the back of the bathroom door and slip into my ratty but comforting
bathrobe. For a moment I consider calling Sarah but I
don't want to interrupt Nick asking her to marry
him . . . again. "Okay." I take a deep, shuddering breath
and say, "Get yourself under control!"

I do for about three seconds and the wailing re-
sumes. I stomp into the kitchen and almost rip the re-
frigerator door off the hinges while looking for
something to eat. I'm hungry but of course nothing
looks remotely appetizing, so I open the freezer and
pray for ice cream. I know . . . cliché to drown my sorrow in rocky road but I don't give a damn. It's either
that or bourbon and if I drink I'm certain I'll call
Tommy and say stupid stuff or even forgive him for
thinking that I'm a coldhearted liar.

I stomp into the living room and plop down on the
sofa so hard that I bounce and then dig into the ice
cream. After a frazzled search for the remote, I turn on
the television and shovel ice cream into my mouth . . .

really big bites until I start to get a headache and I realize that I don't even taste it. Great . . . I just consumed about a million calories without the pleasure. And if that doesn't beat all it isn't until after a full fifteen minutes that I suddenly realize that I'm watching the Spanish channel and of course can't understand a word of what they're saying.

Instead of changing the station I get ticked off at the television as if it was somehow the TV's fault and then decide to give it all up and just shower and go to bed. I cry in the shower and I cry in bed while thinking sad and angry thoughts instead of reveling in the success of Tricked Out Trucks.

"Damn you, Tommy Tucker. How *could* you?" Of course I hear Tommy's voice say, "Put yourself in my shoes . . ."

Suddenly I sit up straight in bed. "Ohmigod!" I put a hand to my thumping heart. I forgot to call Bailey! What if Tommy is still lying there out on the cold, wet ball field? In pain? What if those stupid sprinklers came back on? What if a raccoon comes along and takes a bite out of him? Okay that last one isn't likely, I tell myself and try to calm down. And Tommy said himself that he would be okay in a few minutes.

But I forgot to call Bailey! I was so caught in my own drama . . . my own self-pity that I forgot! I shove my fingers through my curly hair while wondering what to do. I reach for my cell phone lying on the nightstand while wondering if I should call Bailey or maybe his sister? But then I have to explain how I left Tommy flat on his back, twitching and defenseless against the forces of nature. I stare down at the phone in indecision.

"Oh, I am such a bad person!"

"No you're not."

At the sound of the unexpected voice a scream bubbles up in my throat and I'm prepared to hurl the

phone at the intruder, but I quickly realize even in the
dim light that it's Tommy standing there, leaning one
shoulder against the door frame, and looking calm
and collected while my heart is about to jump out of
my chest.

"So a raccoon didn't get you after all. Thank God!"

"What?"

"I was imagining all sorts of terrible things happening to you lying there defenseless. I'm sorry I left you
like that. I'm a selfish, horrible, *terrible* person."

"Candie, I told you I'd be okay."

"But I should have made sure. I let anger get the
best of me."

"And I let fear get the best of me."

"Fear?" I squint at him in the semidarkness.

Tommy rakes his fingers through his hair. "When I
thought about you leaving I panicked. Then, instead of
coming into the shop I stood there and listened to your
conversation and in my fear I came to all the wrong
conclusions. It was stupid. It was wrong." He swallows and takes a step closer to the bed. "Will you forgive me?"

I open my mouth to answer him but when I get
emotional my vocal chords cease to function, leaving
me with nothing but squeaky croaky noises, so I decide that showing is better than telling anyway. I
scramble to a standing position in the middle of the
bed and sort of catapult myself into his arms. He
catches me, thank goodness, and staggers backward
from the sheer force of my body slam, but suddenly
we're kissing feverishly and saying silly stuff to each
other.

"I was such an idiot," he says, and then nibbles on
my neck.

"I should have listened," I tell him before sucking
his earlobe into my mouth. He groans and kneads my

butt cheeks that are cupped by his big hands beneath my oversized T-shirt.

"I should have known better," Tommy tells me, but then leans his forehead against mine. "I sat on your front porch for a long time before gettin' up the nerve to come in. By the way you really need to lock your door . . . just give *me* a key." He sighs and then says, "No more should haves, okay?"

"I'm all for that."

Tommy lifts his forehead from mine. "I want to make love to you, Candie," he says, and slowly lowers me to the bed. He tugs my T-shirt over my head and then shimmies my panties over my hips. For a long heated moment he simply looks down at me and I lean back on my elbows, no longer shy. I know I'm not perfect—my breasts are small, my hips are wide, and my legs are short—but Tommy has a way of making me feel good about the way I look . . . as though I *am* perfect in his eyes.

Tommy makes quick work of removing his shirt and shorts but I sit up and slowly peel his boxer briefs over his hips, sucking in a breath at his sheer male beauty. He pauses for protection and then threads his fingers with mine as he eases his weight onto the bed.

Tommy makes love to me with tender intensity with slow but deep strokes, full of love and passion. My pleasure blossoms and builds into a sweet ache that becomes almost too much . . . and then shatters. Afterward, he holds me in a full body embrace and for a long suspended moment we cling to each other.

"I love you, Candie," he says, but before I can say it back he kisses me. When he rolls to the side I'm about to tell him again but my doggone phone rings. I would ignore it but I just know it's going to be Sarah with her news and I can't bear to disappoint her.

Tommy hands me the phone and I try to answer in

a regular voice that doesn't sound like I've just made love but my hello comes out breathless and husky.

"Candie? Guess what?" she squeaks.

"What?" I grin at Tommy and put her on speaker.

"Nick proposed!"

"Ohmigod!" I force a note of surprise in my voice since I know she would be ticked if I knew before she did that Nick was going to pop the question. Tommy shakes his head at me and grins.

"Where? Give me details!"

"Well, he wanted to take me someplace nice but I was so starved that I begged him to take me to Biscuits and Burgers instead of somewhere that would take a long time. But guess what?"

I start to say *what* but she keeps right on talking.

"He let me eat my bacon cheeseburger and okay half of his fries and well most of his milkshake and while I was contemplating dessert because I had already blown it so why not, he got down on one knee right there in the middle of the restaurant and proposed!"

"Oh Sarah!" I look at Tommy and my eyes mist over.

"The Red Hat Ladies were there—I guess it's their hangout or whatever—and they stood up and cheered! I think the motive was because they all wanted to give Nick a hug but it was so amazing. They brought out dessert for free after that. And guess what else?"

I'm not going to say *what* this time but she waits for me to say it. "What?" I shake my head at Tommy.

"Afterward we went to Pete's Pub so I could show off my ring even though it's the same ring but you know we wanted to celebrate and guess who was there?" When she pauses Tommy nudges me.

"Oh . . . who?"

"Carson Campbell. Candie, he came up to me and you know what he said? He said that Tricked Out

Trucks was genius. *Genius!* I've never been called that before have you?"

"No."

"Anyway, he was real nice. I so wanted to ask him about the drink-in-his-face incident but you will be proud to know that I refrained."

"Good for you," I tell her, and glance at Tommy. His mouth is twitching as if he wants to laugh.

"So," Sarah says, "did you tell Tommy-the-Hottie that you love him?"

I feel my cheeks grow warm. Tommy mouths Tommy-the-Hottie at me and I make a face at him. "Yes—well, I was about to. He got the message."

"Oh Candie!" she cries so loud that I grimace. In a lower tone she says, "So, did he say it back?"

"Yes I did." Tommy leans closer to the phone to make sure that Sarah hears him.

"Candie Montgomery, do you have me on speakerphone?"

"I do."

"You rat!" she accuses, but then says, "Was this not the best day ever?"

"One for the record books," I reply, smiling at how much we think alike.

"You think we might have a double wedding like Mama wants?"

Tommy's eyes widen and I feel my face grow warm. "Sarah!"

She chuckles. "That's what you get for putting me on speakerphone."

"I'm hangin' up now," I tell her, and then look at Tommy. "That was Mama talkin'. She's desperate for grandbabies but I don't want you to think—"

Tommy puts a finger to my lips. "All I know is that I love you. The rest we'll take a step at a time."

I blink away the moisture gathering in my eyes and say, "Sarah was right. This *was* the best day ever. Well, except for the sprinkler incident but you've already made up for that."

Tommy glances over at the digital clock on my nightstand and I follow his gaze. "In five minutes we can make tomorrow even better. You ready to try?"

"You betcha. Tomorrow and the next day and the next day . . ."

"You sure know how to put pressure on a guy."

"You up for it?"

"Oh . . . *yeah.*"6 of 8 for teaser

Will the sexy football coach
end up with the curvy hairdresser now
that she's in Nashville?

With

A LITTLE LESS TALK AND
A LOT MORE ACTION,

everything is possible.

Turn the page for a sneak peek of
LuAnn McLane's next sweet and
sexy Southern romance.

"Everybody help yourself," Tammy announces when trays of food start arriving. "We're getting a little bit of everything and I said to keep the barbeque comin'."

After Tammy waves her hand in a small circle over her head, the crew cheers and noisily shoots chairs back from their tables. Luke and I hang back from the rush to the buffet, and I put my hand on his arm and say, "I'm sorry you got roped into this, Luke. I'm sure you're tired after last night and a long drive to Nashville was the last thing you wanted to do."

Luke looks at me long enough for my defiant won't-listen-to-my-head heart to go pitter-patter. "And maybe you don't know what I want as well as you think you do," he teases in a lighthearted tone, but there's something in those blue eyes of his that gives me pause. When I'm hoping he'll say more we're suddenly at the buffet table and my typical scared-to-go-for-it mode kicks into high gear.

"Have you tried the ribs?" Luke asks as we eat and chat with the band and crew. He cuts one from his slab and puts it on my plate. "I love the sauce. We'll have to buy a couple of bottles as we leave. My favorite is the Tennessee Original," he says, holding up the bottle. "How about you?"

"Mmmm, I like the sweet, smoky one."

Luke nods. "Yeah . . . I like that one too. I believe it's called the Kansas City–style. We'll get a bottle of that one, as well. Your dad would like the Texas Sweet Hot."

"Yeah, he would. That man puts hot sauce on everything. Even his scrambled eggs."

Luke laughs. "Yeah, I remember that from fishing with him at his cabin. We'll pick him up a bottle of the hot stuff."

"Good idea," I tell him, and it suddenly reminds me again of how much we've felt like a couple over the last few months while planning Jamie Lee's wedding except, you know, that we've never had sex . . . or have even kissed for that matter. Mercy . . . that last thought—an image of us in a lip-lock—causes me to choke on my sweet tea.

"You okay?" Luke asks with a slight frown. "Go down the wrong pipe?"

With my hand to my chest and my eyes watering, I nod. Lord, did I swallow the slice of lemon?

"You need a pat on the back?"

No, I need my head examined. "I'm . . . okay," I manage. Lilly, who is sitting next to me, doesn't help when she whispers in my ear, "I'd choke on my tea too if he was sittin' next to me." She bumps my knee with hers, reminding me of something Jamie Lee might do: causing me to choke and laugh at the same time. Luke, who obviously thinks I'm going into some kind of seizure, gently pats me on the back.

"Sorry," Lilly apologizes with a straight face, but the laughter in her eyes says otherwise. Unable to speak, I bump her knee back to let her know I'm on to her tactics.

Laughter and easygoing chatter continue and I think to myself that I could definitely fit in to this group of people, so I'm a little let down that after we're finished eating nothing more is mentioned about me coming to work for Tammy or the record studio. I tell myself that it's a good thing since I'd never have the courage to leave Hootertown anyway.

"Thanks again for comin' to my rescue," Tammy

says as we stand up to leave. "You saved the day, Macy McCoy." She slips an envelope into my hand. "Sorry I was so busy during lunch or I would have visited with y'all more but it seems like I'm always on that dog-gone cell phone. Someday I'm gonna toss it right out the window."

"I was happy to be of service and I had fun," I assure her. Thinking that my short-lived adventure is over I give hugs all around the room, even to Boone, who surprises me with a big hug in return.

Tammy hurries back over to us as we're heading out the door. "Nice to meet you, Luke. You two have a safe trip home." When Luke turns away for a moment Tammy gives me two thumbs up and a wink. I quickly shake my head but she mouths, *Go for it*. I mouth, *Oh, stop* just as Luke turns back, causing us both to straighten up, but I know we have guilty we-were-taking-about-you looks on our faces.

With one last wave and another hug for Tammy, we exit the room to a hallway that seems very quiet after all the boisterous conversation. "Thanks again for coming all this way to pick me up, Luke," I tell him to fill in the silence.

Luke stops in his tracks and turns to face me. "Macy," he begins, but then hesitates with a rather serious expression on his handsome face. This is unusual for Luke, who always seems so sure of himself.

My heart beats faster in anticipation but he remains silent. Wondering what's wrong, I put my hand on his arm and somehow find the courage to prompt him. "Is something botherin' you? You do know that you can tell me anything."

While nodding his head slowly Luke gives me a tender smile. "Yeah, I know that, Macy."

"Well then, what's on your mind?"

I wait for him to answer, but he swallows and I swear his gaze drops to my mouth. For a heart-stopping moment I think he might lean in and . . . *kiss me* right here in the hallway of Jack's Bar B Que. After the initial nonbeating shock my heart starts thumping wildly . . . but then again Luke might be staring at some barbeque sauce on the corner of my mouth or something so I discreetly lick my lips in search of Tennessee Original.

When I don't encounter any tangy flavor I'm pretty sure that he's thinking about kissing me so I step closer to give him easy access. I mean, why make it difficult, right? Because he's so tall I tilt my head up and I'm thinking I should stand on tiptoe but just as I raise up to my toes Luke bends his head, tilting to the left. In that instant I realize that he's going to kiss me on the cheek like I'm his doggone sister! Something in me snaps—from pent-up emotion or maybe just the fairy-tale feeling of this incredible day, who knows—and I think *Screw this kiss on the cheek stuff* and turn my head so that Luke's lips land smack-dab against my mouth.

Luke stiffens as if surprised . . . *shocked*? *Oh God, what am I doing?* I want to kick my own ass for being so brazen. When a dreaded nervous giggle begins in the back of my throat I swallow hard. While looking down at the floor I take a quick step backward while wondering how to explain my behavior. When my back meets the rough, exposed brick wall I clear my throat of giggles but I refuse to look up at him while I rack my brain for something pithy to say to lighten the awkward moment. When nothing clever pops into my befuddled brain I decide to simply apologize.

"Luke, I'm . . ." I begin, but my words are smothered when he tilts my head up and covers my mouth with a sweet yet sexy kiss that sends a hot tingle shooting all the way to my toes. I swear that if the wall weren't right behind my feet, one would pop up just like in the movies. My hands take on a life of their own, first fisting in the soft cotton of his shirt but when he deepens the kiss I slide them up and wrap my arms around his neck until my fingers are buried in the silky hair at the nape of his neck. His mouth is hot, his lips are soft, and when his tongue tangles with mine my pent-up desire for him bubbles to the surface. If we weren't in a public place I think I'd have to jump up and wrap my legs around his waist while he pins me to the wall and makes wild and crazy . . .

If we weren't in a public place bangs into my brain and echoes in my head like a gong. Luke must have had the same sudden thought because he pulls his lips from mine and takes a step backward. He looks dazed and confused but then again, maybe it's because I'm looking at him with half-lidded dazed and confused eyes.

"Wow," he says while threading his fingers through his short-cropped chestnut brown hair, which I recently cut. He has great hair, by the way, thick and slightly wavy. I look up at him, trying to decide if it's going to be another good *wow* like with Tammy or a what-the-hell-just-happened kind of *wow*.

"That was . . ."—he pauses to clear his throat—"unexpected."

Opening my eyes wider, I peer at him closely, trying to decide if he means that in a positive way or not, but I don't know quite how to ask. I decide the safe thing to do is to simply agree. "Um . . . yes, it was." My voice is a bit breathless but I think I pull it off.

Luke angles his head as he looks at me for a long moment and then says, "Then again, maybe . . . *not*."